Found You

Book Two in the *No Escape* Series

LK Chapman

To my boys: my husband Ashley, and my little son Felix.
The two of you are my whole world.

Jay

1

It was just after dawn. Jay reluctantly opened his eyes and curled up, hugging his knees to his chest to try to get some warmth into his body. He had slept outside all night – or at least, since about three a.m. He hadn't wanted to push his luck too far with the car he'd stolen, so after driving long enough to put a good bit of distance between himself and Tatchley he'd left the car at the side of the road. That's when he set off on foot through the countryside, walking by the light of the moon, until his body was so tired he couldn't take another step.

Angry tears trickled down his cheeks as he thought about the previous day. He'd lost Felicity. He couldn't believe it. She'd been there in the woods with him. She'd been right there, sitting on the ground with her back against a tree, hand resting on her bump. But he'd been distracted with Mark, and when he finally turned round, she was gone. He'd tried to follow her, searching desperately for signs of her on the narrow path through the woods, but it had been useless. She'd melted away into the trees, and disappeared.

He wiped his tears away roughly, and looked up at the grey bricks of the bridge under which he'd sheltered. He couldn't let thoughts of Felicity distract him and put him in danger. He had to assume she'd gone to the police by now, and if so, they would be trying to find him. He'd spent long enough in this place. The bridge spanned a small road, and traffic would pick up now that it was morning. He was fairly inconspicuous curled up in the undergrowth, but nevertheless it was time to go. He slowly sat up, and pulled his bag of belongings closer to him, uneasy as he remembered the bloodstained clothes he'd stuffed inside in a panic. He shuddered. *Blood!* Thick, sticky, repulsive blood, like dirt, but even worse. *Not just any blood. Mark's blood.* An image of Mark's broken body filled his mind, and he gagged, though his stomach was too empty to bring anything up.

He took his gloves off and stared at his hands, convinced they were still smeared with blood, and he rubbed them on his jeans to clean them. *Stop!* He blinked, and the illusion disappeared. Though they were still cut and bruised from attacking Mark, his hands were otherwise clean. He'd washed them, *scrubbed* them in fact, with washing-up liquid, before he left the house. If he'd cleaned them any more, he'd have lost the top layer of his skin.

He put his gloves back on, calmer now. He shouldn't be feeling guilty! Mark got what was coming to him. The bastard had stolen his girlfriend from him. Not just once, but twice. He'd stolen his first love, Sammie, with his tricks and games, and he'd come between him and Felicity too. Mark was better off dead. He deserved to be dead.

And as for Felicity, running away like she had… *No. Don't think about her. Not now. Not yet.*

He slipped the backpack straps over his shoulders and stood up shakily. Where to now? He didn't have any idea where he was, so he couldn't possibly make an informed decision of what to do next. All he could do was keep moving.

As he made his way down through some scrubby grass to a line of trees, Jay's thoughts grew darker and more hopeless. What was the point? He'd lost everything he cared about, and there was nowhere he could go. He was hungry and thirsty, he needed to use a bathroom and he felt filthy. He couldn't believe he'd been reduced to this again. He'd spent time sleeping rough before, and one of the worst things had been never feeling clean. That time he'd managed to get help and a place in a hostel, but there would be no help for him now. Now he was on his own.

He dug his nails into his palms until the pain cleared his head. *Get a grip. You can't give up now.* If he gave up, Felicity won. Mark won. They all won, all the people who'd ever fucked with him. He wasn't going to give them the satisfaction.

In the absence of any better plan, he continued around the

edge of the tree line. After a while, he ventured into the woods, surprised to find a small lake – or large pond – with a path weaving through the trees around it. There was a flock of geese on the still water, but otherwise the place was deserted and silent. He walked until he reached an information board showing pictures of birds and animals, and the name Dudford Wildfowl Reserve. Near the sign was a bench looking out over the water, so he sat down, grateful to be able to rest somewhere other than on the ground. Despite his gloves, his hands were like blocks of ice and he rubbed them together to try to get a bit of life into them. The sun was almost up now, and he was glad. Daylight would help him think clearly. It would help him form a plan.

The geese took off in a flurry of noise and he jumped as they disturbed the stillness of the quiet place. Then a noise behind him made him turn. There was a woman on the path. She was young – early twenties, he estimated, though her plain clothes and total lack of style made her appear even younger; childish, almost. Her limp, mousey-brown hair was tied back in a loose ponytail, and her eyes flicked to his face then immediately away again. She seemed as surprised to see him as he was to see her. He got the sense that she'd been planning to sit on the bench that he was occupying. She pulled her ugly beige coat closer around her, and made to walk off again, so he said, 'Do you want to sit here?'

She stared at him. 'No,' she said, 'I mean, it doesn't matter. There's another further along...' She trailed off, looking as though she was about to cry. Well, this was curious.

'Come and sit down,' he said. He moved to one end of the bench to make room for her, and she did as he asked and sat down a careful distance from him. He didn't speak to her straight away. She seemed timid and he didn't want to frighten her. But she didn't appear to be suspicious of him, so either his face wasn't all over the news as he feared, or she hadn't seen it.

When he glanced round at her again, she was crying silently.

'Sorry,' she said when she saw him looking. 'I just, it's...' She shook her head.

'I'm not having the best time right now either,' he told her. 'My girlfriend just left me.'

'Oh,' she said, 'I'm sorry about that.'

He took a moment to look at her more closely. Her hair was tucked behind her ears, which were unpierced, and her skin was pale with an unpleasant waxy look to it, as if pressing a finger against her face would leave an indent for several seconds after. She wasn't very pretty, that was for sure. Not to his taste, anyway. She was clutching her hands together in her lap; her short fingernails were painted pale pink, but the polish was chipped. Did she bite her nails? How disgusting.

'So,' he said, 'what brings you here so early in the morning?'

Instead of answering she started fussing with a drawstring at the waist of her coat, winding the cord around her fingers, unwinding it, winding it again. 'I was supposed to go home and rest,' she said randomly. 'The hospital told me...' She stopped and took a breath. 'My granddad is in hospital. I've been there the past few days. They said I should go home and rest, but I couldn't face it. I've lived with him most of my life and I don't want to go back to an empty house. That's why I came here, because he likes it here.'

Inside Jay's body, a fire came to life. This woman was lonely, in a house by herself, in a weakened and vulnerable state. He couldn't believe his luck. It was as if God himself was on Jay's side. Not that he believed in such things, but after the nightmare he'd been through, this woman was like the light at the end of the tunnel. He was almost giddy with hope and relief. 'Is there somewhere round here we could get a coffee?' he asked innocently.

She nodded. 'Back outside the main entrance there's a petrol station that does take-away coffees. There's a café inside the nature reserve but it only opens weekends and in the summer holidays. And never this early.'

'Would you let me buy you a coffee?' he asked her.

She hesitated, but it was clear as day to him that she was craving some sort of company right now, and would take a chance on anyone who seemed able to provide it. 'Yes,' she said, 'thank you. That's very kind.'

Stephanie

2

Stephanie tried not to make it too obvious that she kept stealing glances at the man from the bench. He was a bit dishevelled, but surely that was something to do with him just having split up with his girlfriend, as his clothes were stylish and didn't look cheap, even if they were a little crumpled. His eyebrows and nails were well-groomed, and though there was maybe a day's worth of stubble on his chin, she had a sense that he usually looked immaculately turned out. He paid for his coffee and her hot chocolate quickly with cash, and once they were back outside he cupped his take-away cup in both hands like he was trying to warm up.

'Do you like birds then?' she asked as they made their way back into the deserted wildfowl reserve.

He looked at her like he wasn't sure what she was talking about.

'It's just… you're out here ever so early—'

'Oh,' he said. 'No. I mean, I don't *dis*like them. But I didn't know this place was here, I just stumbled on it by accident.' He paused. 'After my girlfriend split up with me yesterday, I walked around for hours. I ended up walking half the night, and then I got lost. It's just luck that I ended up here right when you were here.' He smiled at her, which made her cheeks flush with warmth and she quickly looked away, trying to focus instead on what he'd said about how he'd spent the past few hours. He'd been walking all night? That sounded odd, but then, people did strange things when they were upset. Hadn't she done something similar herself, driving here instead of going home, too insecure to go back to her empty house?

'What's your name?' she asked him. 'I'm Stephanie.'

He paused, then answered, 'Jason.'

They sat down on the same bench where they'd met, and he stared out at the water. Although she was preoccupied with concern for her granddad, she still found herself appreciating the way he looked. He was several years older than her, and he had a serious, thoughtful look to him. She began to blush again, and it was as if Jason knew, because he turned to her. 'How come your granddad is in hospital?' he asked.

'He had a fall,' she said. 'But he's been very unwell for weeks. I… I don't think he's going to come back to the house again. I think he'll need to stay somewhere with people around to look out for him.'

Jason nodded. 'You said you've lived with him most of your life?'

'Yes. He… well, he brought me up.'

'Oh, were you… are your parents…' He paused. 'Sorry, I'm being nosy. You don't have to answer.'

She sipped her hot chocolate and watched a couple of moorhens darting about through the reeds at the edge of the water. What could she tell him? She didn't really know why her childhood had been the way it had. 'I never really understood what happened with my parents,' she said honestly. 'I don't know anything at all about my mum. As for my dad – I know a little about him. He was my granddad's son, so he talked about him sometimes. He got in some trouble with the police, and he ended up in prison. After that, he went off to do his own thing. The idea was that granddad would take care of me initially and then my dad would take over once he'd got himself sorted. But I guess he never did.'

'That must be difficult.'

She shrugged. 'Not really. They say you don't miss what you never had. I suppose I have this sense of *something* being missing, but – I don't really know what it would be like to have known him. I guess I should be angry with him, but I'm not. I just… I don't know.' She did know really, though; she just felt silly saying it. The reality was that she longed for her dad to turn up one day, so much that she'd often daydream about it. Especially now her granddad was so unwell, the fantasy of her dad was something she could cling to. But she couldn't talk about her desire for a fairy-tale ending in front of Jason. It was silly and naive, and she was already fretting that her choice of a hot chocolate rather than a coffee made her look childish.

'My dad died when I was young,' Jason told her. 'I can remember him, though, so I know what I'm missing.'

'I'm sorry.'

'It's not your fault.'

'Why did you and your girlfriend split up?'

'It wasn't just one thing. We hadn't been getting on for a while, then yesterday we had a blazing row and she chucked me out.'

Stephanie nodded and they sat quietly, taking occasional sips of their drinks. The hot chocolate spread warmth through her sluggish body, and the sugar gave her a hit of energy, bringing back a bit of life. Perhaps she could face going home after all. It couldn't hurt to have a shower and put on some clean clothes at least, even if she couldn't get any actual rest at the house. She smiled at Jason. Normally she hated talking to anyone she didn't know – and she didn't know many people – but she felt comfortable with Jason. Liked him, even. She couldn't say exactly why, she just did.

Jay

3

Jay smiled to himself. It was obvious that Stephanie liked 'Jason'. No surprise there; he had a knack for getting women interested in him. It was keeping them that he didn't seem able to do. With a flash of anger, he thought of Felicity. How dare she leave him? She was pregnant with his baby; she didn't get to decide where she went or what she did! She'd broken his heart by trying to run away with Mark, by getting Mark to come and "rescue" her. She hadn't needed *rescuing*. She'd had him to look after her, to wait on her hand and foot. Sooner or later she'd realise what she'd thrown away by betraying him.

Stephanie's face had more colour to it now than when he'd first seen her. She'd lost that pale, waxy look – there was a light in her eyes, and he'd put it there. What exactly was she was thinking about? Was she thinking she wanted to see Jason again? Was she wondering whether Jason liked looking at her as much as she liked looking at him? Whatever she was thinking about, it obviously wasn't her granddad in the hospital.

Not for the first time in his life, it had been useful to have a dead dad to talk about. He couldn't count the number of times he'd profited from telling women about his childhood loss. Sometimes it was so effective he didn't need to add the fact that his mum abandoned him when he was little too, only returning after his dad's death – but if the dead dad wasn't quite enough, then adding this bonus part of his family history would usually seal the deal.

He couldn't become complacent, though. No matter how taken Stephanie was with Jason, her feelings could be shattered in an instant by one wrong word from him. He had to be very careful how he proceeded. He needed her help as soon as possible, but he couldn't come straight out and ask for it because it would scare her off. What else could he do, though? He'd got rid of his phone to make sure it couldn't be traced, so he couldn't give her his number, and he had nowhere to stay. If she left he'd probably never see her again and he'd be back to sleeping rough, waiting for the police to find him. 'When do you need to get back to the hospital?' he asked her.

'I think I'll go home first,' she said. 'I'm not much good to anyone like this. I'm exhausted, and I need to eat some proper food. But I can't... it's hard to think straight. I can't even remember what I have in the fridge at home.' She paused, and then said, 'What about you? Where will you go, if your girlfriend has kicked you out?'

He shrugged, acting casual. He couldn't come across as desperate. 'Don't know. I'll figure something out.'

'Where do you work?'

Her question caught him off guard. 'I...'

'I was just wondering because it's almost nine now. If you need to get somewhere, maybe I could give you a lift, if it's not too far. Or I could drop you at the train station.'

'My... uh... I worked in my girlfriend's family's business,' he lied quickly. 'So... no girlfriend, no job.'

'Oh.'

'Yeah. And she won't let me in the house. I'm kind of stuck.'

'Can you go to a friend's house?'

'I... I don't really...' He paused and rubbed the back of his neck as he thought. 'It's not your problem,' he told her. 'Don't worry about me.'

'So you really have nowhere to go?'

'Honestly, I'll be okay.'

'When did you last eat? I had a sandwich at the hospital last night, but I'd love a hot breakfast. There's a nice little café I know in Wrexton, why don't you come with me? It'll save me trying to make something at home.'

A café. It wasn't as good as her inviting him back to her house, but it was a good start. He didn't like the thought of going somewhere public, but the potential benefit of having her shelter him for a time had to be worth the risk. 'Sure,' he said, trying to guess how much cash he had left in his wallet. 'I'm buying.'

...

They didn't talk much as she drove. She was beginning to sag with exhaustion again, and so was he. He was struggling to think very far ahead, so weary and hungry that he was just grateful to be in the warm car, and on his way to get something to eat.

The café was large, and had an old-fashioned canteen feel to it. They sat on worn-looking chairs at a table by the wall, with a plastic-coated orange tablecloth over it. Jay was dubious about the food offerings available in Stephanie's "nice little café". Ordinarily he would never set foot in a greasy spoon like this. He gave his immediate surroundings a quick scan for mess and dirt, reassuring himself that although everything was dated and ugly, it was clean, superficially at least. He glanced nervously at the other occupants of the café. Had any of them spotted him? No one was paying any attention. Even so, he was glad he was wearing his black knitted hat, which he pulled down a little lower over his forehead. He didn't want to take any chances.

The breakfast was better than he expected, and he ate it all, even the toast and hash browns, which he usually wouldn't touch. Stephanie moved her food around her plate as though she couldn't stomach it, but once she got going her plate was cleared as quickly as his. She sat back sipping her tea, watching him. 'Do you... I was just thinking... if you need somewhere to have a shower, change your clothes...' She paused as though she was unsure about what she'd said, but having made the offer she couldn't take it back.

'I can't ask you to do that,' he said, smiling inside. 'Honestly, you've done so much for me already.'

'Well, you bought me breakfast. I'm just returning the favour.'

'If you're sure you don't mind,' Jay said, 'it would really help me out.'

'It's no problem. To be honest, I'd rather not go back to the house on my own.'

Jay smiled. *Jackpot.*

...

Stephanie's house was at the end of a row of red-brick terraces, on a narrow, congested little street. She just about managed to find a cramped parking space along the kerb, and he trailed behind her along the pavement, praying that they wouldn't encounter anybody. It was a relief to be inside, and he followed Stephanie into the kitchen at the back of the house, which overlooked a small concrete-paved yard.

'How long have you lived here for?' he asked.

'Most of my life. As long as I can remember, anyway.'

Jay only just stopped himself from raising an eyebrow. The place was a dump. It had to be decades since anything had seen a coat of paint, and the yard outside was downright depressing: bare except for an old shed, a washing line, and a single plant pot with a few fossilised leaves draped over the side of it. How did she live like this? The ugliness disturbed him, scratching at his brain, distracting him.

'Thank you so much for letting me come back here,' he said, as he forced his attention away from the yard and back to Stephanie. 'Once I've had a shower and put on some clean clothes, I can make a start on looking for a new job.' Of course, he couldn't really do that, but he was sure Stephanie would be impressed by his conscientious attitude. Realistically, he had no idea what he'd do once the cash in his wallet ran out. He couldn't risk using his bank or credit cards. But that was a problem for another day. He could only take one step at a time.

Stephanie showed him the bathroom upstairs, and handed him a fresh towel. 'If you need shower gel or anything you can use the stuff that's in there,' she told him.

'I don't suppose you have a spare toothbrush?'

'Probably. I'll have a look.'

He waited while she rummaged in a cupboard and then she handed him a bright pink toothbrush still in its packaging. 'Sorry about the colour.'

He smiled. 'It's fine. Thank you.'

She nodded and left him to it. Jay spent a long time brushing his teeth, and got tentatively into the shower. It had a shower curtain around it. He was squeamish enough about germs as it was, but the idea of using a shower in someone else's house, with a *shower curtain* around it, of all things, was almost enough to make him reconsider. What if the curtain brushed up against his legs, or worse still, stuck against his body? God knows what he'd end up catching off of it. But he could hardly go back downstairs and tell Stephanie he considered her shower set-up too gross to use. Besides, where else was he going to get a chance to wash himself?

He tried to be quick in the shower, breaking his normal routine of washing each part of his body at least twice, and he dried himself with an equal disregard for his usual lengthy hygiene procedures. He found some deodorant on the windowsill, which he assumed was Stephanie's since it was flower-scented. He sprayed some on anyway, and put on a clean outfit from his backpack. What should he do now? He'd have to leave – he couldn't justify staying in the house any longer, but he needed to come up with a way of meeting Stephanie again so he could build a relationship with her. It wasn't going to be straightforward, but it had to be his best hope.

When he joined her back downstairs, he could see by her face that something had happened.

'It's granddad,' she said. 'The hospital called and said he's taken a turn for the worse. I've got to go straight back.'

'Oh, I'm sorry to hear that.'

She looked at him. 'I… you're going to have to…'

'Yeah… yeah, I'll go.'

'I'm sorry, it's just—'

'I completely understand. I hope everything's okay with your granddad.'

'Thank you.'

She started towards the front door, and he followed her. 'Stephanie,' he said.

'Yeah?'

'I was thinking… if you need to get away for a bit, perhaps I could meet you at that bird place again. Tomorrow morning?'

Her brow furrowed, her mind clearly elsewhere.

'Only if you want to,' he said.

'Maybe, I… I don't really know what's going to happen right now.'

'Yeah.'

They stepped outside. He thanked her again, but she was already rushing towards her car.

Stephanie

4

Time passed in a blur. The next day, she forgot that Jason had said anything about meeting her until the morning was over and she was talking to her granddad that lunchtime, when he briefly seemed to have a little more energy. She told him about her meeting with the strange man at the nature reserve – not that she'd found him strange, really. He'd seemed polite and friendly; "gentlemanly" was the word she used to describe him to her granddad. She left out the part about him going back to the house to take a shower, though. She wasn't sure what her granddad would make of that. 'He wanted me to meet him again, but I forgot all about it,' she said. 'And I was here, I couldn't have gone. I don't have his phone number, so I can't call him. But anyway, it's not important.'

'Go there again tomorrow.'

Stephanie looked at her granddad in surprise. He was propped up with some pillows, and watched her intently from behind his wire-framed glasses. 'You've spent too much time not thinking of yourself,' he told her. 'If you like him, go and meet him again.'

'I can't think about him right now—'

'Some chances only come along once. You have to grab them when you can. If you want to see him again, I don't want you to miss a chance because of me.'

'But—'

'I'm not going to be around forever. I'd like to know you're not all alone.'

'Don't say that.'

After that he wasn't able to carry on talking with her. By early evening he had deteriorated further, and just before eleven p.m., he died; quietly, and it seemed, painlessly. She sat by his side for a long while, feeling tiny, lost, and completely alone.

...

Stephanie blinked in the early morning light. She was a day late for her meeting with Jason, and although logic told her he wouldn't be there at the 'bird place', as he'd called it, her heart said he would. Her granddad had wanted her to meet him again. Dating was hardly her top priority right now – she was washed out and disoriented with grief – but she'd become fixated on the idea of Jason: of meeting him in the place her granddad had used to enjoy visiting, and of her granddad's desire for her to not be alone.

The truth was, she *had* been alone apart from him. She always got on so well with her granddad – they spent hours talking about music and books, and watching TV and films together – and she'd somehow never bothered to look for any companionship elsewhere. She had some friends online, but "real" people were largely an enigma to her, and she'd never fitted in. Her granddad had told her so many times that she was young and had the world at her feet, but it had never felt that way. She felt old. She knew the world was there, but she didn't know what to do with it.

When she approached the same bench where she'd originally met Jason, she was stunned to see him sitting there again. She paused, overwhelmed with emotions: sadness, grief and loss as she thought of the times in the past she'd sat on that bench with her granddad, mingled with an extraordinary feeling of inevitability, of destiny, of stars aligning. Her granddad had told her to come here again, and he'd been right. Warmth spread through her body, as if her granddad was standing right there beside her. *He* approved of Jason. She was certain of that. As she approached the bench, Jason turned and smiled at her.

'I... I'm a day late,' she said as she sat down. She wanted to say more, to try to explain what had happened, but her words were stolen away as she let out a loud sob. Then another, and another. Tears rolled down her cheeks and she couldn't get any words out.

'Is it your granddad?' he asked softly. 'Has he...'

She nodded, and she was grateful when he put his arms around her. She let him hold her close, and it was such an overwhelming relief to have someone, anyone, hold her and comfort her. She let her tears flow, and he continued to hold her close to him, gently stroking her back. 'I'm so sorry,' he said. 'And I'm glad you came. You shouldn't be alone.'

'I don't know… what to do,' she said into his warm shoulder.

'I'm sure you don't need to do anything right now.'

'I feel so… I can't…'

'Have you eaten?' he asked gently. He let go of her, but he stayed close beside her on the bench, and she was glad. Strength seemed to flow from him, and some of it made its way into her. It stopped her from completely falling apart.

She shook her head. Food was the last thing on her mind.

'Why don't you let me cook you breakfast? I'm pretty good in the kitchen. So people tell me, anyway.'

'I need to call my work,' she said. 'Tell them what's happened. They've been so good with time off and stuff…'

'There'll be time for all that.'

'There's so much to sort out… the… the funeral… I need to tell people what's happened…'

'If there's anything I can help with, I will. But first you need to take care of yourself. I know you probably don't want to eat, but you'll feel better if you do.'

'I can't… I can't believe he's gone.'

She started to cry again, and he held her again. A sense of longing rushed through her, and without thinking she pressed her lips against his. He hesitated briefly, and then he kissed her back, softly, and tenderly. After a few seconds she pulled away again, embarrassed by her actions. 'I don't know what I'm doing,' she said.

He stood up. 'Come on,' he said, 'breakfast. Everything else will get sorted out in its own time.'

He held out his hand and she took it.

Jay

5

There wasn't much in Stephanie's house to make breakfast with, but she was barely in a fit state to pour cereal into a bowl, so he figured she probably wouldn't be fussy. He found some eggs that were still just about in date at the back of the fridge, and there was some bread that looked okay. He'd make fried egg sandwiches. That should make her feel better. Stephanie stayed in the lounge, and he was glad because he was starving and wanted to see what other food he could find. There were slim pickings, but he ravenously tucked in to an old banana from the fruit bowl and a strawberry yogurt from the fridge while he waited for the eggs to cook.

When he joined her in the living room with the sandwiches, she looked up at him with a faint smile. 'I told him about you,' she said. 'My granddad, I mean.'

Jay paused. She'd done what? His mind raced, but he quickly calmed down as he remembered the facts. Stephanie was clueless about his true identity, and her granddad was no threat; the old man was dead. 'Oh yeah?' he said.

'He told me I should meet you again.'

He sat down and took a huge bite of his sandwich. Stephanie picked at hers. 'Why did you want to meet me again?'

'What do you mean?' he asked with his mouth full.

'Don't you want to work things out with your girlfriend?'

Jay swallowed his mouthful of sandwich. 'Hell, no,' he said. 'If I never see her again it'll be too soon.'

Stephanie nodded vaguely, as though she hadn't really listened to his answer. Even so, Jay needed a strategy, and feigning indifference or even hatred of his "ex-girlfriend" was the best plan. It was all fictional, after all – he wasn't actually talking about

Felicity. Felicity wasn't his ex – she was his *current* girlfriend. It was just a case of getting her to remember that. His palms began to prickle, like his hands were desperate to turn into fists. *Felicity.* Anger overtook him as an image of her face filled his mind. She was smirking, taunting him, and he wanted to wipe the smile clean off her face. The little bitch, the little *slut*, how dare she? How could she leave him on his own like this? How could she *betray* him like this? But another part of his mind chastised him. *It's your own fault*, it said. *You made her scared of you. You made her stop loving you.*

He shook himself. He needed to snap out of these sorts of thoughts. He tried to find something else to focus on and settled on the television, which was on quietly in the corner of the room. Almost immediately the current programme ended, and the news came on. Panic rose inside his body.

'Uh... can we watch something other than the news?' he said, 'I find it kind of depressing.'

She pressed a button on the remote. 'I don't like it either,' she said. 'It just makes me worry about stuff.'

Jay finished eating, but Stephanie's plate was still half full as she took tentative bites of her own breakfast. 'I won't be offended if you don't finish it,' he said lightly. 'I'll make you some tea, if you want?'

She nodded and he went back to the small kitchen, where he rested his palms on the counter and took some deep breaths while he looked out across the yard. He didn't know for certain that his face would be all over the news, but it was a fair bet. God, this was a nightmare. He needed to stay here in this house, but with the television and the internet, could he really keep on fooling her? He hoped Stephanie truly meant it when she said she didn't like the news. Hopefully that would mean she didn't go looking for it online, either. Then, in a few days, maybe a week or two at most, his story would die down and he'd be a bit safer.

After drinking the tea he made her, Stephanie curled up on her side on the sofa. Jay sat quietly, not sure what to do with himself, until she said, 'Did you find any jobs?'

'Huh?'

'You said you were going to start looking for jobs, after you came here the other day.'

'Oh, yeah,' he said, quickly. 'Well, I tried. I went to the job centre.'

'I can't believe splitting up with your girlfriend meant you lost your job too. And don't you have stuff at her house – clothes and things? You can't have everything you need in that one bag. Do you even have your phone? You never gave me your number.'

'I left in too much of a rush. It got left behind.'

'She has to let you in to get your phone at least.'

'I'm going to let her cool off first before I go round there. It could take a few more days.'

'She sounds like a pain in the bum.'

Jay laughed, though in truth the questions were stressing him out. 'Pretty much.'

'My laptop is upstairs,' she said, 'it's in the bedroom on the left. You can use it to carry on looking for jobs, if that would help?'

'What will you do?'

'I think… I think I need to lie down, for a bit.'

She followed him upstairs, but she went into the other bedroom, which must have been her granddad's room. He considered following her to see if he could provide some comfort, but she seemed to want to be alone, so he went downstairs with the laptop and settled himself on the sofa. Then, instead of going on any job sites, he searched for his own name. Immediately he was confronted with pictures of his face. He clicked on one of the links and scanned the information.

28-year-old Jay Andrew Kilburn is wanted in connection with the murders of a 28-year-old man and a 16-year-old girl in the village of Tatchley. He is also wanted in connection with the false imprisonment of a 27-year-old woman in a house on the outskirts of Tatchley. Jay, who may also use the name 'Jason', is white, 5'11", of medium build, with light brown hair.

Kilburn has connections with the town of Coalton, as well as Tatchley.

Kilburn is considered dangerous and the public are urged not to approach him, and to dial 999 if you see him.

Jay sat back against the sofa cushions, cold, prickly fear seeping through his body. Why had he given Stephanie the same name he'd used before when trying to hide his identity? He should have realised Felicity would tell the police about that. He closed his eyes briefly, but then forced himself to continue. He typed in Felicity's name, but nothing came up. Was her identity being protected? How was that fair? She'd been spouting all her nonsense to the police, making it so his name was linked forever to all this shit, but he could bet she *wasn't* explaining that she had driven him to it herself. She was making him out to be the bad guy! Instead of saying how committed he had been to caring for her – to cooking and cleaning for her, providing for her and his unborn child – she'd dragged his name through the dirt. *False imprisonment.*

It was ridiculous. It was fucking ridiculous. And *he* hadn't killed Sammie, Mark had. Then Mark had tried to take Felicity from him too. Killing him had practically been self-defence! He hadn't wanted to do any of what he'd done; he'd been up against unbearable provocation from people who were supposed to care about him. He glared at the words on the page.

'This wasn't a one-way street, Flissie,' he whispered quietly. 'You made me do the things I did. *You.* It was *your* fault, and any other man would have acted the same.' He typed in Sammie's name, followed by Mark's.

A body discovered in Tatchley Woods is thought to be that of teenager Samantha Zara Haragan, known as Sammie, who disappeared from her home in Tatchley twelve years ago…

Mark Hutchington, 28, was found dead in Tatchley Woods, a short distance from where missing person Samantha Haragan's remains were discovered…

Jay looked away. He couldn't stand it, and he didn't want to read more. They didn't *understand.* Seeing it in black and white made him look like some sort of maniac. It was unfair. It was so unfair. A sound from upstairs startled him; sobbing, gradually growing louder. Quickly, he cleared his search history and opened up an employment site. He left the laptop on the coffee table with the page still open, to make sure he appeared conscientious if Stephanie should take a look.

He found her kneeling on the floor by her granddad's bed and crying with her face in her hands. 'Come on,' he said, helping her to her feet. 'You need to rest.'

Stephanie

6

The next few days were surreal. She was busy, yet at the same time the days were empty. With no normal routine, she drifted from one thing to the next; talking to various relatives on the phone, answering the door to the neighbours and friends of her granddad's who stopped by. She busied herself with funeral arrangements, and Jason helped as much as he could, though at her own insistence he stayed out of sight whenever anyone visited. She wasn't sure how to explain to people who he was and how she met him, and he didn't appear to mind keeping out of the way, busy emailing out his CV and filling in job application forms online.

The night before the funeral, Stephanie couldn't sleep. She got out of bed and paced her room, desire to be with Jason nagging at her, gently to begin with, then more and more insistently. She rubbed her face with her hands. What was wrong with her? He was asleep downstairs on the sofa – what was she going to do, barge in and wake him up? What for? What would she say to him? Eventually, the need to be near him became too strong and she slipped out of her room and made her way downstairs. She gently pushed open the door to the living room, and the light from the hall illuminated Jason's shape on the sofa, covered by a thick blue blanket. He shifted as she came into the room, and said, 'Steph? Is that you?'

'Sorry… I…' What should she say? She couldn't come out and tell him that thinking of him was stopping her sleeping. She'd sound clingy, desperate, or just downright weird.

He sat up as her words trailed off, and reached up to the light switch.

'I should let you sleep,' she said as light filled the room, revealing Jason's messy bed-hair and tired eyes. He didn't look like he wanted to be awake.

'Are you worried about the funeral tomorrow?' he asked.

She nodded.

He smiled kindly, and warmth spread through her. Coming to talk to him had been the right thing. He would know what to say to help her feel better.

'Well, I know I won't be there with you, but you will get through it,' he told her. 'It might not feel that way now, but you will, and then when it's over it'll just be you and me again.'

'It's… it's not just that. It's my dad. I thought someone might have been able to contact him. You'd think he would want to be at his own father's funeral.'

She sat down beside him, and he put his hand over hers. 'Do you have anything to drink?' he asked her. 'Alcohol, I mean. A little bit of something will take the edge off.'

'I don't really drink. Hardly ever, anyway.'

'This is a time when it wouldn't hurt, though, surely?'

Stephanie went over to the large teak dresser by the dining table. Inside one of the cupboards was an old bottle of single malt whisky and two glasses. She took them over to Jason, who poured a glass for each of them.

'We'll drink to him,' Jason said.

They made their toast, Jason saying her granddad's name, 'Roger Vinney,' while she said, 'Granddad,' and they clinked their glasses together. The whisky tasted utterly revolting, but Jason appeared to enjoy it. He smiled when he saw the disgust on her face. 'Not your kind of thing, then?'

She put the glass down and shuddered. 'It's like licking a wet bonfire.'

Jason laughed, and she moved closer to him. 'Jason?'

'Mm?'

'Do you… do you like being here with me?'

'What do you mean?'

'You're not just trying to get even with your ex, or something?'

'She doesn't know where I am. And anyway, I wouldn't do

anything I didn't want to because of *her.*'

'But… but you needed somewhere to stay. Are you—'

Her words were cut off as he kissed her, and her whole body began to tingle with excitement, anticipation. 'I wanted to be here,' he said, when they broke apart. 'I *want* to be here. You believe me, don't you?'

She nodded. 'Will you come upstairs with me?' she asked quietly.

'Steph, are you sure—'

'I've only done it once before,' she told him. 'I know that sounds ridiculous for a twenty-four-year-old. So I want…' She hesitated. 'Do *you* want to?'

He laughed, not unkindly. 'Yes, of course I do.'

'Do you think it's the wrong time for me to think about something like this?'

He put his hand on her thigh. 'No,' he said softly, 'it's exactly the right time.'

Jay

7

He'd been waiting for this moment to arrive. Not because he was looking forward to it, more because he wanted to get it over with. Neither Stephanie's body, nor her personality, had aroused any desire in him so far. She had a curvy figure, which was not his preferred way for a woman to look. He liked the neat, slim shape of Sammie, or the simplicity of Felicity's athletic body, whereas Stephanie's lumps and bumps left him cold. He'd been with women like Stephanie before, though. He'd had sex with women of all sorts of shapes and sizes, and he was confident that when it came down to it, he'd be able to give her what she wanted.

Sure enough, once she had undressed there was a certain appeal to her naked body. While a part of him yearned for a woman who looked more like Sammie, or Felicity, having sex with Stephanie had a cheapness to it, and dirtiness, that he enjoyed. It was like when he used to go out and pay for it – he certainly wasn't proud of what he was doing, or who he was doing it with, but that very fact ended up turning him on.

Afterwards, Stephanie seemed a little ashamed of what she'd done.

'You can still do things that make you happy, Steph,' he told her. 'If you feel like doing something, and it helps you feel better, how can it be bad?'

'I…' Her voice broke, and when she spoke again her words were rushed. 'I'm just so glad you're here!'

He held her close. 'So am I,' he said. He started to kiss her again, and she didn't resist. 'I want to do it again,' he whispered in her ear. She stiffened briefly, but then she said, 'So do I.'

...

Jay was both listless and on edge while she was out at the funeral. He prowled around the house, sometimes sitting and watching the news on TV, or reading about himself on Stephanie's laptop. It was reassuring that no one knew where he'd gone, but alarming that he was still being talked about. He needed a distraction. He'd helped Stephanie to clean and tidy the house the day before, as some of the guests would come back after the funeral, but he got out some cleaning supplies and gave everything an additional going-over. Cleaning always made him feel calmer.

He stayed upstairs in the bedroom while Stephanie hosted the funeral guests downstairs, though none of them stayed long. Once the house was empty she came upstairs and flopped down on the bed beside him.

'How do you feel?' he asked her.

'I don't know.'

'Did it go well?'

'I guess so.'

'And your dad? He didn't suddenly show up, or anything?'

'What do you think?' She sighed. 'He probably never heard about it. People did their best to get hold of him. They left messages, but all his contact details were old. I guess he's not interested in his family any more. He doesn't want to know.'

Jay stared up at the textured ceiling. The bedroom was hideously decorated, dominated by built-in cupboards which surrounded the bed. There was embossed peach wallpaper on the walls, and in the centre of the ceiling hung a velvety cream lampshade edged with gold fringing.

'Do you think he'd be glad I'm here with you?' he asked her. 'Your granddad, I mean.'

She fixed her hazel eyes on him. Strands of mousey hair hung limply around her face. She hadn't even managed to make herself look presentable for the funeral. If she just used some decent shampoo, blow-dried her hair nicely and put on some makeup, she would probably scrub up quite well, so why didn't she? Did she not know how? It was beyond him that someone could care so little about their appearance.

'Yes,' she said, in answer to his question, 'he'd be glad you're here. If there's one thing I'm certain of, it's that.'

Not long after, Stephanie fell asleep, so Jay made his way downstairs and opened her laptop. Soon he would have to think of a new lie to tell her. The ex-girlfriend thing had worked well enough for getting his foot in the door, but she'd realise eventually that he wasn't applying for jobs, he wasn't getting the jobseeker's allowance he'd told her he was, and he wasn't ever likely to start getting it either. He'd have to tell her he was on the run, but he couldn't tell her the truth about why. He had some ideas of what he could say to keep her on his side. Hopefully he'd got his claws into her sufficiently that she wouldn't be able to bear him leaving, and she wouldn't probe too deeply into anything he said. As long as he convinced her to carry on sheltering him, that was all he needed. Perhaps he could work out a way to earn some money and pay his way, as long as it left no paper trail.

As usual, Jay checked for any new stories about himself, Sammie, Felicity and Mark, but nothing had changed. He sighed. He shouldn't stay downstairs too long. Stephanie could wake up and come down any minute. He cleared his search history and made his way back up the stairs, but his mind was buzzing. Where the hell had Felicity gone? What was she doing right now? Was she thinking of him? He hoped she was. The injustice of it all made him sick. He didn't deserve it.

Stephanie stirred when he got into bed beside her. 'What time is it?' she mumbled.

'Half nine.'

'Did I fall asleep?'

'Yeah. You're worn out, I think. It's not surprising after the day you've had.'

'Hold me.'

He put his arms around her and she snuggled against him. 'You're not going to leave, are you?' she said.

For fuck's sake, what was with this woman? Right now he had no patience for her insecurity, her neediness. But he forced the irritation away and instead asked gently, 'Why would I leave?'

'I don't know. I just… I don't know.'

'You worry too much,' he told her. 'I want to be here. I'm not going anywhere.'

She sighed and he kissed her forehead. *Do you hear me, Felicity?* he thought to himself, willing his words to somehow travel from his mind to hers. *You might not be with me right now, but I'm not going anywhere. You and the baby, you're mine. You're my family. And one day, I'll get you back.*

Felicity

8

'Mummy!' Leo cried urgently, 'Mummy, ice cream!' His eyes were like saucers as he watched a boy and a girl walking down the pavement, each licking an ice lolly. The source of the sweet treats was a brightly-coloured van in the middle of the park, people swarming around it like wasps around a picnic. The size of the queue made my heart sink, but Leo headed towards it at a run, and I stifled a laugh. When I looked at him now, I could hardly believe that this energetic, bouncy livewire of a boy had started his life so tiny and fragile that I would sit nervously beside his incubator in the hospital, scared to so much as touch him. I'd gone into labour less than a week after escaping from Jay, so Leo had been premature. A little shiver passed through me and the bright park faded out of focus as I remembered those bleak days at the women's refuge and then the hospital.

There was a thud, followed by a high-pitched cry of anguish, shocking me out of my memories and back to the present. I ran over to Leo who was now face down in the middle of the path, stones stuck to his plump little palms, a small spot of blood swelling on his bottom lip. I scooped him up and cuddled him, but his tears soon dried as his eyes fixed once again on the ice cream van.

'What do you want to do now?' I asked once he'd finished eating and I'd wiped his sticky fingers. 'We could go in the playground if you like?'

He nodded, and held my hand as we set off towards it. I smiled to myself as we walked. We'd not lived in Alstercombe long, only a couple of months, but it was the first time in a long time I'd felt anything approaching a sense of wellbeing, of normality. Perhaps even a sense of belonging. After all, I had a job now, working part time as a receptionist at a dentist's, and Leo had made some friends at nursery. I could support us both, just about, and that meant the world to me. Jay had drained every last penny from our joint account while keeping me prisoner in the house in Tatchley. He'd forced me to rely on him for everything, and he'd taken my independence, my confidence, along with it. But I was getting it back, piece by piece.

I opened the bright yellow playground gate for Leo, who hurtled inside, and I followed more slowly. Yes, the little coastal town of Alstercombe was beginning to feel like home, but I could never entirely relax. Even here, I kept to myself. Almost as soon as I'd escaped from Jay I'd changed my name from Felicity Greenwood to Felicity Hart, dyed my blonde hair to chestnut brown and cut it short, and generally tried to draw as little attention to myself as possible. The police kept me in the loop about their investigations but it gradually became clear to me that they had nothing. The trail to Jay had gone cold. It had been over two years now, so unless he made a mistake or somebody recognised him, who knew how much longer he'd stay hidden for? The very thought scared me, so I tried not to think about it too often.

Having completed a quick circuit of the playground, Leo opted to ignore the shiny new play equipment, which had been put in only a few weeks before, in favour of the big sandpit around the bottom of the slide. I hovered near him, making sure he didn't go near the end of the slide as other children came down, and he contentedly picked up handfuls of sand and watched it fall through his fingers. He eventually tired of that game and made off to a different area, clambering up onto one end of a wobbly rope bridge, while another little boy was making his own way across. I could see what was going to happen before it did – the two boys, Leo small with fluffy blonde hair and a dinosaur t-shirt, the other a little bigger, with dark hair just visible under a bright blue sunhat, met in the middle and fell over each other in a heap, and both began to cry. I rushed over, and once the two boys were disentangled they sat looking at each other warily.

'Maybe we should go across one at a time,' I suggested to Leo. 'The other little boy was already on here.'

Leo frowned, and a deep voice from behind me said, 'Yours can go first.' It was the other boy's dad, and I looked round at him, a little startled, as Leo got straight back to making his way across. 'Thank you,' I said, and despite myself, I took a closer look at him. He was tall, his hair dark like his son's. He had a stubbly beard, and was very tanned. That, along with his outfit – a burnt-orange t-shirt, knee-length shorts, canvas shoes without socks – gave the impression of somebody who spent a lot of time outside, and I found that I liked that idea. Something about him put me at ease. He looked so comfortable with himself. He looked the way I wanted to feel.

'Fearless little guy, isn't he?' the dad said, as Leo negotiated the wobbly surface. I laughed. 'Yeah, aren't they all?'

'What's his name?'

'Leo,' I said hesitantly. I was nervous about giving out our names, even to other parents. 'What about yours?'

'Dennis.'

'That's a cool name.'

The dad laughed, and I smiled tentatively. Was he laughing at me? Had I said something stupid? I soon understood as he said, 'You learn to brush off the Dennis the Menace jokes eventually.'

'Ah, I hadn't thought of that.'

Leo reached the end of the bridge, and I lifted him down. The man helped Dennis up, and unthinkingly I checked his left hand for a wedding ring. There wasn't one. Suddenly, despite the warm day, I was cold all over. What on earth was I doing? What was I *thinking*? I couldn't be here talking to a stranger like this, letting my guard down. All of a sudden I didn't want to be there. I didn't want to be in the playground, and I certainly did not want to be talking to this man. Ripples of unease spread through my body, and I looked around me, feeling exposed, vulnerable. Was I about to have a panic attack? That happened, sometimes. Please, not now. I had to escape this situation.

'I think it's time to go home,' I told Leo.

'Not go home. Play.'

'We'll come another day.'

'Play,' he insisted.

I grabbed his hand. I didn't want to go into meltdown right here in the playground. Why wouldn't the man just go away?

'We need to be somewhere,' I lied to Leo. 'Let's say bye-bye, shall we?'

Eventually Leo relented and, in his grumpiest voice said, 'Bye-bye' to the man and Dennis.

'Nice meeting you and Leo,' the man said, and he looked straight at me. 'I'm Scott, by the way.'

Avoiding his eyes, I took Leo's hand, mumbling, 'You, too,' but I didn't give my own name. Before he could say anything further, I walked away.

Scott

9

All week Scott had been thinking on and off about the woman in the playground. Partly because he was a little worried about her. She'd been happy to begin with, and then she'd changed in a split second, turning nervous and uncomfortable. It had to be something he'd said; it was obvious she'd left because of him. She hadn't been at the playground long – he'd seen her come in, so he knew it had only been a few minutes. Normally he was good at putting people at ease, so it disturbed him that he might have upset somebody, even if he had no idea how or why.

Since he couldn't get it out of his mind, he spoke about it with his sister Natasha, who'd invited him and Dennis round for her twins' fourth birthday tea.

'You're worrying about a woman you met in the kids' play-ground last Friday?' she said to him. It wasn't so much what she said, though. It was the look she gave him.

'It's not like that.'

She gave him a little shove. 'Yes, it is!' she said. 'I've known you all your life. You can't get anything past me.'

Scott busied himself sorting out drinks and pouring crisps into bowls ready to take back in for the party in the living room. Natasha was still watching him. One of her eyebrows was raised, and she looked mischievous.

'You know you've got something in your hair,' he told her. It was the kind of thing he used to say to distract her when they were kids. Somehow, even now he was in his thirties, his big sister could still make him feel like he was about seven years old.

She was checking the ends of her black hair, which was tied back in a ponytail. He let her fuss around with it for several seconds before he said, 'Got you.'

'Oh, for God's sake. How old are you?'

He grinned and picked up the bowls of crisps. At least he'd got Natasha to change the subject. But as he turned she said, 'Perhaps she'll be at the playground again sometime. That woman you fancy. You never know, you might be lucky.'

...

He spent the rest of the day thinking about what she'd said. If the woman and Leo lived locally, they probably *would* be at the playground again sometime, though the chances he'd be there at the same time were slim, surely. But tomorrow was Friday, so he could go there at exactly the same time again, just in case. It was perfectly innocent, after all, just going to a playground. She wouldn't be there anyway, he was just being ridiculous. Why was he making such a big deal out of this? She almost certainly wouldn't be single, and besides, she'd left as soon as he started talking to her. She didn't even like him. She'd probably like him even less if he started bothering her again. He gave himself a shake. *Just forget about her.*

All the same, when Dennis asked to go to the playground the next day, he agreed instantly. Once there, he got stuck in with enjoying his time with Dennis, and when little blond-haired Leo ran over after a few minutes he looked round in surprise, trying to see where she was. She hung back a bit from her son, eyeing Scott uncertainly. She looked wonderfully summery, in a knee-length denim pinafore dress, a bright floral t-shirt underneath, and a pair of sunglasses pushed up into her short hair. 'Hello again,' she said eventually.

'I think Leo and Dennis are pleased to see each other,' he said, taking his eyes away from her to focus on the two boys, who had settled in to playing alongside one another in the sandpit.

'Yeah.'

She was twisting her hands around in front of her body, eyes flicking between him and Leo.

'I... I didn't say anything to upset you, last time, did I?' he asked before he could help himself.

She was taken aback. 'No, of course not. What makes you think that?'

'I… I don't know. Sorry.'

'I just had somewhere I needed to be, that's all.'

'Yeah, of course.'

The two boys went their separate ways and though he wanted to talk to her further, he had to go after Dennis. When he glanced around she was over at one of the pushchairs lined up near the gate, giving Leo a snack. He made a mental note of which pushchair it was. Before he left, he scribbled a note on a piece of paper, and slipped it inside the fabric bag hanging over the pushchair handles. Maybe the note would completely put her off. She'd probably burst out laughing when she saw it. He shrugged to himself. It had to be worth a try. He'd feel worse if he left without doing something.

Felicity

10

I sat down at the breakfast bar that separated the kitchen from the living room in my little flat, and read the note again. It was a phone number, followed by the words: *Scott Driver (the guy at the playground with Dennis!)*

I got up and took it over to the bin, but in the end I didn't throw it away. I folded it in half and put it inside one of the kitchen drawers – the one with the spare keys, box of matches, a few odd screws and other miscellaneous objects that were soon to be forgotten.

A week passed. I didn't call or text the number, but neither did I forget about it. On Friday I went to the playground at the same time again, and sure enough he was there. He looked a bit embarrassed when he caught sight of me, as though he wasn't sure whether to speak to me, so I made the first move. I walked over to him and said, 'I found your number. In my bag.'

'Oh, yeah,' he said awkwardly. 'I'm sorry if I made a mistake. I didn't even ask if you're with somebody. I've been a bit of an idiot.'

'I'm not with anybody.'

He didn't answer, and I tried to work out what to say, how to explain the fact I hadn't got in touch with him before now. 'There's nobody but me to look after Leo,' I said. 'I can't go out anywhere with you, if that's what you were thinking.'

His eyes lit up at the idea that the only thing holding me back was Leo's childcare. It wasn't entirely true, but I couldn't explain to him why I was so nervous around people, men in particular, not when I barely knew him. 'Well, Leo and Den get along together,' he said. 'Perhaps we could go somewhere with them during the day. Next Friday, if you wanted to? Have you been to Spingledown

Farm? They have animals there for Leo and Den to look at, and a nice café.'

I hesitated. I was deeply unsure, but equally, why had I bothered coming over to talk to Scott unless a part of me wanted to get to know him a bit more? I had to admit, the idea of having another adult to talk to, something different to do, another child for Leo to play with other than his friends at nursery, was very appealing. 'That sounds good,' I told him. Leo started to tug at my t-shirt, wanting me to go somewhere with him, so I said, 'I'll text you. My name's Felicity, by the way.'

'Okay,' he said, and he gave me a warm, genuine smile that I couldn't help matching. My eyes lingered on him, despite Leo's insistent tugging on my clothes. I liked looking at Scott, and talking to him too. I couldn't remember the last time I'd given a man a second glance. Mostly I tried to avoid interacting with anyone at all. He was also looking at me somewhat longer than was necessary.

Leo screamed, 'Mummy! Mummy! Mummy!' at the top of his voice. 'I… yeah. I'll message you,' I told Scott again, as Leo dragged me away.

…

When the day of the farm trip arrived, I woke up and a wave of nausea washed over me. I'd had a restless night, and my anxiety must have showed because Leo became clingy and unsettled as I gave him his breakfast and got him ready to go out. I'd told Scott I'd meet him at the children's farm at eleven, but as the morning progressed I struggled to finish getting Leo ready, let alone myself, until at half ten I was still in my pyjamas, my heart pounding. It was all too much. And yet, I'd be cross if I didn't manage to go. I'd been looking forward to it.

'Leo?' I said. He looked round at me from where he was stood in front of the TV watching one of his favourite programmes. When I didn't speak straight away, his eyes fixed on the screen again, so I knelt beside him. 'Do you remember Dennis? From the playground last week?'

He nodded.

'Do you want to see him today?'

He nodded again.

I took a deep breath. Leo would love it at the farm, and as for me, well, maybe I could just get ready quickly and treat it as a day out for Leo. I wouldn't put any pressure on myself over Scott; I'd just dress how I normally dressed and try not to think about him. I certainly wasn't about to put on any special kind of act for him.

I dressed, if anything, slightly scruffier than usual, in faded denim shorts and an old blue t-shirt that was starting to go bobbly. I surveyed my reflection in the mirror with mixed feelings. Was I subconsciously trying to put him off me? I wasn't sure what I found scarier: the idea of him losing interest, or the idea of him continuing to want to spend time with me. Whatever the reason, I had no time to change my outfit. We needed to get going.

As we left, I checked several times that the front door was locked, and then made my way out to the car park, awkwardly pushing the pushchair along in front of me with one arm and holding Leo's hand with the other. I was a few metres from my car when I stopped dead in my tracks. There was a man, coming towards me along the pavement. He was wearing a hat, and sunglasses, but there was no mistaking that face, the shape of his body. *Jay!*

My breath caught in my throat. I drew in air raggedly and painfully, and I darted over to my car and tried to conceal myself and Leo behind it. Tears stung my eyes and I began to shake. 'Mummy?' Leo said. 'Mummy?'

I peeked out over the top of the car, and caught sight of the man again, just before he turned his back to me as he waited to cross the road. It wasn't Jay. His face was nothing like Jay's, neither was his posture, the way he walked – nothing about him matched. It had all been in my imagination.

I turned around and sagged back against the car, struggling to hide the tears in my eyes from Leo. It wasn't the first time this had happened – when I got stressed, my "sightings" of Jay, or my suspicions that I was being followed, and the nightmares, always got worse. I clutched Leo to me and reassured him. I took my phone out to text Scott to tell him we wouldn't be coming, but in the end I found myself typing, *running late, should be there in twenty minutes.*

I put my phone back in my pocket. I was still shaking, but I was pleased with myself. I didn't want Jay to win. I didn't want to always have to be scared.

Scott

11

Scott was relieved when the text only said she would be late, not that she wasn't going to come at all. It had seemed like she might back out. He passed the time waiting for her by chasing Dennis around on the grass at the entrance to the farm, and when she arrived she looked tired and, if anything, a little unwell. Her hair was untidy, like she'd barely looked at it before leaving, and her clothes were scruffy. Not that he minded what she wore or what her hair was like, but he didn't want her to struggle through the day if she wasn't feeling well, yet also he didn't want to broach the subject by having to say she looked ill. He'd spent longer than he would care to admit choosing his own outfit, which was ridiculous since he didn't even have that many different clothes to decide between. She was hardly going to care what colour his t-shirt was, or which pair of cargo shorts he put on, but he'd agonised over it nonetheless.

'Sorry I'm a bit late,' she said. 'I didn't sleep very well, and the time just got away from me.'

'It doesn't matter. What do you want to do first? Den is desperate to go and see the rabbits and guinea pigs.'

'Okay.'

She was subdued as she walked along by his side. Had the whole thing been a mistake? Perhaps he'd got the wrong end of the stick, and she really did see it as nothing more than an opportunity for her son and his to play together. Once she got involved with looking at the animals with Leo and Dennis, her weariness, and the downtrodden expression she'd had, slipped away. When she caught his eye she smiled, a proper smile, not one she was just putting on for his benefit, and his heart leapt.

'So, you haven't been here before?' Scott asked as the two boys

44

watched the guinea pigs in silent fascination.

'No. I haven't lived round here long. Just a few months.'

'Where were you before?'

'I… here and there. I haven't really been… settled for a while.'

He was intrigued by her answer, but didn't press her further as a crease had formed across her forehead at his question. 'I've always lived in Alstercombe,' he told her. 'But when I get a chance I like to have a change of scenery. I do a bit of rock climbing – well, me and a couple of friends. We used to go places all the time, all over the UK, but since I've had Dennis I haven't done quite as much. I'm thinking perhaps I'll try and make it up to Scotland soon. There's some great climbing up there. I'm not a big fan of the cold, though,' he added jokingly.

She laughed, and then looked at him curiously. 'Don't you get frightened, when you're climbing?' she asked. 'I think I'd just freeze and not be able to move. I've never liked heights much.'

'Yeah, I get scared. That's part of it, though. Thinking clearly when you're under so much pressure, and then the feeling when you get to the end of an exciting climb, when the adrenalin has been pumping, it's like nothing else.'

'I know it's not the same thing,' she said, after a pause, 'but I used to do a lot of metalwork. I made jewellery, and other little things. While I was working I'd be concentrating so intently, all this time would pass, and then when I managed to achieve something really cool and I looked back at all the processes it took to get there, it was a great feeling. Not so adrenalin-packed as climbing, I'm sure.' She laughed suddenly. 'It's not entirely without risk, though. I burned myself pretty badly on a soldering iron once. I've got a big scar and everything.'

'So… you don't do it any more? You said you *used* to do metalwork?'

She froze, and a shadow passed over her face. Instead of answering him she said, 'How did you get into it? Climbing, I mean?'

'One of my friends, Martin, his dad was a keen rock climber. There's a big indoor wall not too far from here, so me and Martin used to go there a lot. I pretty much grew up with it, I guess. We both still go there now.'

She nodded, but he'd lost her. Something about talking about her metalwork had upset her, but he had no idea why, just as he had no idea where she had lived before she came to Alstercombe. She'd been deliberately evasive. It was odd, but he shrugged it off. There were things he wouldn't want to blurt out to somebody he barely knew, and that must be how she felt about him.

Leo and Dennis moved on to a rabbit enclosure, where they watched, entranced, as a large white rabbit made its way lazily from one end of the pen to the other. Felicity still looked unnerved, but then her face brightened and she said, 'You must know lots of people in Alstercombe then, if you've always been here?'

'Yeah, that's kind of an understatement,' he said, with a laugh.

'Really?'

'Nearly all my family are here, too: my sister and her family, cousins, aunts and uncles, plus my parents run a fish-and-chip shop in town. They get involved in all sorts of stuff in Alstercombe on top of having the shop, with the church and charities and things. Dennis is with his mum at the weekends so I help them out in the shop on Friday and Saturday nights, and I swear my parents know most of their customers by name.'

'That's so nice, though.'

'Yeah. It gets me a bit of extra work, too. I restore furniture, but my parents like to loan me out to people who want anything from a shelf putting up, right up to fitting a kitchen.'

She smiled, and then said, 'Which fish-and-chip shop is it? There are a couple in Alstercombe, aren't there?'

'It's the one near the beach. Driver's Plaice.'

'I've been in there. It's good.'

'My parents will be happy to hear that. I'll tell them when I'm next there.'

She gave him a funny look, and he got the sense she was going to say something, but Leo and Dennis had got bored of the rabbits, so their conversation was cut short as they followed the two boys to the next area.

...

The rest of the day passed quickly. He enjoyed talking to Felicity. She was friendly and funny, most of the time anyway, until she had these moments where she seemed strange – preoccupied, or perhaps anxious, or sad. His arm brushed hers by accident at one point and it made her jump, and somehow he found himself feeling guilty about it. Towards the end of the day, he tried to satisfy some of his curiosity about her.

'Is… sorry, it's just, you said you have no one to look after Leo except you. I was just wondering, is his dad…?'

Felicity looked up sharply. They were in the café, having coffee and cakes before they headed home. A crease formed between her eyebrows.

'Sorry, you don't have to—'

'No, I… I kind of wanted to tell you. I was going to earlier; it's just not a very pleasant topic. My ex… Leo's dad… I had a bad relationship with him. I mean, that's an understatement, really. He was very controlling, and jealous. I don't want to go into detail, but it's better if you know, I guess. I…' She hesitated. 'I'm finding it a bit strange, being here with you. I've not… I mean, I've been on my own ever since it ended with my ex.'

'Thank you for telling me.'

She smiled slightly. 'He's never even met Leo. I'm hoping he never will. What about Dennis's mum?'

Scott thought about Vicky, and how he could best explain their relationship. 'We weren't ever together, really. It was over before I knew she was pregnant. It's kind of strained between us, sometimes, but it works out okay, for the most part.'

'You said she has Dennis at the weekends?'

'Yeah, she works in a call centre in the week. Den goes to nursery a couple of days but the rest of the time he's home with me. I don't really have to do set hours, so I just fit work in whenever. I like it better that way; I was never really one for nine-to-fives.'

She glanced over at the two boys, who were making faces at each other across the table. 'Look at them,' she said. 'Leo's having the best time.'

'Perhaps we could do it again? We could visit somewhere else, or just go to the beach?'

'Yeah,' she said, 'yeah, definitely. I'd like that.'

Scott

12

Scott was in a happy bubble, until he dropped Dennis at Vicky's house for the weekend.

'Is it true, then?' she demanded, after placing Dennis down in front of the TV. 'You were out on a *date,* with Dennis with you?'

Scott stared at her. How on earth had she heard about it? 'Vicky…'

'Is it true?'

'How can you possibly know what I was doing today?' he said, annoyed. 'Sometimes it feels like you're stalking me.'

'One of my friends was at Spingledown Farm with her daughters. She called me earlier, and told me you were there with some woman.'

Of course it was one of her friends. They somehow managed to be everywhere. It was like she had a whole network reporting back to her. He needed to tread carefully. Vicky could be volatile at the best of times, and that was over everyday things. Scott hadn't been on any dates, let alone had any relationships, since he'd had Dennis, and he knew that Vicky never wanted him to start. Until now, he'd not found anybody he was interested in. Now that he had, the last thing he wanted was for Vicky to interfere and mess things up with Felicity before it had a chance to get started.

'It wasn't just me, Dennis, and her,' he explained carefully, 'Felicity had her son with her too. He's about the same age as Dennis, they enjoy playing together. It was… it was a play date,' he said, seizing on the idea with a hint of desperation. He wanted this conversation to be over. 'It wasn't a *date* date.'

'No.'

'What do you mean, no?'

Vicky put her hands on her hips and Scott steeled himself for a long argument. Her outfit – pink jogging bottoms and a black t-shirt with the word "relax" written across it in glitter – made a bizarre contrast with the furious expression on her face.

'I'm not having this, Scott. I don't want you seeing her again.'

Scott wanted to keep a cool head, but he couldn't. 'Do you know how unreasonable that is?' he exploded. 'You've gone on God knows how many dates since we've had Den—'

'So now you're calling me a slapper?'

He took a deep breath. He couldn't let her get to him. She knew how to press all his buttons. 'No,' he said. 'Of course I'm not. My point is, I don't mind what you do, Vix. I *want* you to be happy. But *I* want to be happy too.'

'So it *was* a date?'

Scott was silent for a moment. Admitting it would make her jealous, but lying would infuriate her. Besides, he didn't like lies. They never did anyone any good. 'I'm sorry,' he said, though the word grated on him. He wasn't sorry. 'Maybe I made a mistake. I didn't mean to cause all this upset.'

'Stop it!' she said. 'You always do this to me! You try to make it sound like *I'm* the one being unreasonable.'

'What do you want me to do, then?'

'You should know the right thing to do.'

'Okay, look, I'm not going to stop seeing her altogether. But I won't meet her while Dennis is with me. Not until I know if it's going somewhere or not, anyway. I only met her with Dennis because Den gets on so well with her son, they're friends. I'm not trying to confuse Den, or anything – to him she's just his new friend's mum.'

She was quiet, then she said, 'You're so fucking infuriating! What is wrong with you?'

'I'm trying to do what you want!'

'You're making it sound like you're doing me a favour. *I'm* not the bad guy here, Scott. I suggest you remember that. And I told you not to see her again *at all*. You're trying to get me to compromise.'

Scott shook his head helplessly. With Vicky, it was best to pick his battles. But he couldn't let her win about Felicity. Keeping Dennis and Felicity separate for the moment was doable. In many ways, it was a sensible thing to do. But he couldn't agree to stop seeing Felicity. And she had no right to ask him to.

'Vix, my personal life has nothing to do with you.'

'It does when it involves Dennis!'

'And I just told you I'll keep Dennis out of it. You can't ask me for any more than that.'

Her eyes glittered darkly, but she didn't say anything. He was far from reassured by her silence. His problems with Vicky went back years, and he had the feeling this argument was only the start of what was to come if he insisted on seeing Felicity.

…

'So, you're never going to be able to have a relationship, then?'

Scott looked up from his drink to his friend Martin, who had just posed the question. It was Sunday night and they were at the Royal Oak, where Scott met his friends for the weekly pub quiz, just as he had done religiously nearly every week for years. The quiz had finished and the others had gone home now, leaving just him and Martin. They'd moved to a quieter table in the corner, and Martin's usually jovial face had clouded over the second Vicky's name had come out of Scott's mouth.

'It's not going to come to that,' he said.

'Really? You think Vicky's going to suddenly change?'

Scott didn't answer, and Martin started adjusting the dark grey beanie hat that he wore near-permanently, whether he was indoors or out. Most people assumed it was a fashion choice, but Scott knew it was because Martin had started losing his hair from his mid-twenties, and was sensitive about it. He didn't really want to answer Martin's question, and he was beginning to regret bringing up the topic of Felicity and Vicky. The whole thing made his head hurt.

'Vicky's just… I don't know. Shocked, or something,' Scott said finally. 'She'll come round.' It was a weak answer, and didn't convince Martin for a second.

'If you believed that, you wouldn't look like you do,' Martin said.

'What do you mean?'

'I mean you look miserable.'

Scott nodded. 'Thanks for that.'

'Look, I know why you let Vicky do this to you. But none of the problems she's had have ever *really* been your fault. Even Tim's death—'

Scott looked up at him sharply.

'Well, that's what a lot of it boils down to, right? She thinks it's your fault that he died, because you were out climbing with him. But there's nothing you could have done to prevent it. Everybody knows that. Even she knows it, deep down, not that I imagine she'll ever admit it. And anyway, she needs to get over it. It's been getting on for three years—'

'You can't put a timeline on grief, can you? She calls him the "love of her life". You don't just get over something like that.'

'He was not the love of her life. That's complete bullshit. She says that *now*. But remember what she was like with him? She didn't treat him like he was the love of her life, she suffocated him. I don't believe she could really have loved him.' Martin looked at him closely. 'You should tell her the truth about him.'

'I'm not going to do that. It wouldn't achieve anything. It would just be cruel.'

'I bet you've been tempted.'

'Yeah. When we've argued, and she winds me up, but it wouldn't help. She probably wouldn't even believe me. She has this idea in her head about how they were going to live happily ever after. How could I walk up to her and say, "You know he was just about to split up with you before he died, right?" She's had a lot on her plate dealing with having Den while she's still grieving, and I was the one who did that to her. I'm not going to stick the knife in.'

'You can't keep beating yourself up about that. It was the fact that you were so cut up about his death that made you jump into bed with her, and anyway, it takes two. It wasn't only your doing, was it? You've always been a great dad to Dennis, and you've always been there for her. Don't keep letting her be so unreasonable. You're allowed to have a life of your own. Don't let her do to you what she did to Tim.'

'I'm just going to have to talk her round somehow, about Felicity.'

'What if you can't?'

Scott shrugged. He didn't know what he'd do.

'Well, it's up to you,' Martin said. 'But your eyes lit up when you told me about Felicity, so if you let Vicky mess it up because of all this crap about Tim's death, I don't think you'd ever forgive yourself.'

'It's not just Tim's death, though, is it?' Scott said. 'It's all sorts of things. It's like… I feel like I've always let her down. You know what I'm talking about.'

Martin drained the last of his drink. 'You're talking about ancient history,' he said. 'It's time to move on.'

Scott

17 YEARS AGO

13

'Did I say that you guys are my best, *best* friends,' Vicky slurred, trying to gather Scott, Martin and Tim in for a giant hug. Scott exchanged a look with Martin. It had been fun since they'd met Vicky a few weeks ago, but the way she'd latched onto them was becoming a bit irritating.

'Yeah,' Scott told her, carefully extricating himself from her grasp. 'I'm going to get another drink.'

By the time he got back from the kitchen, Vicky was looking distinctly the worse for wear. She was leaning against Martin on the sofa in the corner, though he wasn't paying much attention to her. She'd invited herself to the house party, managing to tag along with them like she always did, whether they wanted her to or not. None of them had the heart to tell her to leave them alone – she didn't know many other people, if any, and they felt a bit sorry for her.

Scott sat down on the sofa arm next to her. 'Are you okay?' he asked her. Her eyes were half-closed, but at his words she sat up and brushed some stray hair away from her face. 'I... I'd better... you know,' she said.

'I don't know,' he said.

'I need to get home,' she explained. 'I don't feel so good, and my mum... she's being such a pain. She says once I'm eighteen next month I can do what I want, but it's like until then she's trying to make the most of being a total bitch to me.'

Scott didn't reply.

'Can you... can you walk me? I feel weird. It's only twenty

minutes. We could… talk and stuff. It'll be fun.'

Twenty minutes each way. Scott looked towards the window. There was rain misting down through the streetlights outside. He was pleasantly drunk and happy to be inside the warm house. The prospect of walking Vicky home was not appealing, and her suggestion that it might be fun to "talk and stuff" did nothing to sweeten the deal. He groaned. 'Vix, come on. Just stay. What's your mum gonna do, really?'

She got up abruptly, staggering in her heels. 'Fine,' she said, 'screw you.'

'Vix—'

'Just leave her,' Martin said. 'She'll be fine.'

. . .

In his eighteen years of life, Scott had only been in a hospital once or twice. His palms were sweaty as he made his way through the corridors, Martin and Tim at his side, following signs to Vicky's ward.

'It's not like we knew she was going to get fucking *stabbed*,' Martin said under his breath to Scott. 'Nobody can really blame us, can they?'

Scott jumped as a door to his left opened suddenly, and he moved aside as a couple of doctors emerged and made their way rapidly down the corridor. He rubbed his sweaty palms against his jeans to dry them. What if those doctors had been called to go and help Vicky? Maybe she'd got worse. Perhaps she was dying! Martin was waiting for him to answer, the expression on his face echoing how Scott was feeling. 'It's not our fault,' Martin said again, 'is it?'

'I don't know,' Scott mumbled. He wasn't sure whether he was to blame for what had happened to Vicky. He'd been too ashamed to tell his parents that she had asked him to walk her home. Why had he been so lazy and told her no? If only he hadn't gone to the stupid party at all! He could have spent his Friday night helping his parents out at Driver's Plaice like they'd asked him to. Instead, he'd wasted his evening at what was, in reality, a pretty boring party and had woken up the following morning to the news that Vicky was in hospital. He'd stayed away initially – she was too ill for visitors and had needed surgery – but now she was awake. She'd messaged all three of them asking them to come and see her. Scott hadn't recognised the number; she must have borrowed someone else's phone.

When they eventually found her, she was lying on her side with her eyes closed, an untouched tray of food on her table.

'Should we… should we come back another time?' Tim whispered to Scott.

Scott put his hand gently on Vicky's shoulder and she opened her eyes. 'Oh, it's you guys.'

'Yeah, we… we wanted to…' He faltered. What on earth should he say? 'How do you feel?' he asked finally.

Vicky pulled herself up to a sitting position, and Tim helped her with her pillows and the controls for her hospital bed.

'So, how do you feel?' Scott asked again.

She fixed him with a glare. 'Like I've been stabbed.'

'What… what actually happened?'

'Well, I was at a party with my so-called friend, and he couldn't be arsed to walk home with me when I said I needed someone to.'

'I meant what happened with the…' Scott swallowed. Of course she knew he was asking about the attack. She was letting him know she blamed him. 'I'm sorry,' he said weakly.

'I don't remember it clearly,' she said. 'He took my phone. And he took my purse, not that he would have found much in there.'

'Vicky…' Scott said, but he gave up. What could he possibly say that could make up for her being stabbed?

'I thought you were my friends,' she said. She was starting to cry. To Scott's embarrassment, she lifted up her hospital gown, under which she was wearing nothing but a pair of underwear, and showed them all the big dressing covering the wound on her side. 'Look!' she said.

Scott exchanged a glance with Martin and Tim, who both looked as embarrassed, guilty and uncomfortable as he did. None of them had had to deal with anything this heavy before.

'You'd better go,' Vicky said. 'My mum went to get a sandwich. If she comes back and finds you here, she'll give you all a slap.' She fixed her eyes on Scott. 'Especially you. You're the one I actually asked to walk me.'

Scott's insides began to hurt. 'I've said I'm sorry.'

'Yeah,' she said. 'You can all fuck off now. I'm tired.'

Felicity

PRESENT DAY

14

When Scott sent me a message saying how much he'd enjoyed our day out together, my stomach filled with little butterflies. He suggested meeting at the beach at the weekend, while Dennis was at his mum's. I frowned when I read those words. Had something happened? He'd seemed keen before that we should all meet up again, Leo and Dennis included. I shrugged. It didn't really matter, and I quickly replied to tell him I was looking forward to it.

On Sunday afternoon the three of us sat on the shingle, Scott helping Leo sort through different pebbles and shells with genuine enthusiasm. I smiled to myself. I wasn't sure which of them was having the most fun.

'I think Leo really likes you,' I told him as he sat back down beside me.

'I like spending time with him,' he said. 'You know, it's funny, when I found out Den's mum was pregnant I wasn't sure what I'd be like with a little kid. I thought I might be a disaster, but I actually really enjoy it.' He grinned. 'Or maybe I just like having an excuse to do daft things and play around all day.'

I smiled as my eyes fell on Leo, playing a little way down the beach from us. He was bashing at the sand chaotically with a toy rake and exclaiming excitedly to himself. 'Not too hard,' I called out to him. 'You don't want sand to get in your eyes.'

Scott was watching me, and a shadow fell over me. Not because of his gaze, but because his experiences weren't much like mine. I loved Leo more than anything, but the past couple of years had been overwhelming and lonely.

'It's hard, though, isn't it?' Scott said. I stared at him in surprise, and he smiled. 'What I said just then – I didn't mean to make it sound like I find it easy or that things never go wrong. Any parent who says that is lying.'

A wave of relief washed through me at his words. I'd so rarely spoken to other parents. Leo was running around in circles now, stopping occasionally to scoop up some pebbles in his spade. 'It's… I think because it's always just been me and him, I…' I trailed off. What was I trying to say? There weren't any words big enough for the turmoil I'd been through since becoming a mother. Would he understand if I said sometimes I could barely remember who I used to be? That giving birth to Leo so soon after escaping from Jay had turned my world inside out and upside down? That I'd never known isolation like it, that once I'd left the women's shelter and started out on my own, I had no friends, no family, nothing but a tiny person who relied on me for everything at a time when I barely had any energy even for myself. Scott couldn't possibly know what that was like. He'd told me himself that he was surrounded by relatives and friends here in Alstercombe.

'Don't you know anyone round here?' Scott asked. 'Someone who could give you a bit of time to yourself every now and again?'

'No.'

Scott looked at me sympathetically. 'Well, like I just said, nobody enjoys it all the time, being a parent, and I only have Den part time. I can't imagine what it's like to do it completely on your own. You've done an amazing job. Leo is a great kid. You shouldn't beat yourself up about finding it tough sometimes. You should be proud of what you've done.'

A lump formed in my throat and I didn't reply straight away. 'It means a lot to hear someone say that.' My voice came out a bit squeaky. Scott moved closer to me, and hesitantly put his arm around my shoulders. I stiffened. Did I want him to touch me? I never let anybody touch me. The weight and warmth of his arm around me was alien, unsettling. I took a deep breath in, and out. He gave me a little squeeze and his arm dropped away again. To my surprise, I missed it. But I couldn't exactly ask him to put his arm around me again, could I? He probably thought I was odd enough as it was.

'So you really don't have any support around you? No one to talk to?' he said.

'It's just me and Leo. I've learned to rely on myself, after my ex. I have to… that's how it needs to be.'

'Yeah, I can understand that.'

'You can?'

'You had such a bad experience with him, of course it's going to shake you a bit. But… most people are good. I know that sounds a bit stupid, but I believe it.'

'So you're "good", are you?' I teased him. He grinned, and out of the corner of my eye I saw a blur of movement. Leo was hurtling headlong towards the sea. I scrambled to my feet and ran to catch him before he dashed straight into the waves. He kicked his legs and said, 'No, Mummy, no!'

'You can go in the sea,' I explained, 'just let me help you. We don't want the waves to knock you over.'

I held his hand and helped him have a little paddle. Scott was watching us and I started to smile back at him, but then I hesitated. His eyes were kind, yet they seemed to bore into me. I didn't like being watched like that. I felt like he could see right through me. Had I let my guard slip too far? I'd said things about my thoughts, my feelings. People could exploit that kind of thing. I'd let him reach in and grab a piece of me, and I never wanted anybody to do that again.

Leo started to cry so I looked down at him. The sea had come up over the top of his wellies and got his jeans wet. It was a summer day but it was cool and breezy on the beach, and a couple of big tears rolled down Leo's cheeks. I rushed back over to Scott, who stood up to help. He tipped the water from Leo's wellies and smiled at him. 'You trying to take half the ocean home with you?' He turned to me, but instead of smiling I said, 'I want to go home now.'

'We haven't been here long,' he said, startled by my sudden

change in mood.

'I want to leave.'

He frowned. Was I being over the top? Well, whether I was or whether I wasn't, I needed to go. My anxiety played by its own rules, and once it took hold, all I wanted was to hide away. Despite his obvious reluctance to leave, Scott helped to gather Leo's beach toys together into a bag, and he followed behind me as I walked back up to the road.

'Did I do something?' he asked me as I paused by my car. I held Leo's hand tightly, my cheeks beginning to burn. I'd made myself look ridiculous. Why couldn't I just be normal? His eyes were full of concern.

'Scott, I'm sorry,' I said. 'You didn't do anything. I have these moments, sometimes. Anxiety. I know it sounds daft and I feel embarrassed now. I think I'm just used to being on my own, and I… I don't know. I just freaked out for a second. But it's nothing you did.'

'Don't worry about it,' he said kindly. 'It doesn't matter.'

'It does, though. I am sorry, Scott. Truly. I know… it's not that I think you're like him. My ex, I mean, I just…' What could I say? I couldn't explain myself. I'd just unnecessarily marched us off the beach on some paranoid impulse and I wished I could turn the clock back five minutes.

'Well, I can go, if you want me to,' Scott said. 'Or, we could do something else instead. Once you've dried Leo off.'

I looked down at Leo. He was no longer crying, just staring longingly back at the ocean. I had spare trousers for him; there was no reason we couldn't carry on with what we were doing. 'Let's go back down to the beach again,' I said. 'I think I'm okay now.'

…

We spent another half-hour or so down on the shore, kicking a ball about and helping Leo paddle in the sea. Once Leo was tired out, we retreated to a small café near the waterfront.

'I should probably tell you,' Scott said, 'the reason I said we should meet on a day I don't have Dennis, it's because his mum realised I was seeing you. She doesn't want me to do it while Dennis is with me.'

I glanced up at him. He looked very troubled.

'That's a shame,' I told him. 'Leo likes Dennis. But I can understand her point of view.'

'So can I. I just didn't expect to have to talk about it so soon. It felt like all we did was go for a day out so Leo and Den could play together – it was all pretty innocent. But, I mean, I guess if we… if this might become a… thing, I should take it slow with Dennis. I don't want to confuse him and make problems between me and Vicky. That's her name, by the way, Den's mum.'

I was about to reply when Leo started to stick bits of sandwich onto my arm and I turned to him. 'Did you enjoy going to the beach today?' I asked him. He nodded, and went back to eating. Scott's hand was resting on the table. I kept looking at it. I wanted to touch him, but if I touched him, he'd know how much I liked him. Did I want him to know? It was safer if he didn't. But would I kick myself for not grabbing the opportunity? A small war sprang up inside my head, until finally I reached out just at the same time as he lifted his hand. My fingers landed on the table instead. I started to move them away, but he must have realised what I had been trying to do, because he put his hand over mine, and he smiled at me.

Scott

15

'I still feel bad, you know, about some of the stuff that went on with Vicky.'

At his words, Natasha looked up from the pan of pasta sauce she was stirring. In the living room Dennis, and Natasha's twins, Kathryn and Rory, were hurtling around chasing one another, and Scott was keeping an eye on them through the doorway.

'Is this why you were so desperate to come round and see me today?'

'Me and Den come round for lunch every week.'

'Not two days in a row.'

Scott didn't reply and Natasha rested her hand briefly on his shoulder. 'Look, I know yours and Vicky's... history, inside out. I know *your* side of it, I know *her* side of it, I know Martin and Tim's side of it. Yes, you made mistakes; some small ones, some big ones, some stupid ones, but she's made some pretty big ones too. You and her... I mean, if things hadn't worked out so tragically in a lot of ways, it would read like a comedy of errors. But you've never purposefully set out to hurt her. You don't have a nasty bone in your body. And if you're going right back to her being stabbed, I mean, a teenage boy feeling like he can't be bothered to walk somewhere in the rain, it's not the crime of the century, is it? You weren't holding the knife that night. And who knows, if you had been with her, that man might have attacked you both. It could have ended up even worse than it did.'

'You know it's more complicated than that.'

Natasha frowned, then turned off the hob and turned to face him. 'Is it because of Felicity? Is she why you're second-guessing yourself like this?'

'Her ex really hurt her. I don't know all the ins and outs of it, but the fact she's had such a bad time in her last relationship, it makes me wonder if it's going to do her much good to get drawn into all my crap.'

'It's pretty early on to start worrying about that, isn't it?'

Scott shook his head. It was early days, but he'd never meant for Vicky to know anything about Felicity yet. The fact that she did was forcing him to face these questions now.

In the living room, the children had all piled onto the sofa in a heap of arms and legs. 'I should probably…' he said, inclining his head towards the door.

'They're fine,' Natasha said, after she'd peeked around the door to see what Dennis and her twins were up to. 'No one's screaming or crying. So you can't get out of this conversation, not yet anyway.'

'She's invited me round for dinner later this week.'

Natasha beamed. 'Well, that's great! You're obviously doing something right.'

'Yeah, but other times…' How could he explain her sudden changes in mood? He was only just beginning to understand her himself. 'It's almost like she's scared of me,' he said.

'What… do you mind me asking, what sort of bad time did she have in her last relationship?'

'She just said he was controlling. I'm wondering if there's more to it than that, but she hasn't said. She's been on her own since she's had Leo, and she seems very private. Like… anxious, about getting to know me – or anybody, I think.'

Natasha nodded. 'And you think that once she realises Vicky is going to cause problems for you both, that might be a deal-breaker?'

'I've already told her a bit about it.' He made a noise of frustration. 'Man, I just… it's like, sometimes I wish I'd never met Vicky. I love Den, but Vicky, she just won't take her bloody claws out of me. She's just always… there.'

'When I heard you were having a baby with her, I'm not going to lie, I was absolutely horrified,' Natasha said. 'I could have strangled you for being so stupid. We all saw her suck the life out of Tim before he died, and I was so scared she would do the same to you.'

'Yeah, well, Tim loved her, at the beginning at least. I don't… God, I don't even *like* her that much. That's an awful thing to say, isn't it?'

A high-pitched scream rang out from the living room, and Natasha wiped her hands on her apron as she rushed to see what was going on. She wasn't gone long. 'They're okay,' she said when she joined him again. 'They're just starting to get a bit silly. I told them to calm it down or there won't be any ice-cream after their pasta.'

'Was it Kathryn who screamed?'

'Yeah. Rory sat on her. She's not hurt, though, and he's said sorry now. God, that scream she does, it makes my blood curdle. You'd think someone had let a pack of rabid dogs into the house.' She shuddered, and then fixed her eyes on him. 'Scott, listen to me. I know this all feels like a mess, but you'll find a way through it. Just like you did with Dennis. You proved me wrong about how that would end up, that's for sure.'

Scott remembered very clearly the talking-to Natasha had given him about having a baby with Vicky. Her words still rang in his ears now. She'd told him he couldn't possibly look after an infant when he could barely look after himself, that he was far too irresponsible and impulsive. She'd apologised as soon as the words were out of her mouth. She said she was just worried about him. They both laughed about it now, but it was the worst argument they'd ever had.

'If Felicity makes you happy,' Natasha continued, 'and if you make her happy, you'll find a way to make it work. I'm sure she won't be put off by Vicky any more than you're put off by her ex.'

Natasha turned back to the hob, and Scott peered around the doorway to check on the children in the lounge. Maybe Natasha was right. Maybe he was worrying about nothing.

Scott

14 YEARS AGO

16

Vicky clung to his arm with a force that showed she was truly frightened. 'Can't you wait a bit longer?' she said. 'We'll be back at mine soon.'

'I… not really, Vix,' he told her.

She looked around anxiously at the bustling shopping centre, shrinking away as some people passed close beside them.

'Perhaps coming here was a bit too much,' he said. 'It's good you're challenging yourself, but there's challenges and there's' – he gestured at their surroundings – 'this.'

She followed his gaze, her fingers still closed tightly around his arm. 'I told you, the wedding is today,' she said. 'I have to get something to wear to the evening reception tonight. I had no choice but to come here!'

Scott nodded, but he didn't necessarily believe her. It wasn't that he thought she was faking her agoraphobia. Her anxiety was plain to see, and he was sure that if he'd been stabbed in the street it would probably have a lasting effect on him, too. Nevertheless, he sometimes had an uncomfortable feeling that he was being used. There had been the time a couple of months ago when she'd phoned up in a panic because it was her mum's birthday the next day. Vicky claimed that her mum had asked for a specific necklace from a shop in the middle of Alstercombe, but she'd forgotten to go and buy it and needed to Scott to go into town with her, because she didn't like leaving the house alone. He was happy to help, until he discovered inadvertently that Vicky's mum's birthday had already been and gone.

Another time, she called him away from a date, saying that he needed to take her to the hospital because she'd cut herself badly while chopping an onion. Sure enough, she had a large cut on her hand, but when he spoke about it in passing to the two other women she was house-sharing with, neither of them could recall ever seeing Vicky cook anything more elaborate than beans on toast.

Today, Vicky had called and told him that she'd been invited at the last minute to the evening reception of her boss's wedding. She said she was desperate to go because she wanted to stay in her boss's good books, but that she had no smart clothes to wear. In other words, Scott had to take her dress shopping, and then accompany her to the celebration itself. He'd agreed – Vicky's job was very important to her, since it was one of the few things outside of her home that she could still do.

However, as Vicky walked around the shops, sticking close to him among the dresses and shoes, he had started to wonder. Had she *really* been invited to a wedding reception and given so little notice that she had to buy the clothes the same day? He wasn't against helping her to go out – she could just about brave going to the shops if she had somebody to help her – but was it really a coincidence that she'd called him just when he was supposed to be leaving on a trip to Snowdonia with Martin and Tim?

Her current distress had been caused by the fact he'd stopped by some public toilets inside the shopping mall and said he needed to use them. Vicky would have to wait outside on her own for him, and being left alone in a public place was something she couldn't cope with. She squeezed his arm, 'Don't make me wait out here on my own. I can't… I just can't.'

'I'll be, like, two minutes.'

'No, Scott.'

He looked at her, and the panic in her eyes made his mind up. He couldn't bear to add to her distress. He sighed. 'All right,' he said. 'All right, I won't go here, but we need to go back to yours straight away.'

She nodded and they walked quickly, making their way back to the car park. 'I couldn't have stayed any longer anyway,' she said. 'It was too much. I'm sure I've got shoes at home that'll look okay with one of these dresses I found. I would have liked new shoes…' She trailed off and then looked round at him. 'Are you mad at me for making you miss your trip?' she asked.

'It's not your fault. And I'm going to drive down and join the guys tomorrow, anyway.'

Was that a flash of disappointment on her face as she heard he would still be able to go? He didn't want to believe the whole shopping trip, and the wedding, had been a deliberate ruse. On the other hand, wouldn't he want someone to punish if he was her? Someone to blame? Not only had she had the ordeal of the attack, the agoraphobia that had developed a year or so after had consumed her life, and her world had shrunk dramatically. If he was her, he'd be angry too. But would she really put herself through a day like this just for the sake of messing up his plans?

They made it back to her car, and Vicky's face brightened a little once they were inside and she'd closed her door. 'I do appreciate you helping me,' she said. 'I feel so stupid that I can't just do things for myself.'

'It won't be this way forever. You're getting help now. It's a process, isn't it? Small steps. You'll get there.'

She gave him a strange look, and started her car.

Vicky

14 YEARS AGO

17

Back at her house, Vicky disappeared into her bedroom, telling Scott she wanted to try on her new clothes. Instead, she threw them down on the bed and sat cross-legged on top of her duvet. Her heart rate hadn't completely calmed down after the trip out. Shopping centres were one of the worst places; they were so big – big open spaces between the shops, the people rushing by her, making her panic. And they weren't easy to get out of quickly, that was the problem. Once you were right in the middle of a place like that, well, you were pretty much stuck. There was nowhere to hide, and it left her feeling completely exposed.

And when she started feeling uncomfortable like that, she was convinced people could see it. She could feel their eyes on her, and the breathlessness would begin, the racing heart, the shaking, the lump in her throat, the nausea, the tears pricking her eyes. She had to find a way out before she went into meltdown. She was always on the lookout for escape routes – she needed to know the quickest way out of a place and back to her house, where she could close the door behind her and shut it all out.

Having Scott with her was a bit like having an anchor. She could stick close to him, and she wouldn't feel quite so strange then, and her thoughts wouldn't run away with her so quickly. But he didn't want to always be helping her. He visited her often to check she was okay, but it wasn't like he was her boyfriend. He had his own life, and he was slipping through her fingers.

Not surprised he doesn't want to hang around with a nutcase like you, a little voice piped up in her head. *You're no fun to be around. Just hassle. What man would choose a woman who gives him endless hassle?*

'Shut up,' Vicky muttered under her breath, desperate to quiet the critical little voice that was her near-constant companion. She'd started this plan now – this made-up wedding – so she had to follow through. She put on one of her new dresses, a figure-hugging purple one that made her cleavage look amazing, and then she picked up her phone. She wasn't sure whether Scott could hear her, but she couldn't take any chances. It had to be convincing. She went through to the sound settings on her phone and played her ringtone for a few seconds, and then she stopped the sound and pretended to answer a call.

'*Really?*' she said after a few seconds. 'I'm so sorry to hear that. That's awful, I hope he's okay.'

She waited a few moments. 'Yes, please give her my love. See you on Monday, bye.'

...

She kept a close eye on Scott's face as she told him that one of her boss's elderly relatives had had a heart attack right after the wedding ceremony and the evening do was off.

'We could have a drink here instead,' she said. 'What do you fancy?'

Scott shook his head. 'I'll probably just get on the road tonight...'

'I'll go and see what I've got in the fridge,' she said, ignoring him.

'So,' she said when she came back, holding a bottle of vodka and two shot glasses, 'you never told me what you think of my dress.'

She turned from side to side, modelling it for him. He barely looked at her. How could he not be interested? She glanced down at herself, reminding herself that she did look as good as she thought she did. What the hell was wrong with Scott? She was putting on quite a display for him; surely any man in his right mind would at least *look*.

'I'm going to go,' he said.

She opened her mouth, and then closed it. Her cheeks flushed hot with anger. 'I'm dressed up now. We can have our own party here. Don't just run out on me, it's a Friday night, I want to have some fun.'

He was frowning.

'What is it?' she snapped. 'Why do you look so miserable?'

He took a deep breath, and her heart sank. This didn't look promising. 'I… okay,' he said, 'I'll be honest with you. I looked at your phone when you were in the kitchen, and the only call you've had today was when *you* called *me,* this morning. There are no answered calls on there. You told me somebody from the wedding phoned you. I heard you talking in your room, but… well, where's the call, Vicky?'

Vicky dug her nails into her palms. How could she have been so stupid as to think this would work? 'You went through my phone? How did you even get into it?'

'I've watched you unlock it before. I only looked at today's calls, nothing else, I swear. Listen, I had no problem with coming to help you today. But I… there never was a wedding, was there? You just didn't want me to go away for the weekend. Vix, you know I'm here for you, but I don't like being used, and deceived.'

She exploded. 'Do you think *I* can ever go away for the weekend? Don't you think *I* want to be able to go out with friends whenever I want, without a care in the world?'

'I—'

'I can't go anywhere!' she shouted at him. 'I wouldn't be able to go to a wedding reception even if there was one to go to! I could barely manage the shops today, even with you there. I felt sick. I thought I was going to pass out!'

'Was it worth it just to hurt me?'

'Yes. Because you did this to me! And I want you to see first-hand how shit my life is! I can't bear that you hurt me like this and yet I'm the one suffering. I'm the one on medication and having to go through all this fucking treatment, while you get to carry on like nothing happened. You can do whatever you want, whenever you want, and you don't even realise how lucky you are.

The only time I go out is to go to work, and I can only just manage that. It does my head in! It's not fair!'

'Vix, I… I'm going to leave now. I can't come round just so you can shout at me. I know you're angry. I also know this isn't the first time you've tricked me. If you *genuinely* need me, that's one thing, but inventing these errands just to call me away from what I'm doing—'

'Are you saying there's nothing wrong with me? That I'm just doing this for attention? My mum used to say that. You know what she used to do? She used to dump me in the middle of town, on my own. In the middle of all the people. She used to shove me out of the car. Said I was being childish. I thought I was going to *die,* when she used to do that. I had to get back to the house as fast as I could before I had a panic attack in the middle of the street! That's why I had to move out, to get away from the old witch.'

'I know. You told me she did that.'

'I'm supposed to try to face it, you know, the… the anxiety, whatever, but not… not like fucking *that*! She made me worse!'

'I know. I know, Vix.'

'Then why are you just fucking off? You did this to me, Scott! And now you can't even be bothered to spend any time with me.'

'Can you blame me? It's like you're using your phobia to score points, or something. I care about what's happening with you, but it's like you want me to suffer too. It's starting to really get me down. Perhaps that's what you think I deserve, but that's not what friends do to each other. Friends support each other, they don't try to drag each other down.'

'That's what we are, is it, friends?'

The look that passed over his face said it all. 'You don't even like me, do you, Scott? Why don't you just admit it?'

'All right,' he said. 'No. When you're being like this, I don't like you very much.'

'You better go then.'

'Vix, I don't want to leave you while you're feeling like this. We can talk about it if you want. Let's try and figure this out. I know you blame me for what happened to you, and I'm sorry for all of it, but surely you don't truly believe that *everything* that has happened is entirely my fault, do you? I mean, three years have gone by since you were attacked—'

She narrowed her eyes at him. 'The stabbing feels like yesterday to me.'

'Yeah, I… nobody expects you to just be able to move on overnight, that's not what I meant—'

She ignored him. 'So, you want to know if I truly blame you for everything, for all of it?'

He waited.

'Yes,' she spat. 'I do.'

He nodded. 'In that case, Vicky, I'm not sure I can be around you any more. This whole situation, it's toxic. I can't be part of it.'

'Fine,' she yelled at him as he made his way towards the door. 'Get out, then. You're pathetic, you know that? As soon as things start to get real, you just run away.'

He didn't answer. Once the front door had closed behind him, she sank down onto the sofa and swallowed a couple of mouthfuls of vodka straight from the bottle. *Look at yourself, Vicky. All dressed up to go out and you're drinking on your own on your living room sofa.*

Vicky let out a cry of fury. She'd show Scott. One day, he'd regret being so dismissive of her. She'd get better again, eventually, and then *she'd* mess up *his* life, and he could see how much he liked it.

Jay

PRESENT DAY

18

'Jason, I've been thinking,' Stephanie said.

Jay reluctantly looked round at her. He knew what this conversation was going to be about, and he didn't like it. After two years, she was becoming a problem for him, rather than the solution she'd been at the start. 'Steph, don't,' he said. 'Don't start all this again—'

'Do you really *like* living like this? Having everything in my name, pretending you don't exist?'

'That's the way it has to be.'

Stephanie put her empty dinner plate down on the coffee table and sat back with a sigh. They'd been eating their evening meal – fish and vegetables, cooked by him – in front of the TV. Stephanie complained about his healthy food sometimes, but she looked a hell of a lot better for it. She must have lost a stone at least, though to his bewilderment she said she wasn't particularly interested in weighing herself and didn't seem to care that much about her appearance. Jay did, though. She might look better, but there was still room for improvement.

She didn't reply to him straight away. Hopefully the topic was closed. He certainly didn't want to talk about it any further.

'What if we want a future together? A family?'

I already have a family. He put his hand on Stephanie's leg and gave it a squeeze, trying not to let his irritation show. 'Why worry about that now? We've got plenty of time yet, we can just enjoy ourselves.'

'Can we? You avoid going out with me, you only leave the

house to go running or when you're out in your van. *My* van,' she corrected herself. 'You can't even do a proper job. Moving people's furniture and clearing houses for a bit of cash here and there can't be how you want to spend the rest of your life. And as for your…' She struggled for the word and gestured vaguely at his face and hair. 'I can't remember what you really look like any more, and I bet you can't either.'

Jay tried to block her words out. He didn't want to think about it. He hated the way he looked now – he'd dyed his hair black, and bought a pair of glasses with thick plastic frames. He wore scruffy jeans, and cheap t-shirts with clichéd designs on them. When he looked in the mirror, he knew the person looking back wasn't really him, but he couldn't clearly recall his old appearance any more. At least, not unless he reread the old news stories about himself online, with his photo plastered at the top of the page in the hope that people might still spot him. He still checked occasionally in case there were any recent news stories about him, but there was never anything to be found. Presumably this meant the police were winding down their search for him, focusing on other things. He hoped so, anyway.

'Steph,' he said softly, 'this is our life. I don't know what to say to you. We can't change it.'

She looked at him meaningfully.

'No,' he said quickly. 'No, it's not an option, Steph. I don't want to talk about it.'

He stood and picked up the plates, but she followed him to the kitchen. In a fit of temper he slammed the plates down beside the kitchen sink. 'You want me to go to prison, do you?' he said, 'or to end up dead? Do you want to end up dead yourself?'

He glared at her, but she stood her ground. 'After it was all over, you could be free.'

'I'd never be free.'

'Why won't you even think about it?'

'Real life isn't like the movies. The good guys don't always win.'

Stephanie sank down onto one of the chairs at the small kitchen table. He stood behind her and started to rub her shoulders, but she pushed him away. He hovered by her chair, unsure what to do. Could he really not have come up with a better story to explain why he had to stay hidden? He asked himself this question frequently, always coming to the same conclusion. No, he couldn't have come up with anything better. There was only so much he could sugar-coat having to hide from the police, and he'd done the best job he could. He'd explained to her not long after moving into her house that Jason Marriot, the name he'd used to introduce himself, was not his real name. He'd never told her his real name. It was safer for her not to know. He said "Jason" had fallen in with the wrong crowd, got himself mixed up in some dangerous situations, and eventually he'd got in way above his head. Now, not only were the police after him, but also members of the "criminal gang" he'd run away from.

When he'd first told her, Stephanie had listened all wide-eyed, especially when he peppered his story with some gruesome details, claiming he'd witnessed the gang murder one of their members – somebody they suspected of informing on them to the police. She'd been frightened, and he told her he could leave her house if that's what she wanted, but he knew she wouldn't make him go. After her granddad's funeral, she'd come to need him and rely on his company. She barely knew anybody else in the world, and apart from her colleagues at Penny Pinchers – the discount store where she worked – and a couple of people she spoke to online, she had no interactions with the outside world at all. He also knew she was more affected than she cared to admit by the fact her dad had never made it to her granddad's funeral.

Their current argument – one they'd had many times before – was about him turning himself in, and trying to negotiate a "deal" for his freedom, or at least a reduced sentence, in exchange for giving up the names of people higher up in the food chain of the criminal underworld she believed he'd been tangled up in. Every time they argued about it he would tell her that he'd still end up in prison anyway, and that on top of that her life would be in danger as the gang would use her to try to get to him. So far he had always managed to get her to back down, but it was tough, and becoming tougher every time she brought it up. On top of that, he didn't have any more idea what he was talking about than she did. He might have just used the argument that real life wasn't like the movies, but the closest he'd come to organised crime was watching programmes about it on TV.

He sat down opposite her at the table. Time to change tactics. If trying to outmanoeuvre her in an argument wasn't working, he'd tug at her heartstrings instead. 'I couldn't live with myself if anything ever happened to you,' he told her. 'In all honesty, part of me *wants* to go to the police, to pay for what I've done in the past; because I've hurt people, I've threatened people. I've told you the kind of shit I used to do. And that's how I know what will happen to you if anyone from my old life gets even a sniff of where I am or what I'm planning. They *will* come after you, and they won't think twice about hurting you. And if, against all my better judgement, I did speak to the police, don't you think *they* will wonder where I've been all this time? The police were closing in on me before I left, they want to catch me, and if they do, sooner or later they will realise you were deliberately helping to keep me hidden. You'll get in trouble and I can't do that—'

'I've already got in trouble. I had to pretend that speeding ticket you got in the van last year was me, remember? I had to pay a fine—'

'A speeding ticket is a hell of a lot different to this. Do you want everyone to know you've been keeping me here? Imagine what people would think of you hiding a criminal in your house.'

'People *know* you're here, the neighbours see you sometimes—'

'They don't know who I am! And your colleagues at Penny Pinchers, they don't even know you have a boyfriend, do they? Imagine what they'd say if they found out what you've been doing! They'd think you must have been so desperate, to let me live here, that you must be so gullible, and naive. It's only us who know what it's really like.' He reached across the table and took her hand. 'Steph, I love you. You're the love of my life. Isn't that enough? So our lives aren't like other people's, but other people might not ever have the sort of love that we do. We just… there's a price we have to pay. You understand, don't you? I mean, what's the alternative? Do you want me to leave?'

'Of course I don't.'

'So… what do we do, then? We can't keep having this conversation. *I* can't keep having this conversation. It's driving me crazy.'

'I know. It's just… this situation, it makes me so unhappy sometimes.'

He went over to wrap his arms around her. 'I love you,' he whispered. 'I love you, Steph.'

'I love you too,' she said. His body flooded with relief, and also a little prickle of contempt for Stephanie. Although he desperately needed her support and love, her absurd belief that someone like *him* could love someone like *her* was rather pathetic. He was way out of her league. She was deluded. Her delusion served him well, though. He kissed the top of her head, and smiled.

Stephanie

19

Stephanie collapsed, exhausted, onto the bed beside Jason, and he grinned at her. She beamed back at him – she couldn't help it. She had to admit, no matter what other compromises she made to be with Jason, the sex she had with him was like nothing she could have imagined. He always knew just what she wanted him to do, and if there was ever the slightest hint of things becoming stale he'd coax her to tell him things she fantasised about, things she'd never have dared to say out loud in the past, and he would pretty much always deliver. She even loved the smug way he'd look at her in bed, as if he was congratulating himself on how good he was. He deserved those congratulations. Today he was giving her that look again. 'You know the neighbours can probably hear you through the wall. You're so fucking loud,' he teased her.

She gave him a little shove. 'I don't care.'

He began to get out of bed and she reached out for his arm. 'Don't go.'

'I won't be long.'

'It's late and it's dark,' she pleaded. 'Surely you don't really want to go for a run right now?'

He ignored her and started to get dressed in his running clothes, so she sighed and lay back down on the bed. This kind of thing was one of the compromises she had to make to be with him. Not that she minded him going running, but why did he have to spend quite so much time away from the house? Sometimes he was gone from early morning until late into the evening, and gave little explanation as to what he'd been doing. Some days he would barely speak two words to her from when he got up to when he went to bed. Even the sex – it was amazing when it happened, but was he into it as much as she was? Did he truly enjoy it, or was he ticking something off his to-do list, going through the motions to keep her happy? Jason was looking at her now, and he was annoyed. She avoided his gaze. Had her thoughts been written so clearly on her face? Sometimes it was as though he knew what she was thinking.

'It's not attractive, you know, trying to stop me going out. Being all needy. I've got to feel like I have my own life.'

Stephanie sat up, hugging the duvet to cover her bare chest. 'Sometimes I'm not sure how you feel about me.'

God, why had she said that? It was going to infuriate him more. Sure enough, he said, 'I tell you all the time. What do you want me to do?'

'I… I don't know.'

Jason looked at himself in the mirror on the back of the bedroom door, fussed briefly with his hair and put on his cheap black-plastic-framed glasses. 'I don't need this shit, Steph. I'm going out. I might be a while.'

…

The next morning, he was all smiles again. He got up early and brought her a coffee. 'I'm sorry,' he said as she sat up in bed and took the mug from him.

'For what?'

'For last night. I know perhaps I don't give you as much attention as I should.'

She watched his face closely. Did he really mean it? It was impossible to know for sure. 'We don't have to be in each other's pockets,' she said. 'I just feel a bit lonely sometimes.'

'I'm not used to it. To being with somebody. I've never been with anyone for longer than a few months before, and we've been together a couple of *years* now. I love you, but I guess I need a lot of space too.'

Stephanie nodded. He'd told her things like that before. She was never completely sure how honest he was being, though she tended to give him the benefit of the doubt when it came to his past. Or perhaps it went further than just the benefit of the doubt. Perhaps she was being wilfully ignorant, not wanting to press too hard, because she might not like the answers. She shook herself. She couldn't let her thoughts go too far down that path. If she started to question everything too deeply, she'd lose her mind.

'You need things as well, I get that,' Jason continued. 'Perhaps different things to me. We can meet in the middle. I'll try harder.'

'Well, Ellie, from work, she's having a party later this week. For her twenty-first. She's invited everyone from the shop, and their partners, perhaps you—' She stopped when she saw the expression on Jason's face.

'You want *me* to go out with a load of drunk teenagers?'

'They're not all teenagers. I'm not, Ellie's not. There are older people there too, like Rita. She's twice as old as me. At least.'

Jason raised an eyebrow. Stephanie knew what he thought of Penny Pinchers, with its shelves stacked high with budget merchandise and all the staff in their gaudy orange t-shirts. He seemed to think any association with it was somehow below him.

'Ellie only invited you because you were just promoted to supervisor and she's being polite,' he said.

'You don't even know her! You don't know any of them.'

'Whatever. But you know what you're like after a couple of drinks, you'll just embarrass yourself. Then the next day you'll be back at work with them again, and they're hardly likely to take you seriously once they've seen you making a twat of yourself.'

Stephanie's cheeks grew hot. 'You're just worried I'll tell them about you!'

'Steph, they don't like you. You've told me that yourself. I'm only saying what you already know.'

She was silent for a moment. Jason was right, she *had* told him that she suspected no one at Penny Pinchers liked her. They'd go silent when she came near, and she was the butt of every joke. It had been the same all her life, back to her schooldays. It was as though she had a permanent Kick Me sign stuck to her back. Being promoted to supervisor meant a lot to her, but was it just making her a bigger target? Even Jason's comment about her embarrassing herself had already crossed her mind – she tried too hard in social situations and people didn't like it. Ellie could well be inviting her in the hope she'd become the evening's comedy act. She was damned if she was going to admit to Jason that he was right, though.

But before she could say anything, he spoke first. 'I'm not trying to hurt you; I'm only saying this because I care about you.'

Stephanie handed her cup of coffee back to him. 'Keep this,' she said with a stab of anger. 'I don't want it.'

'Now you're being childish.'

'I thought you said we'd try to meet in the middle. So what is it you're trying to do now? You're allowed to disappear off all day and half the night but I always have to be here waiting for you, is that it?'

'We don't need other people. That bloody shop isn't good enough for you. You could do something better than trying to organise a bunch of losers like that lot at Penny Pinchers.'

Stephanie nodded slowly. 'How you can be so judgemental about people and places you don't even know anything about is beyond me, Jason. What right have you got to look down your nose at me, and the place I work, when you used to be little more than a thug?'

Jason's expression changed, softened. 'You're right. You are. Steph, ignore me, I'm being a dick. I just want you to be happy, that's all.'

'I don't... I don't actually *want* to go to Ellie's birthday thing,' she said. 'I don't like big social things; I'd rather stay at home. But you didn't have to be so nasty about it.'

He grinned. 'So stay home then. I'll show you a good time.'

'Okay,' she said vaguely.

'Okay what?' he said. 'Are we all right now? Friends again?'

'I...' She shook her head. She could never stay annoyed with him for long. 'Yes,' she said. 'We're friends again.'

Jason handed her coffee back to her, and she smiled despite herself. His moods were so odd. He got jealous and insecure so easily, and he'd lash out with his words. It hurt sometimes, but she was sure deep down he just wanted somebody constant and reliable; to make him feel secure and give his life more predictability. She liked providing that for him, even if he didn't really provide the same feelings for her.

Jay

20

Once Stephanie had gone out to work, Jay had a shower and got dressed, then sat down on the sofa, unsure what to do next. He had no jobs to go to, and though he kept his phone close by in case he should suddenly get a call, it wasn't likely anybody would phone up about a job they wanted doing that same day.

As was often the case at times like this, he ended up dwelling on Felicity. Where could she have gone? He regularly tried to find information about her online, but his searches were always fruitless. It was clear she'd deliberately made herself hard to track down – she didn't want him to find her. He closed his hands into fists. Christ! She didn't know what she wanted, or what was best for her. He knew, and he needed to remind her, but how could he when he had no idea where she was?

He closed his eyes and let his thoughts drift, and today his mind moved on from Fliss to Sammie. If he tried really hard, he could still remember the way her face had looked – the way it had really looked, in real life, not the way she looked in the news stories about her death, where they said what a wonderful person she had been, alongside photos where she had a smile plastered on her face and she looked posed and fake. *Her death.* A cold shiver went through him and he shook that thought away. He tried to remember her smiling at him, leaning in to kiss him. Then he winced as that image was replaced by another. Her face after he slapped her, when he believed she had been betraying him with Mark. There was blood on her lip, her eyes huge and scared.

Stop! Stop thinking these thoughts.

But more images came crowding in. Her blonde hair wrapped around his fist when he grabbed her by it. Her face turned away from his, eyes glistening with tears, as he lay on top of her, hurting her – *that's when she got pregnant. She got pregnant because you raped her. Just like Felicity.*

'No!' he shouted out loud. He put his hands up to the sides of his head, pressing his temples like he could squeeze the memories out. 'Stop it. Stop it!'

He ran out of the room and into the kitchen, where he turned the cold tap on full, collecting the water in his hands to splash on his face. The sensation of the cool water shocked him out of his cruel memories. Yes, he'd made a lot of mistakes in the past, but he would make up for it when he finally found Felicity. He'd show her he could be a good partner, and a good dad too. He'd be supportive, and loving, so much so that she'd feel guilty she ever tried to run away from him.

He went upstairs to change his t-shirt, which had ended up getting covered in water. He needed to get his head together, take things one step at a time. Trying to find Felicity was doing his head in, but he had to carry on planning for the future. He didn't make much money being a 'man with a van', and some of what he did make was spent contributing towards bills and keeping Stephanie happy, but he'd managed to squirrel away some savings towards his future with Felicity. For the moment he had to try to be content with that. Perhaps once he had changed he would go out to stuff some adverts for his services through letterboxes, try to drum up some more trade.

Just as he was pulling a clean t-shirt over his head, there was a knock on the front door. He froze. He hated it when people came to the door. If Stephanie was in she would always answer it, but when he was on his own he would generally ignore it and make sure he stayed out of sight. He stayed still, barely moving a muscle, though he was almost certainly being overcautious.

The person knocked again, and his pulse sped up. Surely they'd go away now? They knocked a third time, and Jay made his way slowly over to the window, which overlooked the street. He peered directly downwards, and though his view was partly obscured by the lacy net curtains, he could make out a man wearing a scruffy old coat outside the front door. He didn't look like a police officer.

Jay made his way down the stairs, and instead of going straight to the front door he crept across the hall into the living room, where he'd be able to get a better view by peeking out of the front window. But the man outside must have seen him moving through the frosted glass panels on the door. 'I can see you're inside. Please, I just want to talk.'

Jay frowned. 'For fuck's sake,' he muttered under his breath.

When he opened the door, he realised his initial assessment that the man was scruffy was putting it mildly. The man looking back at him was downright decrepit: the face underneath the hood of an old blue anorak had a yellowish hue, one of his eyes was bloodshot, and he had a bulbous, pitted nose that looked uncomfortably red. Though he was undoubtedly not a young man, Jay suspected he looked older than he actually was.

'Does Stephanie Vinney live here?' the man asked.

Jay's mind raced. Surely this man couldn't be... 'Who wants to know?'

'I'm Keith Vinney. Stephanie's father.'

Jay nodded slowly. 'I see.'

'Does she live here?'

'Where do *you* live?' Jay asked. 'Because you look like you're homeless.'

Keith Vinney didn't seem particularly offended or taken aback by Jay's comment. In truth, having resorted to sleeping on the streets more than once in the course of his own life, Jay wasn't entirely unsympathetic. But he didn't like being reminded of it, and just looking at the man was making his skin itch. He'd hated having to live like that. He wished he could scrub it out of his memory.

'I live the other side of town, in a flat in Graycott. I've not been there long.'

'Where were you before?'

'Here and there. Does Stephanie live here?'

'That Graycott estate is a real shithole, isn't it? That's what I've heard.'

Keith was silent, and Jay considered his options. It was time to stop playing around. He needed to get rid of Keith, and fast. And make sure he never came back.

'Stephanie doesn't want to see you,' he said. 'Ever.'

'I'd rather hear that from her, if you don't mind.'

'I'm Steph's boyfriend, and I've had plenty of nights listening to her crying over you, so forgive me if I'm not welcoming you with open arms,' Jay said. Of course, this wasn't actually true. Stephanie did dwell sometimes on her parents, but she'd maintained that she'd love to see her mum or her dad again, and that she'd be more than willing to forgive and forget the past. But Jay was damned if he'd tell Keith that. He might be able to fool a lonely girl several years his junior like Steph, but Keith had been round the block a few times. He'd see straight through Jay's lies if he got half a chance.

'I just want a chance to make things up to her,' Keith said.

'For whose sake? Hers, or yours? I mean, can you offer her anything? You don't look like you have much to offer.'

Keith shifted from one foot to the other. Had his face gone a shade redder? Maybe it was time to change tactics. If Keith took a dislike to him, he might keep coming round in the hope he would catch Stephanie on her own.

'Look, I understand,' Jay said. 'I can't promise anything, but why don't you leave me your details? I'll talk to her about it later. In the meantime, it would be better if you gave her some space. Let her decide when and if she's ready to talk to you.'

'If I could just—'

'She didn't choose to have you walk out on her, so give her the choice of when she's ready to talk to you now.'

'I didn't walk out on her. I was in prison.'

'Yeah, well, you didn't bother coming round after you got out, did you? It's been years, hasn't it?'

'I know I should have come to find Stephanie way before now. I… I didn't know how she'd react. I was a coward, I admit it.'

'I'll tell her you came,' Jay said. 'I'll talk to her tonight. Write your number down—'

'I don't have a phone.'

For God's sake. 'Fine. Write your address down, then. I'll make sure she gets it, and please, if she decides she doesn't want to come round and see you, just respect her wishes. She's been messed around enough in her life.'

Keith didn't answer, so Jay said, 'I'll get a pen and paper.'

He quickly grabbed them from the kitchen, and stood impatiently while Keith laboriously scrawled out his address.

'I'll try to persuade her to give you a chance,' he told Keith. 'I believe in giving people second chances.'

Keith's face brightened as he handed the paper and pen back to Jay. 'Thanks,' he said, 'thank you. I appreciate it.'

'All right. See you, then.'

Jay closed the door and looked at the piece of paper with Keith Vinney's name and address on it. He screwed it up into a ball. Why hadn't he just told Keith that Stephanie didn't live here? That would have been a sure way of getting rid of him. He immediately corrected himself. That wouldn't have worked. Stephanie might not have many close relatives but she did have some. They came to the funeral, they knew that Stephanie had inherited the house, and Keith might be in touch with them. He wasn't convinced Keith wouldn't come back, but he'd done a reasonable job.

He went into the kitchen and opened the bin, but his hand wouldn't move. With a noise of irritation, he closed the bin and smoothed out the paper. Stephanie would love to meet her dad. And despite conning her the way he was, he didn't *hate* her. He'd even go so far as to say he was fond of her. He couldn't tell her about her dad and jeopardise his own position, but he'd hide her dad's details somewhere. Once he found Felicity and was ready to leave, perhaps he could tell Stephanie about her dad then.

Jay

21

Later that day, when Stephanie got home from work, Jay couldn't resist bringing up the topic of her dad – not to tell her that he'd been at the house, but because he was curious and it was something to amuse himself.

'I can't imagine he'd ever turn up now,' she said, when he asked if her feelings were still the same. 'It's been a couple of years since his dad's funeral. If he was going to come any time, surely it would have been then.'

'But if he turned up, you would really forgive him for being out of your life for so long?' Jay pressed her. He'd always found her feelings on the subject mystifying. How could she have such a generous attitude towards a man who abandoned her?

'It's immaterial now, isn't it? He's not going to come. Why are you so interested all of a sudden?'

Jay shrugged. 'I've never forgiven my mum. And she didn't stay gone, she came back for me.'

He waited for Stephanie to reply, but she was filling the kettle and taking the box of teabags from the cupboard, paying little attention to him or his feelings. 'Let's get a take-away for dinner,' she said as she finished making their mugs of tea. 'Chinese. I fancy something different.'

'I don't.'

'Well, you do what you want. But that's what I'm going to have.'

She took down a menu that was stuck to the fridge door, and sat down at the kitchen table with her tea to study it. Jay was irritated. He wasn't sure what he'd wanted from Stephanie, but after her dad had turned up at the door, Jay had spent much of the day thinking about his own dad. While his mum had been absent, he'd had years to soak up his dad's philosophies about life, work, families, and most of all, women. Although sometimes Jay would wake up as a child to inexplicably find a woman in his house – though he'd rarely see the same one more than once – his dad was vocal on the fact that he hated women. Before Jay had even finished primary school, his dad had explained to him that women were not to be trusted, and if you started feeling anything for them they'd just rip your heart out and betray you. Jay understood that his mum's betrayal was more than just the fact that she'd left his dad on his own; it was that she'd left him on his own with the massive burden of a child. He tried to tell his dad he was sorry he'd made him so unhappy, but his dad said, 'It's not your fault. You didn't ask to be born, did you? But your mum *chose* to walk out on you. She *chose* to fuck up my life.'

'You know, perhaps you're too hard on your mum and dad,' Stephanie said, startling him from his thoughts.

'I'm not hard on my *dad*,' he said. 'Only my mum.'

'But like you said, she came back. You should give her some credit.'

Jay opened his mouth to argue with her, and then closed it again. What was the point? Did he really care what Stephanie thought about anything? Once his mum had come back, she'd tried to add some balance to the views his dad had given him. She'd been careful not to bad-mouth his dad, but she'd explained that she'd been very young when she'd met him, only sixteen, and he'd been twenty. She said his dad hadn't liked her spending time with her friends and family, and she'd ended up giving up her education, moving in with him and having a baby way before she could cope with that kind of responsibility.

'I never stopped loving you,' she told Jay over and over. 'But I couldn't look after you feeling the way I did, and there was nobody to help me.' She hinted at other things too, sometimes. She never came right out and said it, but Jay got the distinct impression she'd been frightened of his father. 'I shouldn't have left you with him,' she said once, but Jay had yelled at her when she said that, so she never said it again.

Grudgingly, Jay agreed to getting a take-away. He sat moodily in the kitchen waiting for it to be delivered, while Stephanie went upstairs to read a book. As far as Jay was concerned, Stephanie spent rather too much time doing stupid things like reading or playing games online. She liked such odd stuff, too. The books she read were all fantasy novels, full of strange creatures, magic and weird and wonderful places. Well, not wonderful. Just weird.

When the food arrived, she came down and carried it through to the dining table, busying herself collecting plates and laying out all the various containers. Jay's irritation increased the longer he watched her. He ached for Felicity and resented the presence of this poor substitute. Even Stephanie's clothes were driving him mad. She'd changed out of her work uniform and she was now wearing the top Jay hated on her most – a tight-fitting ruffled cream t-shirt. On a slim, petite woman it would probably look quite pretty, but on Stephanie the effect was alarmingly volumi-nous, the ruffles emphasising her curves and making her look like a giant meringue. By the time they were sitting at the table and she started piling her plate high, he couldn't hold his tongue any longer.

'Do you *have* to wear that?' he snapped.

She glanced at him in surprise. 'What do you mean?'

Her expression was driving him crazy; the innocent surprise at his question, her complete ignorance of the torrent of abuse he wanted to unleash at her. The vile words piled up at the forefront of his mind – he wanted to tell her how annoying, undesirable, boring and idiotic she was. He wanted to make her cry, to pierce through whatever shell of self-confidence she had left and make her feel like crap. But he held his tongue. She was just so *trusting*. It would be like kicking a puppy. A puppy that he needed in order to survive.

'I just… sorry Steph, I'm being moody. Ignore me. I'm really tired. I think perhaps I'm coming down with something.'

'What's my outfit got to do with that?'

'I just… look, that top, it's not my favourite one, that's all. But it doesn't matter, you should dress in whatever makes you happy, it's not about me.' He practically had to choke out those words. Of course she should dress for him; he was the one who had to look at her. But saying that would do him no favours at all.

Stephanie reached across the table and touched his hand. 'You do look tired,' she said. 'You should eat a proper meal for once. Get some carbs inside you. What harm is one take-away going to do?'

His eyes lingered on the trays of food, especially the noodles, the rice; the things he would normally never touch. He must be in a weakened state because the dishes did look appealing.

'Maybe you're right,' he said, and she smiled.

Stephanie

22

Stephanie lifted her head from Jason's chest and smiled at him. 'It was nice to see you enjoying food for once.'

He stroked her hair and she laid her head back down. After devouring the contents of every plastic container, they'd curled up together on the sofa and Stephanie had put on a film. Now it had finished, her mind turned back towards the meal, and Jason's odd behaviour.

'Why are you so... particular about things?' she asked him. 'Not just food, everything you do, the exercise, the cleaning and tidying?'

'I want to look good. And I want to live in a place that looks good.' She sat up, in time to catch him glancing scathingly around the room. 'Well, a place that looks *clean*, at least,' he corrected himself.

She followed his gaze. The decor hadn't changed since her granddad's death, so the room was dated, but everything was in its place, lined up and straightened, polished and sparkling, all courtesy of Jason.

'What's wrong with caring about how things look?' he asked her. 'It's not a crime, is it?'

She touched his cheek with her hand. 'No, it's not a crime,' she said. 'I'm trying to understand you better.'

'When things are messy it's as if there's all this noise in my head,' he said slowly. 'It can make me feel ill sometimes.'

'Do my clothes make you feel ill?'

'What do you mean?'

'You complained about my top, remember?'

'Yeah. I guess that ruffled t-shirt you've got on makes me feel a bit ill. It... how it sticks out all over the place.'

She smiled cheekily. 'Maybe I should take it off.'

'Maybe you should.'

They made love hurriedly, right there on the sofa. Then he pulled her down onto the carpet and they did it again.

...

Stephanie closed her eyes in pleasure as she bit into the huge coronation chicken baguette she'd bought from the sandwich shop next door to Penny Pinchers. She put up with Jason's healthy food at home, but in her lunch breaks – and on rare occasions like the night before when she'd ordered a take-away – she followed her own rules. A lump of chicken fell into her lap so she picked it up and ate it, and then rubbed at the stain. Jason would be driven mad by food falling on him and staining his clothes, but she shrugged it off, grateful that her work uniform was orange and the stain barely showed up.

Jason was strange about so many things. Why did he get quite so upset by mess and disorder? Had there been too many times in his life he'd felt out of control, and so he needed control now? She took another large bite of sandwich. Analysing people wasn't really her thing; it was easier to take people as they came and not dig too deeply. Whatever caused Jason to be the way he was, whether it was his personality, or what had happened to him in his life, she couldn't change it now. She could either take it or leave it.

She finished her baguette and pulled her current fantasy novel from her bag, but before opening it, she paused. Why was it that these lunch breaks were quite so important to her? It was beyond just a chance to take a break and relax. Beyond an opportunity to read her books. It was a little chunk of time when she could be alone with nobody *judging* her. *That* was the truth. *That's* why it mattered so much. It was a time when she wasn't surrounded by rooms scrubbed and tidied to within an inch of their life by Jason. It was when she knew he wasn't suddenly going to start criticising her, hurting her with his harsh words, or making her doubt his feelings for her. It was when she could truly be herself.

Is that how it should be? Shouldn't I feel I can be myself when I'm with Jason? An uncomfortable knot formed in the pit of her stomach. *It's not right. You know it's not right.* She took a deep breath. This line of questioning needed to be nipped in the bud. She couldn't go down that road, not right now. Jason might be odd, might make her feel uncomfortable sometimes, but she loved him. She needed him. He was the one person who'd been there for her after her granddad's death. She couldn't be without him. These doubts had to be swept under a metaphorical rug at the back of her mind, for the moment, at least.

...

That night she was woken by Jason feverishly moving around in bed, tossing and turning, muttering unintelligible words. She propped herself up on her elbow, watching him, wondering if she should wake him because he was so agitated. Her worries from earlier came creeping back into her mind.

Suddenly, he sat bolt upright. 'Felicity,' he said. And then he woke up.

Jay

23

Jay paused in the middle of pulling on his running shoes and stared at Stephanie in horror. 'What did you say?' he asked her, though he'd heard her perfectly clearly.

'I asked you who Felicity is.'

'Where did you hear that name?'

Stephanie raised an eyebrow. Shit. She must be able to hear the concern in his voice. He was making her suspicious. He had to get his head together.

'Last night you sat up in bed and said it,' she explained slowly. 'Don't you remember? You woke up and you were agitated, but then you went back to sleep. I was going to ask you straight away, but I didn't want to have a conversation like this in the middle of the night.'

Jay plonked himself down on the stairs. His mind was racing. What the hell could he say? He needed to answer quickly, so that she didn't suspect he was making something up.

'Are you going to lie to me?' she asked, when he didn't come up with an answer. 'Please don't. Just tell me the truth. Is there someone else? You're away from the house enough of the time, and I never really know where you are or what—'

'I'm not seeing anyone else.'

'Then who is she?'

Jay sighed. Then an idea struck him. 'Somebody I used to date,' he said. 'It wasn't particularly serious – at least, it wouldn't have looked that way to anyone on the outside. I don't think she was that into me. She can't have been, or she wouldn't have...' He let his words trail off for effect.

Stephanie came over to sit beside him and he shuffled up on the stair to give her room. 'What did she do?' she asked gently.

'Well, like I said, she obviously wasn't that into me. I guess I was more into her than I wanted to admit. I… I loved her. Not as much as I love you,' he said hurriedly, 'but—'

'It's okay. I get it.'

'One day I went round to see her. Her front door wasn't locked, so I went inside her flat, and I found her. She was in the shower, and my…' He broke off theatrically again. He was almost beginning to enjoy himself. Stephanie's brow was furrowed in sympathy. Or perhaps her frown was there because she still doubted him. He couldn't take any chances; he had to convince her. 'One of my closest friends was in there with her,' he continued. 'They were having sex. I was so shocked I cried out her name. I still dream about it sometimes. That's what I was dreaming about last night. I don't think I've ever got over it, not fully.'

Stephanie put her hand on his thigh. 'Why didn't you tell me about this before?' she asked. 'You've always said you've never really had relationships in the past.'

'Like I said, it wasn't really a proper relationship. Not from her perspective, clearly.'

'But it was from yours?'

Jay searched her face. She wasn't convinced. In the past she'd lapped up his stories about his former life, but this time he wasn't so sure. Was she beginning to wake up and realise he wasn't what he seemed? 'It wasn't just the fact she cheated,' he continued. 'It was the way they looked together, the way her clothes were thrown about all over the place. It had never been that… heated, between me and her. She was much more excited by him than she had ever been about me. I think that's the thing that hurt the most.'

Stephanie didn't reply. What was she thinking? Did she believe him? He wasn't sure. 'I need to go out,' he said, 'clear my head.'

She nodded. 'I'll see you after work, then.'

…

Jay made sure he went for a long run, venturing right down to

Wrexton canal. He jogged along at a leisurely pace, watching the water and stopping every now and again to cool off in the shade of the bridges that crossed over the path. It was a pleasant day, bright and clear, and he was glad that through luck he'd ended up in another town with a canal he could run along, as he'd enjoyed doing when he'd lived in Coalton with Felicity.

He began to feel tired, so he stopped and sat on a bench. He was still rattled by Stephanie hearing Felicity's name. If he'd said her name, had he said other things in his sleep too? There were worse things he could say than a name, far worse. Things that could land him in jail. He shook that thought away. If he'd said anything else, Stephanie would have told him – she wouldn't keep secrets from him. Hopefully his explanation was enough to put her mind at ease.

In truth, he'd been dreaming about finding Felicity – he'd seen her in the street right in front of him, so close he could touch her. That must be when he'd cried out, though he hadn't realised it at the time.

He put his head in his hands. The whole thing was driving him mad. He had to find Felicity, and sooner rather than later, or his dreams would probably keep on coming. Maybe they would get even more intense. Why had she made herself so difficult to track down? How could she prevent him from seeing his own child? Yes, he'd hurt her, but he regretted it. He wanted a chance to apologise. And anyway, shouldn't *she* take some responsibility for what happened? *She'd* badly hurt *him*. In fact, the emotional hurt she'd caused by rejecting him and messing with his feelings was worse than any physical pain he'd inflicted on her, no doubt about that. Cuts and bruises could heal up, but his feelings never would.

If he could just talk to her, he'd make her understand. But it was hopeless. Utterly hopeless. She was gone, and unless something miraculous happened… He sat bolt upright as an idea struck him. The corners of his mouth twitched upwards in a smile. How had he not thought of it before? He got up from the bench and made his way quickly back down the towpath and towards home, his body tingling with excitement. It was the best idea he'd had so far, and if it worked, Felicity would be his.

Felicity

24

'How about we go and see Scott?' I said to Leo. 'We can have chips for dinner.'

Leo clapped his hands together and said, 'Chips!' We'd fallen into a routine now of staying at Scott's flat over the weekend, and sometimes we'd go down to say hello to him at Driver's Plaice, where he worked on Friday and Saturday nights. Even though I'd done the journey many times before, when I started driving my chest tightened with anxiety and my palms began to sweat. This happened to me sometimes. Ever since I'd escaped Jay, anxiety and fear had been my frequent companions, but today was worse than usual. There was a white van a couple of cars behind and my skin prickled uncomfortably as it reminded me so strongly of him. *It's not Jay,* I told myself, *there are vans everywhere. It's not him.* Instead of easing my fear, it intensified as the van followed me at every turn I made. I couldn't get a clear view of the driver. My throat contracted and I struggled to breathe. I opened the window, hoping a blast of fresh air would clear my head. It didn't. In desperation, I pulled over, to see what the van would do. It sailed on by me, and I sneaked a look at the driver. It was a woman.

I shook my head, cursing myself for being so paranoid.

'This isn't the chip place,' Leo said.

'I know, sweetie,' I told him. 'We'll go there now.'

My nerves had mostly subsided by the time I parked on the street near Driver's Plaice. Leo scampered over to the door with me following on behind, and the warmth and familiarity of the chip shop wrapped around me as I stepped inside.

Spanning two buildings, Driver's Plaice had a small restaurant area to one side with several tables and chairs, while on the other was a traditional take-away. Although the green and white wall tiles reminded me of a public toilet – in fact the shop really should have looked ugly with its canteen-style tables, checked curtains at the window and old laminated menus – I found I loved being there. The place had an air of homeliness, and something about its faded charm was reassuring to me. It certainly didn't put off the summer crowds, who packed the place so full on hot days in July and August that the decor could barely be seen.

Scott's mum smiled at me from behind the counter. She gave Scott a nudge, and he beamed at me. He was busy with a customer so I sat down at one of the tables.

'Do you want the same as usual?' he asked when he came over.

'Yeah. Thank you.'

He hesitated. 'Is something wrong? You look a bit—'

I glanced at Leo and he followed my gaze, nodding as he understood that I didn't want to talk about it in front of him. 'How's it going, Leo?' he said. 'Have you come to get some dinner?'

'I've got lots of teeth,' Leo proclaimed.

'Is that right?' Scott said enthusiastically. 'How many?'

Leo bared his teeth and simultaneously tried to count them, touching each one with his finger. 'Lots,' he concluded.

The door opened and several people came inside, so Scott kissed me and went back behind the counter. 'We'll talk later at home,' he said.

. . .

'You're not losing your mind,' he told me when I finished explaining about the van, and said how daft I now felt about my fears. 'If I'd been through what you'd been through, I'd get anxious too. It's only natural. I mean, I've told you what Vicky was like, after she was stabbed and she was frightened of going anywhere on her own. She's a lot better than she was, but stuff like that, it leaves a mark. It makes you scared of the same thing happening again – it's only natural.'

I nodded uneasily. 'I know you're right. I get so frustrated with myself though. I thought... I want all this to be getting better now; the nightmares, the flashbacks, the anxiety.' I paused. 'He's always *there!*' I said, with sudden venom. 'He... he fills my head. He makes it so I can't even *think!* I want it to stop. I want to be *normal!*'

'You are normal, Fliss.' Scott said calmly. 'Perhaps it could be helpful to get some extra support, though, if you feel you need it. I mean, if you thought it was a good idea to talk to somebody, or something like that...'

'I did,' I said. It was true, I'd talked to a counsellor after escaping from Jay, but I'd given up on it almost immediately because I didn't want to relive my experiences. I wasn't keen to try again.

Scott didn't push it further, and I sighed and rested my head back against the armchair. We were in the living room of his flat – a cosy room, overstuffed with furniture as he couldn't help bringing pieces home with him from the small workshop that he rented. The chair I was currently occupying was an old wingback, reupholstered in jazzy bright green fabric with pheasants on it. He'd been intending to sell it but I'd persuaded him against it, and it was now my favourite piece of furniture in the flat, while Scott's was the enormous rustic dining table.

'I love looking at you sat on that chair,' he said. 'It suits you.'

I looked over my shoulder at the fabric. 'Really?'

'Yep.' He came over and planted a kiss on my lips. 'Beautiful,' he said.

'Stop being daft,' I said, though I smiled at him.

'You are beautiful, though.'

Out of nowhere, a heavy feeling settled in my stomach. 'Don't say that.'

'Why not?'

'I just... I don't like it, okay?'

'Because your ex made you feel like you're not?'

Suddenly, I wanted to be away from Scott. I got up and he touched my arm gently. 'Did I say something wrong?'

'I... no,' I said. 'No, it's okay. I'm just... I'm being silly. It's nothing.'

'Well, the thing is, I wanted to ask you something. Maybe this isn't the best time, but I've been meaning to ask you for days. I think I just need to say it.'

I smiled nervously. 'Spit it out, then.'

'Okay. What it is, I mean… I thought we…' He made a noise of frustration at himself. 'I want us to live together. All the time. Me, you, Leo. And Den when he's with me during the week.'

I opened my mouth but no words came out. *Beautiful.* The word kept echoing in my ears. Why did it make me so uncomfortable? Multiplied with his idea of us moving in together, with the van I thought was following me, it was a perfect storm. I made a little noise in my throat, but I still couldn't speak.

'It was a stupid idea,' he said, 'ignore me. It's too soon for us, please forget I said it.'

I tried to get past him, to escape from him and this conversation. 'Fliss, I'm sorry. Say something, please.'

'I'm all right.' I told him. 'I just want to… I need some space for a second.'

He let me go and I ran to the bedroom. My skin was crawling, and I only wanted to be alone. I curled up on my side, and closed my eyes.

Scott

25

Scott gave her twenty minutes or so, not wanting to intrude on her privacy, but he was going crazy. Had he messed everything up? Was she going to say she never wanted to live with him? Was she going to say it was *over?* 'Felicity, what's wrong?' he said, when he joined her in bed. 'Was it something I said?'

He expected her to refuse to talk about it, which was what she usually did, but to his surprise she said, 'You called me beautiful.'

'And that's... a problem?'

She took a deep breath. 'And then you asked me to move in with you.'

'Please forget I asked that—'

'Just listen for a second.' She paused to gather her thoughts. 'Jay would sometimes say I was beautiful,' she said at length. 'When he was trying to control me.'

'You think that's what *I* was doing?' he asked in horror.

'No, I... it reminded me of it. That's all. Jay would say it, and it's like he thought it justified whatever he was about to say to me. Once, he said it when he was talking to me about my jewellery, back when I was trying to turn it into a business. He said people would never buy what I'd made, and that when I wore it, it didn't do me justice. That it looked tacky, because I was beautiful and the jewellery wasn't. He tried to make it sound like he cared about me, but really he just didn't want me to make jewellery.'

Scott nodded. He was beginning to understand. 'But why didn't he want you to make jewellery?'

'He didn't like me having any interests that weren't him, or that took time away from me being with him. It's hard to explain what it felt like, when we were together. It was... claustrophobic. He didn't just want me in his life; he wanted my whole life to be his.

Everything else, friends, work, hobbies, anything at all, he saw it as a threat. I had to be wary of every word that came out of my mouth.'

Scott let her words sink in. 'That's not who I am,' he told her. 'I can't even imagine being that insecure. That *possessive*.'

Felicity didn't reply for a long while, and when she did, her words surprised him. 'I'm not against it,' she said, 'us living together. When it feels right. But I need to be sure, and I don't feel sure yet.'

He nodded. 'Thank you for telling me that stuff about Jay.'

'I had to try to understand him in order to survive,' she said. 'I had to see the patterns in his behaviour, so that I'd know what to say to him. You're right about him being insecure. Everything I did that wasn't with him seemed to hurt him. And everything I said that he didn't want to hear. And if he felt hurt, he...' She trailed off.

'That's when he'd hurt you.'

They were silent for a long while, and then an idea occurred to him. 'How do you feel about coming to meet a few more of my friends?' he asked. 'At the pub quiz tomorrow night? Everyone would love to see you. Natasha can come round and babysit Leo, and Dennis will still be with Vicky.'

She hesitated. 'Leo doesn't really know Natasha that well.'

'We wouldn't have to stay late. We can leave really early if you want to.' He studied her face. She worried about Leo, understandably, and he was asking a big thing from her.

'So it would just be me and a whole bunch of guys?'

'I'd let the guys know to bring their other halves. Those that have them, anyway.'

'How many people would that be, then?'

He did a quick count in his head. 'Depends if everyone can make it. Could be anything from six or seven up to fourteen or so. We'd maybe have to split into two teams.'

Felicity didn't answer.

'I'd make sure we didn't end up on different teams,' he said lightly, though he knew that wasn't really what she was worried about.

'Okay, I… well, maybe. It does sound fun. I'd like to meet more of your friends, but my head's spinning right now. I think I just need a good night's sleep.'

…

The next day he was delighted when Felicity told him she'd like to come along to the pub quiz. She was initially nervous about leaving Leo with Natasha, but once they left his flat she brightened up and the evening passed quickly and enjoyably, Felicity impressing everybody by providing several of the answers to the music round, until it got to eleven and they started walking back home.

'You were great tonight,' he said.

'What do you mean?'

'You knew the names of all those songs.'

'Oh that,' she said with a laugh. 'It's probably all the time I used to spend with my dad in his workshop, listening to the radio while we worked on stuff. He always used to sing along, even to the cheesiest tunes. Whenever I hear Dolly Parton, I can almost hear him rumbling away her lyrics in his deep voice – it takes me right back. I like remembering those times. Well, it's a bittersweet feeling, because it reminds me how much I miss him. But hearing those songs tonight with so many friendly faces around me, I don't feel so alone any more.' She linked her arm through his and smiled at him. 'I had a really good time tonight. I'm so glad you suggested it, and it was nice to meet your friends.'

'I'd love to meet some of yours one day,' he said, without thinking. He could kick himself. He knew why that couldn't happen. 'I don't know why I said that,' he told her. 'I know you don't want to contact anyone from your life before. Anyone who Jay might pressure to tell him where you are.'

She nodded. Not for the first time, he got the sense that there was even more to her history with Jay than what she'd told him. In truth, she'd never told him much. She always spoke in very general terms. Once their relationship started getting more serious, she'd confided in him that on top of being controlling and emotionally abusive, Jay had been physically and sexually violent. She'd never given any explicit details of anything he'd done – her opening up about how he'd reacted to her jewellery-making was as close as she'd ever come to describing a specific moment in her relationship with Jay. He couldn't blame her for not wanting to relive it. But was there something beyond that? Did she believe that her dealings with Jay weren't over? That was the impression he got at times, and it unnerved him.

They weren't far from home when his phone rang, and he sighed when he saw Vicky's name.

He answered it, and Vicky's loud, panicky voice filled his ear. 'You need to come round right now! It's Dennis, he's ill, he's really ill…'

'What do you mean? What's wrong with him?'

'I don't know. I don't know! Just… just come round.'

'I'm on my way,' he told her. 'Have you called—'

Vicky hung up and Scott stared at Felicity. 'She said Den is really sick. I need to go and help.'

'Did she say what's wrong?'

'No,' he said, struggling to gather his thoughts. Vicky's home was about fifteen minutes' walk away – less if he ran, which he was planning to – but it was in the opposite direction to his own flat. Felicity would have to walk back on her own.

'Don't worry about me,' she said. 'Go to Dennis. I'll be all right, it will only take me a few minutes to get back.'

Despite her words, her true feelings were written all over her face. She was frightened. 'Fliss, I don't want you to walk on your own,' he said.

'You need to go to your son. Has she called an ambulance? If he's that sick…'

'I don't know. She hung up before I could ask. She's not good with things like this.'

'Go to your son,' Felicity said. 'Don't worry about me. I can walk on my own. I can.'

'Text me as soon as you get inside,' he said. 'Vicky could be exaggerating about Den, she's done that before, but I need to see him for myself, check he's all right.'

'Go,' she said. 'Now.'

Scott didn't need telling again. He turned around and started off at a sprint towards Vicky's house.

Felicity

26

The darkness and my sudden aloneness descended on me like a dense fog. As Scott's figure disappeared in the distance, I made my way quickly down the pavement. It was a well-lit street, but I found it difficult enough to walk around during the day sometimes, so at this time of night it felt like evil could be lurking in every shadow. I sped up, my flat ballet pumps making a light pattering noise as I moved at a near run.

I turned a corner, and started down the next street. I was close now, very close. A couple more minutes and I'd be inside Scott's flat, where Natasha would be waiting and Leo would be safely tucked up in bed. A cat ran out onto the path, startling me, and I tripped on a paving stone which sent a shooting pain through my ankle. I cried out, struggling to get back on my feet, then I froze. There was a man beside me. He held out his hand. He was saying something, but I couldn't make sense of the words. It was Jay! I scrambled away from him. 'Don't touch me!' I said. 'Don't touch me, don't touch me!'

I backed into a low garden wall, almost falling over it into the flowerbed, but somehow keeping my balance. Where could I go now? Running was hopeless, Jay was too fast. My blood turned to ice and I braced myself for him to yell at me, to grab my arm, or my hair... but then the illusion fell away. The man in front of me was not Jay. He didn't look like Jay at all.

'Are you all right?' he asked. 'Do you need help?'

I shook my head, angry at myself. 'Sorry,' I muttered. 'I'm sorry, I thought you were someone...' I didn't finish the sentence. I crossed the road at a near run, the pain in my ankle now forgotten, and covered the final metres to Scott's flat. I ran up the stairs to the front door and when Natasha came to greet me in the hall, I practically fell into her arms.

'Felicity? What on earth's happened? Are you okay? Where's Scott?'

'He had to go to Vicky, she said Dennis is sick. I thought… I thought I saw Jay…'

Natasha let go of me to lock the door carefully behind me, and she watched as I obsessively checked it a couple of times.

'*Thought* you saw, or *did* see?'

'It wasn't him. It was just a man trying to be kind to me. I hurt my ankle tripping over a paving slab…'

'Come inside and sit down—'

'He looked *nothing* like him, Natasha! The man – he looked nothing like Jay at all! But I still saw him, I *saw* Jay. I'm losing my mind. I'm losing my mind!'

Natasha led me through to the living room and we sat together on the sofa.

'So Vicky said Dennis is ill?' she asked me.

'Yeah,' I said, trying to remember the conversation Scott had been having on the phone. 'I'm not sure what's wrong with him. It sounded like Vicky was really worried.'

I couldn't read Natasha's expression. She didn't appear unduly concerned about Dennis's condition. 'Funny timing,' she said.

I frowned. What did she mean by that? I didn't have enough mental energy to try to figure it out. In fact, I couldn't concentrate on her very well at all. My head was all over the place and my hands were shaking. 'Is Leo okay?' I asked.

'Yes, he's fine. He slept all evening.'

I nodded. 'Sorry, Natasha, I…'

'It's no problem.'

'I feel ridiculous!' I cried, emotion overwhelming me. 'I can't believe I thought some stranger in the street was Jay.'

'Well, it's dark outside, you've had a few drinks, and you were rattled by Scott having to go off like that. Your mind showed you what you were afraid of rather than what was really there.'

'I know you're right,' I said, 'but I feel like I'm getting worse. I thought being with Scott would help, but I feel even more anxious.

I sometimes… I sometimes wonder whether I'm doing the right thing.'

Natasha looked at me kindly. She was a calming person to be with. Sensible, patient and practical, she never lost her cool, even with her young twins, who could be demanding at times. She looked a lot like Scott with her dark hair, and a slightly mischievous look to her face when she smiled. She dressed a bit like him too, always in clothes that looked like she was about to dash off for a hike or some other outdoor adventure. She rarely wore makeup or jewellery, apart from the small, plain gold band of her wedding ring.

'Only you know whether you're doing the right thing,' she told me. 'But a new relationship is a big deal. Even good things can be stressful – it's a change in your life, when you've got used to relying on yourself. I know I'm biased, but you honestly can trust Scott. He's crazy about you. I'm not saying he's perfect, nobody is, but his heart is in the right place. He's kind, and he loves you and Leo. I don't think I've ever seen him as excited as when he told me about this house he's found.'

I stared at her blankly. 'What?'

She looked surprised, then concerned. 'He… hasn't told you about the house?' She didn't give me a chance to answer before she continued. 'He maybe thought it was too soon. Sorry, Fliss, I've put my foot in it, haven't I?'

Ripples of unease spread through me. What house? Scott had talked about living together, but he hadn't said anything about a *house*. Had he already found somewhere he wanted us to move to? Why was Scott talking about his plans to Natasha behind my back? What else did they talk about? I began fidgeting around with my hands in my lap as I considered the other thing she'd said – that Scott loved me. He hadn't said it to me. We'd not been together long. Did I want him to love me? Did I want to love him? My head was spinning, and I wanted it to stop.

'I can't imagine what you went through with Jay,' Natasha said. 'I…'

'I don't want to talk about it,' I said automatically. It was generally what I said to anybody who asked. I didn't mind Natasha knowing about Jay and the basics of what had happened – Scott had asked me if I was okay with him telling his family, and I'd said he could tell his parents and Natasha, and his friend Martin. Scott struggled to keep things hidden, and the support of family and friends was something of central importance to him. For me, though, I felt safer holding back as much as I possibly could. Showing anyone my real self was like letting somebody begin to pull at a loose thread. Once they got hold of it, if they chose to, they could pull it and make me completely unravel. It was safer to let nobody that close – they could have the headlines, if they had to, but I didn't want them to have the whole story. I couldn't bring myself to think about those times. I might relive my time with Jay involuntarily in the nightmares and flashbacks that were occurring with increasingly frequency, but I was damned if I was going to speak about it, or think about it, when I didn't have to. Even if people sometimes told me that talking would help.

'I can tell you something about Scott,' Natasha said, 'he would *never* be violent, or cruel. It would go against every fibre of his being. Even if he was angry with you – which one day, he probably will be, because no relationship is ever going to be perfect – he would never, ever harm you. Whether you want to be with him or not, that's up to you, but Scott is not the same as Jay. You can be certain of that.'

Vicky

27

'Where's Den?' Scott asked frantically when he got inside the house. 'Is he okay? What happened?'

She stood out of the way to let him go further into her house, but she didn't give any indication of where Dennis was.

'Vicky!' he pleaded, when he'd established that Dennis wasn't in the living room or the kitchen. 'Where is he? Is he asleep upstairs?'

She nodded dumbly. Now that Scott was here, she didn't know what to say. Why had she done this? Why was she always such an idiot about things? Scott was going to see right through her. He rushed up the stairs and into Dennis's bedroom, and she followed him slowly.

'He looks fine,' he said quietly, when she joined him in the darkened room, lit only by a small nightlight. 'Well, he's not fine,' she snapped, irritated by his quick dismissal. 'He stopped breathing.' *Oh God, why did I say that?*

'He stopped *breathing*?' He rushed over to Dennis and listened to his breathing. Having satisfied himself that Dennis was okay for the moment, he guided her out of the bedroom. He closed the door softly behind them and they stood together in the hallway.

'Why…' he said, struggling to control his voice. 'Why is he still here, if he stopped breathing? Didn't you call an ambulance?'

'He started breathing again.'

She thought Scott was going to start yelling, because he looked so worried and frustrated, but he just said, 'When did this happen?'

'Just before I phoned you.'

'So, Dennis wasn't breathing, but you phoned me, rather than calling 999?'

'I told you, he started breathing again before I called anyone. I thought about calling for an ambulance, but I don't like to waste people's time…'

He stared at her in confusion and disbelief, and then he pulled himself together. 'Let's get him out of bed and drive him to the hospital now. We can explain what happened, and they can check him over. Are you okay to drive? I can't do it, I've been drinking.'

'Of course you have,' she snapped.

'What's that supposed to mean?'

'You've been out getting drunk with that *woman,* while your son could have died.' Vicky's heart was hammering. The words were coming out before she could stop them. What was she doing? She wanted to stop, but when she was with Scott she lost control. He made her feel so angry and hurt and betrayed. He made her feel stupid, too, and she was sick of people making her feel stupid. Perhaps if Den really was sick it would teach him a lesson. *No, I don't mean that. I'd never wish that on Dennis.*

Scott was still staring at her. 'So you knew I was out with Felicity tonight.'

'You're always with her at the weekend, aren't you? She stays at your flat.'

He narrowed his eyes. 'I'm not arguing with you about my girlfriend while Dennis needs to go to hospital.' There was an edge to his voice now, like he was testing her. 'Are you going to take us there? Otherwise I'll call for an ambulance. I'm not happy just leaving him, even if he seems okay now.'

She didn't answer, so he took out his phone. 'They'll need to speak to you,' he told her. 'I wasn't here, I can't explain what happened.' He dialled the number and handed her his phone. 'I'm going to check Dennis again, you—'

Her head began to pound. She had to stop this. Jabbing a stiff finger at the screen, she ended the call.

Something must have shown in her face, because he said, 'Vicky… what is it? Something about this doesn't seem right.'

She didn't answer. What could she possibly say?

'Vicky, did he actually…' He paused. 'Did he really stop…'

She still didn't speak. *What have you gone and done now?* The hated voice from her past spoke up in her head. *You've really made a mess of things this time.*

'Vicky, please tell me you didn't make this up,' he said.

'What, so you want your son to be sick?' she spat at him, suddenly furious. 'You should be relieved he's okay, not disappointed.'

'That is *not* what I meant! Of course I don't want Den to be ill! I can't... I can't believe you've done this.'

He began to make his way down the stairs. 'If you lost him it'd make your life easier, wouldn't it?' she shouted at him. 'With him out the way you wouldn't have to deal with me and you'd be free to spend as much time as you like with your new girlfriend.'

Scott ignored her. When he reached the bottom of the stairs, he started making his way towards the front door without a backwards glance. She ran after him.

'Scott, I'm sorry,' she said. 'I didn't mean to scare you. I opened my mouth and... the words just got away from me.'

He still didn't speak.

'For God's sake, say something!'

He turned to her. 'This isn't the first time you've done things like this,' he said quietly. 'But I never thought you'd stoop so low as to tell me my son had stopped breathing, just because you're jealous of me being with somebody else. If you can't see for yourself how wrong all of this is, I don't know what I can say to you. But I can't deal with it any more. You need help.'

'You do *not* get to say that to me,' she said. 'Not that. Not when it's your own fault.'

'No, Vicky. You chose to tell me lies about Dennis to get me to cut short a night out with Felicity. That is not my fault. That's a decision *you* made. I wish you would just admit it.'

'I wanted to see if you'd care enough to bother coming round.'

Now he lost his temper. She flinched as he yelled, 'Of course I care enough to come round! Why would you test me like that? I know you don't like me being with Felicity, but this is sick, Vicky. You – you're messed up in the head.'

She grabbed his arm. 'You wouldn't be this angry if you didn't feel something for me.'

'I'm not having this conversation. I'm going home.'

'Fine, walk out when I start saying something you don't like.'

'You say a lot of things I don't like. You say a lot of things that a lot of people don't like. Like Tim. Or that guy before him, what was his name, Ollie?'

'Don't talk to me about Tim! Don't talk to me about *Ollie*!'

'You let paranoia and mind games infect both of those relationships. It's one thing when it's just about two people, Vicky, but we have Dennis. We have to make this work.'

She wanted to scream at him, but before she could speak he said, 'Goodbye, Vicky. I'll see you when you drop Dennis round tomorrow.'

She stared at him as he opened the door and stepped outside. He wasn't even cross with her now. He was just fed up. Disappointed in her. It was worse than him being angry – at least when he was here arguing, he was actually in the house with her. But what had she expected? He was obviously going to see through her flimsy lie. She slammed the door in his face and made her way back upstairs, emotions bubbling dangerously inside her.

She checked on Dennis, and then she went and sat on her bed, and cried a few hot, lonely tears. *I'm not surprised you've driven him away,* that droning voice from her past continued. *Who would want you?* Vicky cried out in rage. She picked up a framed photo of herself, Scott and Dennis from her bedside table, and threw it across the room.

Vicky

6 YEARS AGO

28

'Just give me a break, will you?'

Vicky fixed her eyes on Ollie. His face was flushed with anger, making him look slightly ridiculous – the same as in the summer when his pale, freckly skin got sunburnt and he'd go lobster-red.

'Well, just tell me why you put your phone away so quickly whenever I walk into the room? Why—'

'Because I want some fucking privacy!'

Vicky recoiled like she'd been slapped. Why was this happening to her? She'd moved away from Alstercombe to be with Ollie – he'd been so good for her, and he'd helped her go a long way towards overcoming her agoraphobia. She still had good days and bad days, but it was so much better than it had been. Yet now she felt like he was torturing her. Something was going on. She *knew* something was going on. *It would make sense for him to have found someone else. He'll be bored of you by now.*

'Why do you need privacy if you have nothing to hide?' she said. 'I would let you read my messages.' She threw her phone towards him. 'Here, read them. I've got no secrets from you.'

Ollie sank down onto the sofa. He put his face in his hands, and she waited for a second, two, three. Finally, he raised his head to meet her eyes. 'I don't want to read your messages. I trust you, so I don't need to. You should be able to trust me. But you don't, do you?'

'Show me then! Show me what you were looking at just then.'

'Fine,' he said. 'Here. Knock yourself out.'

She took his phone and opened his messages. A hot ball of

guilt settled in her stomach. There was nothing there – just work emails, a couple of messages from his mum, his brother, a few friends. He'd had no time to delete anything; he was on his phone when she came in, smiling at something. That was what had made her suspicious, the way he'd been smiling.

'I'm sorry,' she said. 'I'm so sorry Ollie, I just… my mind, it runs away with me, I imagine things. It's just that I don't know what I'd do if I didn't have you. I love you so much, I…'

Her words trailed off and he put his arm around her. 'I love you too,' he said. 'It's all right. But I need to feel like you trust me. Please, just trust me, okay?'

She nodded. Her body flooded with relief. She'd stop now. She would make herself stop – the checking, the obsessing. It had to end, she knew that deep down. 'I will,' she said. 'I do.'

She couldn't stop, though. Whenever he was out of the house, her mind couldn't switch off. What was he doing? Who was he with? She'd message him, and often he didn't reply straight away, or not at all, and she felt like she was losing her mind. Every time he was at home and on his phone, every time he smiled at something and she didn't know what it was, or whenever he was distracted, a kind of itch started in her head and no matter how many times she forced him to show her his phone, or she looked through his messages secretly, the itch never got scratched.

One night, he said he was going out with some work friends. She spent the evening pacing around the house, getting drunk and worrying. One moment she'd convince herself that she was just being silly, the next she'd be certain she was right to be suspicious. She texted Ollie, over and over. He didn't reply. *Of course he's not replying. He's found somebody better. Someone easy-going, someone fun, someone pretty.* She stood at the top of the stairs. She was so drunk that the landing was blurry, the steps down to the hall moving in front of her eyes. She brought her foot to the edge of the top step. It would be so easy just to slip.

…

'What happened?' Ollie said urgently. 'Oh my God, Vix, what have you done?'

She squinted up at him. What the hell was going on?

'You called me. You said you'd fallen down the stairs! I got here as quickly as I could…'

She looked round at the stairs. There was red wine all over the carpet. It looked like a crime scene. In fact, she'd called him before she 'fell', faking panic before ending the call and throwing herself down, hoping she would pass out at the bottom, which clearly she had.

'Where were you?' she asked.

'I'm going to call an ambulance.'

She blinked a couple of times, and he came into better focus. 'Why's your shirt done up wrong?' she said.

Scott

6 YEARS AGO

29

Scott struggled to make sense of Vicky's torrent of words. 'So...
he told you he's met somebody else?'

'He said it was *my* fault! He said he was happy until I kept
questioning him all the time. He said I stifled him and in the end
he decided he might as well find somebody else since I thought
that's what he was doing anyway!'

'You... you'd better come inside and sit down,' he said, leading
the way to the living room. He hadn't seen Vicky in years – he'd
thought perhaps she would never contact him again – and yet here
she was in his hallway, drenched after walking from her car up to
his door in the rain, pouring out a long, muddled story about her
break-up with a boyfriend that Scott had never even met.

'I'll make you some tea,' he said gently. 'You can start from the
beginning.'

'The beginning!' she said. 'Is that the beginning where you told
me our friendship was toxic and you couldn't be around me any
more, so I ended up looking for comfort with a creep like Ollie?
Or the beginning where I got fucking *stabbed*.'

Scott closed his eyes briefly. *Don't let her get to you. That's what she
wants. That's why she keeps bringing it up.*

'You're going to help me,' she said. 'You're going to let me stay
here until I get myself sorted out.'

'Vicky...'

She glared at him. Her makeup was smeared down her cheeks,
her red-blonde hair so wet it was almost black. Her situation was
pretty bleak; could he really turn her away? The answer was

simple. He couldn't. 'You can sleep in the spare room for a few days,' he told her, 'just until you find somewhere else to go.'

She fixed her gaze on him, her eyes full of old rage. It sent shivers down his spine. 'I'm not going to say thank you,' she said coldly. 'You owe me. This is the *least* you can do.'

. . .

He slept badly, and woke the next day to find Vicky sat in the living room looking at her phone, a cup of black coffee on the table beside her.

'How long have you been up?' he asked her.

She shrugged. Then she held her phone out to him. 'Look at this,' she said, 'look what he's said about me.'

Scott scanned through the text on the screen, trying to figure out what she was referring to. 'It's just people saying they're sorry you and him broke up,' he said in confusion. 'Why would that...'

'Look at what he *replied* to one of them.'

'Vix, perhaps it would be better if you didn't look at this stuff—'

She snatched the phone back out of his hand. '"I'm not sorry we broke up," she quoted, "it feels like a weight has been lifted."' She waited for his reaction, eyes glittering. Her eyelids were puffy and red. Had she been up all night crying?

'Like I said, just don't read it. It's only going to make you feel worse.'

She threw her phone down beside her on the sofa, and he noticed a large bruise on her arm. 'How did you get that?' he asked.

'I fell down the stairs.'

'When?'

'Night before last. Ollie took me to hospital after he found me passed out in the hall, but I'm not badly hurt.'

Scott shook his head. This story just got stranger and stranger.

'His shirt was done up wrong when he came in and found me. That's how I realised what he was up to. He broke up with me the second I got out of hospital. Not that I would have wanted to be anywhere near him anyway. He makes me *sick*.'

'My God, Vix. I'm sorry.'

'I can cope with a few bruises.'

He sat down beside her, just as she reached for her phone again.

'Don't look at it. It's not worth it.'

'Look! Look what he said!' she cried, the moment her eyes fixed on the screen. She held her phone in his face, and he read the words. 'He shouldn't be saying this stuff where you can read it,' he said. 'Stop following him, then you won't have to see it.'

A couple of tears spilt down her cheeks. Scott considered the words he'd just read. The language and tone didn't much endear him to Ollie, but he had to admit the man's suspicions matched up with his own experiences with Vicky.

She's fucking nuts. Wouldn't be surprised if she threw herself down the stairs to get some attention.

Scott

PRESENT DAY

30

Scott arrived home from checking on Dennis just as Natasha was on her way out.

'What happened?' she said.

'Don't ask.'

'I just did. Tell me what's going on. Is Dennis okay?'

Scott reluctantly explained and Natasha shook her head. 'I knew it!' she said, 'I just knew it! You can't let her keep doing this to you.'

'How can I stop it?'

'She makes me so angry! I mean, is nothing sacred to her? You don't tell somebody their kid is sick to spoil their night out. It's messed up.'

'All I can do is try not to give her what she wants. She wants a reaction, and… well, she got a bit of one, but I walked away before things got out of hand. Fighting with her makes it worse.'

'You can't just accept it.'

'I'm sure once she gets used to the idea of Felicity she'll calm down.'

Natasha gave him a long, sceptical look.

'How is Felicity?' he asked. 'Did she get back okay?'

'She had a bit of a scare on her way home. She thought she saw her ex. She didn't,' she added quickly, 'but she was shaken up. She said her nightmares and things are getting worse.'

'They are.'

She touched his arm briefly. 'I need to get home, Scott, I'm wiped out. Are you going to be okay?'

'Yeah, I'm all right. Thank you for helping out, I appreciate it. I just want to see Fliss, now. Check she's all right.'

'I might... I might have accidentally told her something.'

'What?'

'About the house. I didn't realise you hadn't told her. I thought you were going to talk about it this weekend.'

Scott's heart skipped a beat. She'd told Felicity about the *house?* That wasn't good. He'd concluded it was too soon to bring it up, after her reaction when he mentioned living together, but now she'd found out about it from Natasha he was curious to hear her reaction. 'How did she take it?' he asked.

'I'm not going to lie to you, Scott, she didn't exactly look thrilled.'

Scott nodded. He wasn't surprised.

'I'm really sorry if I put my foot in it. For what it's worth, I told her that she could trust you. That you're nothing like that ex of hers. I know I'm biased, so perhaps she won't pay any attention to me, but she's nervous of being in a new relationship. I just wanted to try to help.'

Scott found Felicity curled up on the sofa, half covered by a fleece blanket. She was awake, and she sat up when he came into the room.

'How's Dennis?' she asked immediately.

'Fine.'

'That's good. Was it just a false alarm—'

'Vicky made it up. He wasn't ill. She wanted me to drop everything and rush round there.'

He sat beside her on the sofa, and she gave him a look which unsettled him. It was like she wanted to be sympathetic, but something was holding her back. 'Natasha told me what happened,' he said, 'that you thought you saw Jay on your walk back.'

Felicity nodded but didn't speak.

'And she said that she'd accidentally told you something.'

Felicity wouldn't meet his eyes. Instead she pulled the blanket closer around herself and stared down at her lap.

'All it is,' he began to explain, 'my parents told me last week about a house an old family friend is selling. It's a bungalow with a loft conversion. That's what made me start thinking about us moving in together, because I bet they'd let us have it for a good price. But it doesn't matter now.'

'You want us to *buy* a house together?'

'Is it really that crazy an idea? I know you don't have any savings, but I have some – I got an inheritance a few years back – and one mortgage will be less than the two lots of rent we pay now...' He trailed off. Felicity was staring at him as if he'd just suggested they walk out in front of a bus together.

'Look, we can just forget it,' he said. 'You already told me it's too soon, and that's fine. We don't have to rush into anything.'

'Natasha said that you love me,' she said flatly.

He sighed. Was there anything Natasha *hadn't* said? 'That's true,' he said simply. There was no point in hiding it. He wanted her to know. He just hadn't meant it all to come out like this. 'I do love you. I have done... almost from the start.'

'So why did you tell her and not me?'

'It just sort of came out. You know how close me and Tash are. I got excited about the house; I got carried away talking about it—'

He reached out for her hand, but she stood up abruptly. 'I need to go to bed. I'm exhausted.'

'Fliss, the only reason I didn't tell you that I love you is because we haven't known each other long. I didn't want to come on too strong, and I didn't want to make you feel like you have to say it back.'

'Why does Vicky hate you so much?' she asked bluntly.

'There are a lot of reasons. Some of them valid, some... not so much.'

'I don't like how you've been talking behind my back, Scott. I feel very uncomfortable.'

'Let's... perhaps we should get some sleep. Talk about it another time.'

She left the room silently, and he waited a few minutes before joining her in bed. They held each other briefly, but then she shifted away from his embrace, and it was a long time before either of them slept.

...

He woke sometime in the early hours of the morning. Felicity was moving around in bed, making a moaning sound. He sat up and watched her in the dim light of the bedroom. She was writhing and scratching frantically at one of her wrists. 'No,' she said quietly, 'no, Jay, no, no!', her voice becoming louder, more urgent.

He turned on his bedside lamp, and she awoke with a cry. Her eyes were huge and terrified and fixed on him, but she wasn't seeing him properly and the dream still clung to her. 'It's Scott,' he told her. 'You're with Scott. You're safe.'

Finally, recognition filled her eyes and she covered her face with her hands. 'You're safe,' he told her again. She rolled onto her side, curling up into a ball, and as she moved he noticed that she had drawn blood from her wrist. 'Everything is okay,' he said. 'You don't need to worry about anything.'

He stroked her back and she jumped. 'Don't touch me!'

He took his hand away. What had she been dreaming about? Jay, obviously, but what had he been doing in her nightmare that had made her cry out like that, and attack her wrist so viciously? He was disturbed by the fact she'd scratched it so hard that she'd made it bleed, but now she didn't even seem aware that she'd done it. 'When is it going to get better?' she asked.

'I don't know.'

'I can't... Why won't it ever go away? Why won't *he* ever go away? I hate him. I hate him. I hate—' She burst into tears. He lay helplessly by her side. Should he try to hold her again? Before he made up his mind her tears stopped, and she got out of bed. He followed her into the kitchen, where she got herself a glass of water and sat down at the table.

'I don't like surprises,' she said finally. Her voice was calm, measured, like she'd been rehearsing the words for the past few minutes. 'I know it was well meant, and I know how close you are to your family, but hearing about the house and how you feel about me from Natasha was like being ambushed. And then she started singing your praises, and it made me feel very... I don't know. Like I'm being... managed. Handled.'

'I promise you that's not what it was. Natasha made a genuine mistake, and then she was trying to reassure you. It shouldn't have ended up that way. I wanted to be upfront with you, and I screwed up. I know I should be honest with you. In fact, there are more things I should tell you about Vicky. I only left it because—'

'Please. No more revelations tonight. I'm not sure I need to know.' She took a deep breath. 'I'm sorry, Scott. I don't think we should be together. I think... I think it's over.'

Scott's stomach dropped though the floor. She turned away from him, so he stared at her back, her shoulders hunched under her pale blue pyjama top, the ends of her chestnut brown hair sticking out messily in a halo around her head.

'Why... why would you say that?' he asked. 'I made one mistake, Fliss! All this is new for me too, but I thought everything was good, wasn't it? We have so much fun together; you, me, Leo. I... we were happy! We *are* happy—'

She turned to face him. 'Good?' she said. 'Happy? I'm getting worse! Natasha says it's because a new relationship is a big change. And perhaps she's right, but that doesn't mean it's a change for the better. The nightmares, and the flashbacks, they might be warnings. It might be my mind telling me I'm making a mistake! It might... it might be telling me I'm in danger!'

Felicity

31

I couldn't bring myself to continue looking at Scott. He was crushed. I didn't want to see it. I hurt too, just as much, but I was doing the right thing. I had to be. I couldn't just ignore the signs. I couldn't take the risk.

'Fliss, it's not a mistake.' He rushed over and sat beside me. 'You're not in danger.'

I couldn't concentrate. I was thinking about the house again, and I got lost in a memory. Suddenly, I could hear Jay's words as clear as day. 'I think I might have found us a place,' Jay said to me. 'A house, in the country, away from all the noise and people.' I tried to shake the memory away, but it was all-consuming. I was there in bed with Jay again, back in our old flat, where he said those words to me. Fear gripped me. I had to pretend I was happy with Jay's news, terrified of his reaction if I told him the truth. 'When you're there, you'll like it,' Jay continued, 'and it'll be better for when we have a family.'

Scott's hand was on my arm. He was speaking. I heard the word love. I heard the word trust. His face was so kind, so quick to laughter. There had been many, many times I'd felt happy with him. Times I felt free. Times I let my guard down. And that was what was so alarming.

I shoved Scott's hand away, tears prickling my eyes. 'No,' I said. 'I'm not moving anywhere with you! I'm not going anywhere! I'm not... I'm not...'

Scott was speaking. His words faded in and out, but I caught a sentence here and there. 'The house was a stupid idea,' he said desperately. 'It's too soon. Forget I mentioned it.'

I staggered into the kitchen, where I leant against the worktop and tried to catch my breath. I gazed intently at Scott's handmade spice rack on the wall by the cooker, trying to read the label on each jar to calm myself, to reconnect with where I really was, and distance myself from the memories.

'Felicity, I don't want to break up—'

'Jay trapped me in a house,' I said, cutting off Scott's words. 'He told me he'd found somewhere for us to live. He took me there in the back of his van and when I woke I was chained by my wrist to a bed in one of the rooms upstairs. That's why I scratch my wrist. I... I still have nightmares about it, I can still feel the handcuff. I...' I drew a deep breath before continuing. 'He'd lock me in all day while he went out to work. Even once he got me pregnant he left me for hours on end. I thought I'd have to give birth on my own. I thought I was going to die.'

Scott's face turned white with shock. 'He did... he did *what?*'

'He thinks he did it because he loves me. He thinks he was looking after me!'

'I didn't know. Fliss, I didn't know he did that to you. I can't believe—'

'I was there for the best part of a *year...*' I trailed off, choked with fear and horror.

'And nobody found you? Weren't the police—'

'Nobody told the police! My parents are dead and my friends had deserted me. My work colleagues probably didn't bat an eyelid. Nobody even knew I was gone.'

'Fliss, listen to me, what that man put you through was unforgiveable. It was... it was *monstrous*. But he's not normal. He needs help. That isn't what normal people do to each other. You were just incredibly, incredibly unlucky that you were involved with somebody capable of doing those things. I would never do something like that. You must know that, surely—'

'Do you think I would have had a relationship with Jay if I thought *he* was capable of doing that?'

'*I've* never done anything to hurt you, have I?'

'Neither did Jay at the start! He didn't act that way to begin with. I used to like him. I used to love him. I used to *trust* him.'

'Felicity, you have to have faith that you won't choose somebody like that again. You can trust your judgement.'

'Of course *you* would say that!' I said, panicking. The walls felt like they were closing in on me. By going into the kitchen I'd backed myself into a corner. I couldn't leave the room without going past Scott, who was standing in the kitchen entrance. 'I want to leave,' I told him. I took a step forward but Scott didn't move.

'Don't let him do this to you,' Scott said. 'I am *not* Jay! I'm not Jay.'

I tried to dart past him and he caught my arm, only gently, but it was unbearable. 'Get off me!' I screamed. 'Get off me, get off me!'

He let go, but he followed me out of the room. 'I'm leaving,' I said, 'I'm taking Leo and I'm going home. I don't want you to try to stop me.'

'I won't. I'll help you. I can pack his toys and things.'

'Just stay out of my way,' I said. I was shaking now. Every nerve was screaming. I just needed to get somewhere safe.

He did as I asked and stayed in the living room while I gathered mine and Leo's things together. I peeked around the door at one point, and he was crying. For a second I wanted nothing more than to throw my arms around him, tell him I'd made a mistake, but I steeled myself against those impulses. I wouldn't give in. For all I knew he could be crying to manipulate me.

'I'm leaving now,' I told him once I'd finished packing our bags.

'Please, take some time to think about it,' he said, once he'd rubbed at his eyes, composed himself a little. 'Not straight away, but once you get home. I'm not trying to trap you, I just want to be with you, and with Leo too.' He reached out to touch Leo, who was fast asleep on my shoulder, having been taken from his bed. Scott let his hand drop again. 'It hurts that you can't trust me,' he said. 'I understand why you feel you can't, but I don't like being compared to your ex. You and Leo, you mean the world to me. I'm not the bad guy, Fliss. I don't deserve this.'

His words cut through me. But I couldn't afford to weaken my resolve. Right now I was scared, and I wanted to be at home safe with my little boy, with every lock triple – *quadruple* – checked, and nobody trying to contact me.

'Leave me alone, Scott, please.' I told him. 'I need space. I need time to… think.'

'I'll give you space.'

'Thank you.' I grudgingly let him carry my bags down the stairs because I couldn't do it while holding Leo, but then I got in my car and drove away, without a backwards glance at him.

Felicity

32

It didn't take long before I started regretting what had happened between me and Scott. Had we really broken up now? Was it truly over? It was all a blur – I'd been so unnerved by finding out about Scott's feelings and plans for our future from Natasha. Now, I realised that I had hugely overreacted.

Scott did as I asked and made no contact with me. At times I was glad, at others I missed him desperately. But what was worse? Being with him and feeling terrified that one day he'd change and I'd be trapped, or being without him and being safe, but lonely? Leo missed him too, but I tried to keep him distracted.

A little over a week passed, and one day I looked up from the reception desk at the dentist's and found Martin standing in front of me.

'Martin,' I said politely, 'I didn't know you were a patient here.'

'I'm not,' he said.

'I thought as much.' I sighed. I knew what he had come to see me about, and I couldn't face him telling me what an amazing man Scott is and how silly I was to throw it all away.

'I've not come to try to talk you round or anything,' he said, as though he'd read my mind, 'and Scott doesn't know I've come here. But there are things it might help for you to know.'

The bell above the door chimed as a young woman came inside with two small children. She stood behind Martin.

'Look, I know you can't talk right this second,' he said, as I opened my mouth to tell him to go, 'but could I come back and talk to you in your break? What time—'

'Come back in an hour. At twelve-thirty.'

'Thanks Felicity. I'll be here.'

I was thankful that it was only an hour I had to wait to see what

Martin had to say, because I had to admit I was curious. He was waiting in the small car park outside, immersed in looking at his phone, so that he didn't notice me until I was only a few paces away.

'What's this all about, then?' I asked him when he looked up.

'It's going to take more than a few minutes to explain.'

For a second I wanted to turn around and go back inside. Did I really want to do this? Did I want to know anything else about Scott when I wasn't even sure if I should see him again? Despite myself, I nodded my agreement, and we walked to a small café down the road. After ordering some sandwiches, we settled ourselves at a quiet table in the corner. 'I know this isn't really my business...' he started.

'How is Scott?'

Martin folded his hands on the table. 'I'm not going to lie to you Felicity, he's in bits.'

I was surprised by quite how much this news hurt me. I'd been expecting to get an answer like that, but hearing that Scott was in such a bad way because of me was like being punched in the stomach. I fixed my eyes on a deep scratch in the tabletop until the uncomfortable sensation subsided. 'I didn't mean to hurt him,' I said finally. 'But I found out he wanted us to buy a house. It came out of nowhere. It was overwhelming.'

'Yeah, he told me about that. He said you ended up hearing about it from Natasha, or something? He wasn't trying to ambush you. He got overexcited at the thought of the four of you being a family and ended up getting ahead of himself. Tash got mixed up and thought he'd already told you about the house.'

'Martin, did you really come here just to tell me second-hand everything Scott told you? If I wanted to know all this, I could ask him myself. It's not that I don't appreciate what you're trying to do, but—'

'No, I didn't come for that. Scott does tend to get overexcited about things, though. He's always trying to jump ahead of himself. That's all this was.'

We paused as our food arrived, and we didn't say much as we

ate. I got the feeling Martin was building up to saying something, and I thought it best to let him get to it in his own time.

'Did Scott ever tell you that Vicky's former boyfriend died?' he asked eventually.

I put down my sandwich and looked up at Martin in surprise. I hadn't been expecting that. 'No. He never told me that.'

'He blames himself for what happened. There have been several things, over the years, that have made a lot of bad blood between Vicky and Scott. But the thing Scott finds the most painful is what happened to Tim. Tim was Vicky's boyfriend for a couple of years before he died, and he was close friends with Scott, and with me, too. We've known each other since school.'

'I'm so sorry,' I said, 'I didn't know. Why would Scott blame himself?'

'Because Tim died while he was out rock climbing. With Scott.'

I pushed the plate containing the rest of my chicken and avocado sandwich away from me. I'd lost my appetite, and a wave of sympathy for Scott washed through me. Why hadn't he told me?

'Scott doesn't talk about it much,' Martin said as though he'd heard my thoughts. 'Most people round here know what happened, and he's spoken about it more at length with me, and with Vicky. He probably would have told you, except that anything to do with Vicky is just opening up a whole can of worms.'

'He told me about her being attacked when she was seventeen, and the agoraphobia.'

'He did?'

'Yeah.'

'Don't get me wrong, we all felt terrible about what happened to her back then, but she got this... *fixation* on punishing Scott for it. There have been problems ever since.'

I struggled to take it all in. Vicky's boyfriend Tim had been Scott's friend. Tim was dead. Vicky was obsessed with punishing Scott, and yet she had had Scott's child. How had that ended up happening? I decided to tackle one thing at a time. 'So, when did... Tim die?'

'The accident happened a little over three years ago.' Martin paused and I glanced at his face. Was it upsetting him to tell this story? He looked okay, but I tried to help him find the words. 'So… something went wrong while they were climbing? Did Tim fall?'

'Basically, yeah. Scott was the lead climber, so he was ahead of Tim, and then when he reached the top of one of the sections of their route, he set up an anchor to bring Tim up.'

Dread crept through me. Part of me didn't want to hear what happened next.

'There were other pairs of climbers doing the same route,' Martin continued, 'and one of the pairs above them dislodged some rocks. Scott thought it was just a few little ones to start with – he shouted out a warning to Tim, but it seemed like they would be okay. Then a larger rock came down. It landed on the rope between Scott and Tim, and severed it. Tim fell, and he died.'

I sat silently for a moment. 'A rock fell down?'

'That's right.'

'That's not Scott's fault! I thought you were going to say he made a mistake, but a *rock*… that's nobody's fault. I mean, what are the chances—'

'Scott knows it's not really his fault. But he feels responsible. He was the more experienced climber – he felt like Tim was trusting him and he failed. Also, Tim had a lot of stuff going on with Vicky around that time, and his head probably wasn't in the right place, but Scott said a change of scenery would take his mind off things. He'd talked Tim into going, so he feels responsible that way, too.'

I took a moment to digest this information. 'So… what other things have happened between Scott and Vicky?'

Martin took a breath, and I expected him to start talking, but instead he pushed him plate away and stood up. 'Do you want another coffee? This is going to take a bit of time to explain.'

I paused. Did I really need to know all of this? My mind was already in turmoil. 'Yeah, okay, thanks,' I said uncertainly. I settled back in my chair as he made his way to the counter. I was curious, yet apprehensive. If Martin thought it was important I understood Scott and Vicky's history, then I'd hear him out. But I wasn't too sure it would make any difference to my feelings.

Scott

6 YEARS AGO

33

'How are you feeling?' Scott asked Vicky, as he sat down beside her on the sofa. She'd been staying in his flat for a few days now, doing little but watch TV or lie in bed. It was clear she'd found the break-up with Ollie traumatic, but keeping herself shut away was starting to do more harm than good.

In answer to his question, she shrugged, and pulled her duvet right up to her neck. She'd taken to dragging the duvet out of the spare room and huddling under it on the sofa. 'Why don't you come out later?' he asked her. 'It's quiz night.'

She raised an eyebrow like he'd asked her to go out and scrub toilets. 'No,' she said. 'I'm not doing that.'

'You might enjoy it. Or at least, it would be a distraction. Distraction is what you need right now. You don't want to let Ollie win, do you?'

'He already has won.'

'You know what I mean.'

Vicky didn't reply. In actual fact, he wasn't sure whose side he was on. Vicky was cut up about Ollie, but she was still obsessed with him – where he was, who he was with, what he was doing. She constantly looked at her phone, as well as sending him messages and trying to call him. Had she been possessive and paranoid while they'd been together? That's what Ollie seemed to think, and though Vicky had occasional moments where she acknowledged that she might have been overbearing, on the whole she railed against Ollie, claiming that all her actions were justified – his final act of cheating on her proving in her mind that she was justified about every moment of suspicion that had gone before.

'Come on,' he said. 'Come with me. You can see Martin and Tim, they'll be there.'

'Why would I want to show them what a loser I am? It's bad enough you've seen me like this.'

He gave up. What use was it? He couldn't make her do anything. If she chose to stay here and make herself feel worse, he'd have to leave her to it. He began to stand and she pulled him back down. 'I'm not that bad, am I, Scott? Did I really deserve all this? Am I *that* unattractive?'

He glanced at her. Her hair was bundled up into a messy heap on top of her head, and she was wearing a baggy pink pyjama top with cats all over it. He wasn't sure she'd had a shower since she arrived at the house, and there was a half-finished sharing bag of crisps beside her on the sofa.

'Vicky, I don't know exactly what went on between you and Ollie. Sometimes relationships just don't work out.'

'You didn't answer my question.'

'No, because what I think about you shouldn't make any difference to how you feel.'

'So you *do* think I'm unattractive?'

He sighed. 'Vix, no, I don't think you're unattractive. Of course you're not. You just—'

His words were cut off as she leaned in to try to kiss him. He moved out of her way. What on earth was going on in her head? 'Just… just come out tonight,' he told her, since he had no idea what to say about her trying to kiss him. 'I know it'll help you feel better. It'll help a lot more than *this,* anyway,' he said, gesturing vaguely at himself, the TV, and her duvet.

…

'Don't rush to wish me well all at once,' Tim said.

Scott exchanged a look with Martin.

'I know you and Vicky don't exactly see eye-to-eye, Scott…'

Tim began.

'That's an understatement,' Scott replied. She'd put him through hell. She tried to kiss him a second time, a couple of days after the pub quiz, and he had politely suggested that she find somewhere else to stay. She had, but not before telling anybody who would listen that he had slept with her and then thrown her out on the street. In fact, she'd just gone to stay with another old friend, and before long had got back on her feet with a new job, and had surprisingly quickly made a whole circle of new friends. What he and Martin hadn't realised until this moment, however, was that one of the changes she'd made was starting up a relationship with Tim.

Scott faced Tim squarely. The quietest of the three men, Tim looked uneasy having to talk to them about Vicky, his eyes nervous behind his glasses, and he'd run his fingers through his sandy hair several times so that some of it now stuck out sideways. 'How did you and her get together, anyway?' Scott asked.

'I just went to see her a few times, to check she was okay after everything that happened. I never intended for it to become anything more than that, but we just seemed to hit it off.'

'You know she tells people that I slept with her and then threw her out of my flat?'

'Yeah.'

There was a burst of laughter from one of the tables near them in the Royal Oak, and Tim managed to get out of saying anything further. Scott wasn't too worried about his silence. He was pretty sure his friends knew him well enough to know he wouldn't treat a woman like that.

'Tim, it's not that I'm not… happy… for you.'

'I'm not happy,' Martin said. 'Scott's just being polite. Vicky is a nightmare. A full-on nightmare. You're making a big mistake.'

Tim was about to reply, and Scott jumped in to try to stop an argument breaking out. 'It's just that she's not long out of a relationship that didn't end so well,' he said. 'Her head may not be in the right place.'

'She seems okay to me,' Tim said. 'She's told me about Ollie.

He was cheating on her, she said she's glad it's over.'

'That's not quite the same as what she was saying to me.'

'She's had a chance to see things more clearly since then.'

'Well, great, then,' Scott said, without enthusiasm. He exchanged a second look with Martin. He could see his own fears written in his friend's face. This was going to end badly. He just knew it.

Felicity

PRESENT DAY

34

'So,' I said to Martin, struggling to get it straight. 'Vicky made up some stuff about Scott sleeping with her and kicking her out, and then he upset her by not supporting her being with Tim?'

'Yeah...' Martin looked shifty.

'That's still not all of it?'

'I mean... no. There was some other stuff that went on.'

'What other stuff?'

'You should probably ask Scott.'

I gave Martin a long look. 'Did Scott have an actual relationship with her?' I pressed him. 'Are you saying it wasn't just one night?'

He looked genuinely confused, and then he said, 'Oh, no, I'm not saying anything like that. No. Scott never had a relationship with her. It was the... disagreements we had about her being with Tim, it ended up getting a bit out of hand. But we were his friends and she wasn't making him happy. He completely changed while he was with her, but us – me and Scott – interfering, it made things worse. I'm not proud of what happened, and neither is Scott.'

I was about to press him further, and then I thought of my friend Leanne. The way she'd been so against Jay and me being together. But she'd ended up pushing me further towards him when her interventions backfired.

Martin was watching me curiously. 'You seem like you can relate.'

'My friends didn't like my ex.'

'No,' he said. 'I... I was sorry to hear about what happened to you.' He shifted awkwardly in his chair, unsure what to say to me. I smiled at him.

'You know, Scott doesn't know every little thing about my past, and I don't know every little thing about his. I knew there was more to this Vicky business. That's not why I broke things off.'

'Why did you break things off?' he asked directly. 'Sorry. It's nothing to do with me. But I've never seen Scott like this before. He's… he's crazy about you. And he misses your son too.'

'He misses Leo?'

'Yeah.'

I looked at the time on my phone. 'I've got to go.'

'Okay. Look, I'm not going to go on at you about Scott, and I won't bother you at work again, but I want to say that just because something frightens you, it doesn't mean it's the wrong thing to do.'

I let his words sink in, and I smiled. 'Perhaps you're right,' I told him. I made my way slowly back to work, my mind full of conflicting thoughts, and confusing feelings.

. . .

Once I'd finished work for the day and picked Leo up from nursery, I headed back to my flat with Martin's words still running through my mind. I was on autopilot until I checked the mailbox on the outside of my block, and was surprised to find a small package inside. I took it out tentatively; I didn't like anything unexpected to happen, and I wasn't expecting any deliveries. Leo tugged on my hand, eager to get inside and out of the spitting rain. Turning the package over, I was filled with a mixture of relief and sadness when I recognised the handwriting as Scott's. He must have delivered it by hand, as it didn't have my address on the front, only the names 'Felicity and Leo'.

I didn't open the parcel straight away. We went upstairs and I placed it on the breakfast bar, and tried to forget about it while I gave Leo his evening bath. Curiosity soon overwhelmed me, so before putting Leo to bed I carried him into the kitchen with me and opened the package.

'Cars!' Leo said when he saw the contents. I helped him to take out two of his toy cars, which he examined with delight, and then I slid out the note that came with them.

Found Leo's cars under the sofa, I know how much he loves them so I wanted to return them to you.

I miss you. I know I made a mess of everything. I'm sorry I got it so wrong. Scott x

I stared at the note for perhaps a minute, barely breathing, and then I put Leo gently down on the floor, where he started pushing his cars around and singing to himself. I ran into the hall, where I took in a great gulp of air and then began to cry in huge sobs. I put my hand over my mouth to stop Leo overhearing me, and after allowing my emotions to overtake me for a minute or two I dried my eyes and went back in to sit beside him.

'Isn't that nice to get your cars back?' I said. 'I was wondering where they were.'

'Daddy's house,' he said.

I froze. What had he just said? For a terrible moment I thought he was talking about Jay, but then I realised that of course he meant Scott.

'Daddy?' I said, 'Do you mean Scott? Dennis's daddy?'

'My daddy.'

I put my arm around him and he sat down on my lap. 'Leo, would you like it if we lived with... with Daddy?'

He didn't seem to understand the question, so I said, 'Would you like it if Daddy was with us all the time?'

He paused, then gave a little nod. I kissed him on the top of his head. 'I think... I think I might like that too.'

With Leo in bed fast asleep, I sent Scott a message asking if he could come round to see me. I waited impatiently for his reply, and he soon told me he was on his way. I stood at the window overlooking the car park, watching for his arrival.

I rushed to let him inside and though I tried to form some sort of sentence that would explain how I felt, instead I just kissed him. He kissed me back without a moment's hesitation and before I knew it we were shedding our clothes in a frenzy until we ended up in the living room and he pushed me down on the sofa. 'Is this okay?' he asked softly. 'Tell me if you need to stop.'

'It's okay,' I reassured him. 'It's good. I want to, I really want to.' I realised as I said it that this was about the first time in our relationship that I truly had a strong desire for sex. Although Scott and I had made love from time to time since we'd been together, and I'd taken some amount of pleasure in it, it had always been difficult for me after my experiences with Jay. It had ended up more as something functional I'd done to grow and maintain the relationship, not because I felt like it. Now I needed and wanted it desperately. I wrapped my legs around his to pull him closer to me. My heart was pounding, my breath short, and I clung to his back, pressing my fingers into his skin, until I cried out at the intensity of my orgasm.

Afterwards, it was as though he couldn't believe what had happened. 'That was… I never thought… that was just…' He stumbled to a halt.

'I loved it too,' I said. I rested my head against his chest, and closed my eyes.

…

Before long I got too cold on the sofa and went to retrieve my clothes, and his. 'You have Den at the moment, don't you?' I said as I handed him his jeans and t-shirt. 'Where…'

'He's round at Natasha's. She was happy to take him for the night when I said we might… that I hoped we might…' He gave up, then said, 'I just told her you'd invited me round. I said I didn't know what for.'

'But you hoped we'd get back together?'

'Yes,' he said simply.

'And I guess Natasha wants us to?'

'Well, yeah.'

'Your family and friends really want us to be together,' I said. 'They really want you to be happy.'

'Don't feel pressured by them. We're all in each other's business, it's always been like that. We all sort of come as a package. But it's not about what they think.'

'Martin came to speak to me today.'

Scott paused in the middle of pulling on his jeans. 'Oh, for God's sake,' he said, 'I didn't tell him to do that, I promise.'

'He told me about Tim's death.'

'Oh.'

'I'm sorry.'

He nodded, and I gave him a little nudge. 'He also told me that just because something frightens you it doesn't mean it's bad.' I finished dressing and sat on the sofa. 'And I realised he's right. You know, sometimes it's brave to move on from a relationship and be on your own. I thought I was being brave by isolating myself. But actually, I think what takes more courage for me right now is to trust my feelings. And I know how I feel now. I… I love you.'

'You… you do?'

'Yes.'

His delight and excitement were written all over his face, but he said, 'We don't have to rush anything.'

'Well, I've thought about it, and I know it's early days, but I think I'd like to take the next step and move in together. And Leo… Leo called you Daddy.'

Scott stared at me. 'He did?'

'You dropped off those cars for him, and when he saw them he said they were at Daddy's house.' I studied his face. 'Are you okay with him calling you that? I can try to stop him, but he was quite determined.'

'I'm more than okay! I was missing *both* of you so much. You know how much I enjoy being with Leo. As long as you're comfortable with it, I'd love for him to call me Daddy.'

I curled up in Scott's arms once again, and after a while he put on the TV. It was so cosy being snuggled up to him, so normal to just watch something together, that I began to doze off, lulled to sleep by the drone of the TV and the warmth of his body. He gave my arm a squeeze. 'Let's go to bed,' he said.

I nodded, but then my gaze fell on the TV screen. There was a police drama on – the kind of thing I'd never usually watch. There was a crime scene in the woods. My eyes fixed on the police tape, the trees, the disturbed ground, where presumably they had found a body.

'Pretty gruesome, this,' Scott said. 'Pair of teenage girls murdered on their way home from school. I don't really want to watch any more of it, to be honest.'

My mouth was dry. I couldn't move, or speak. What the hell had I been thinking? If Scott found a fictional crime on a detective series too unpleasant to watch, what would he do when he discovered the truth about Jay's crimes? I couldn't keep it from him forever. Sooner or later, the truth would come out, and when it did, I wouldn't see him for dust. It didn't matter what he felt for me and Leo; nobody in their right mind would risk a run-in with Jay.

Scott turned off the TV and held me close, smiling down at me. I couldn't smile back. As the baby monitor crackled to life with a little cry from Leo, I leapt up, grateful for the distraction. 'I'll go and check on him,' I said, rushing out of the room. I hesitated at the doorway, looking at Scott. He stretched, and then settled back against the sofa cushions. Leo was quiet again, so I carried on looking at Scott, my heart heavy. I loved having him in my home. I loved him helping with Leo, playing with him, teaching him things. I loved *him*. But I knew who he was. He didn't really know who I was. And when he found out, I could lose him again in a heartbeat.

Scott

35

It was midnight. He was still awake, and so was Felicity. She kept tossing and turning, until he asked her, 'Are you all right?'

Silence.

'I thought we were okay.'

'I…' Her voice cracked. 'Scott, there's something…'

'What is it?'

She got out of bed, and went over to Leo's bed against the wall in her room, bending down beside him to stroke his hair. As she straightened again, she turned to him. 'Let's go in the other room.'

He followed her tentatively out of the bedroom. What was going on? Everything had been good – what had suddenly changed? She sat down on one of the stools in the kitchen, and instead of talking, she folded her arms on the breakfast bar and buried her face in them.

'Felicity?' Scott said softly. He went over to her and placed his hand on her back. 'What is it? What's wrong? Is it something to do with Jay?'

She raised her head. 'I don't want to tell you,' she said. 'Because when I do, it'll be over. But if I kept it a secret you'd find out one day. If things have to end between us, it's better it happens now, not a year or two down the line. And anyway, I don't want there to be secrets. There can't be secrets.'

'Fliss, you're frightening me.'

She gave him a sad smile. Well, more of a grimace. 'What I've told you about Jay so far, it's only the tip of the iceberg,' she said slowly. 'It's much, much worse than you think.'

He listened in horror as she outlined her ex's crimes. The words came like blows. *Murder. Teenage girl. Woods.* It didn't stop. Jay had killed a man too, beaten him to death with his bare hands.

'The other man, he was also involved in the young girl's death,' she explained. 'They killed her between the two of them, and then, after I escaped from the house, Jay killed him too.'

'I don't… I can't…' His stomach clenched, and he ran over to the kitchen sink. She sat silently while he was sick, and when he turned to look at her, she simply nodded and said, 'It's over. I knew it would be. There's no hard feelings. I understand.'

He made his way unsteadily back towards her, and plonked down onto the stool next to hers. 'But he's in prison?'

She stared at him. 'No,' she said. 'Didn't I say that already? That's the whole point! He is not in prison. The police never caught him. They don't know where he is.'

'I… I don't understand,' he said finally. 'He's… he's *got away with it?*'

'I suppose, for the moment, yes.'

'How can you be so *calm?*'

She laughed bitterly. 'I am not calm, Scott. But there is nothing I can do. If I don't just accept that this is the way things are for now, I would completely lose it. I have to be patient. And vigilant. That's all I can do.'

'Felicity, when you told me about him trapping you in that house, I just assumed he was in prison now! I didn't understand—'

'Well, now you do.'

He started to stand up, and then he sat down again. Pressure was building inside him. 'He could come after you?' he said, finally managing to articulate his concerns.

'Yes. Theoretically. He hasn't so far.'

'What are the police doing? Can't they protect you from him?'

'I'm not in any imminent danger,' she said. 'Like I said, he's never made contact, he's not threatened me, or come near me. He may never try. If he sent a message to me online, or called me, anything like that, I have a contact at CID that I'd get in touch with. She's in charge of the team looking for Jay. I have her card right here.' She reached towards the noticeboard on the wall – it was mostly covered in paintings that Leo had done at nursery – but she took down a small business card and handed it to him.

There was a name and number written on it. 'Detective Inspector Anne Miller,' he read from the card.

'She's good,' Felicity said. 'She's determined. I trust her.'

'So this… detective, and her team, really have no idea where he is?' Scott said eventually.

'No. They found his van, not long after I escaped. It had been abandoned, but they couldn't figure out where he went next. They think he stole a car – there was a house broken into not that far from where he'd originally left the van – but the couple were on holiday so it wasn't reported straight away. It was all… it was too little too late. After a while, all the leads dried up. Now there's only a small team on his case, and as far as I know they haven't really made any progress.'

He shook his head. How could this be real? This wasn't what happened to people he knew, this wasn't something that could possibly affect his normal, everyday life. This was what happened in stories. Or on the news.

'I thought you'd walk out the door,' Felicity said softly.

'Why?'

'Don't you see? I let you have feelings for me, and I never should have done. If Jay is out there looking for me, and he finds me, and I'm with you… he could *kill* you, Scott. Surely you realise that? What if he tracks me down, and sees you with me? I didn't deserve what Jay did to me, but *you* don't deserve to die just because you fell in love with me.'

Felicity

36

After my heart-to-heart with Scott, my nightmares subsided a little. Though Scott was shocked by my revelations he said he was determined to stand by me, not to let Jay win.

I gave notice to my landlord that I would be moving out soon, and Scott and I went to view the house he'd told me about. It was a little dated inside but Scott was enthusiastic about the prospect of putting in a new kitchen, since he had done that sort of work before, and assured me he had a friend who worked at a bathroom company who could get us mates' rates. It was easy enough to see past the decor, as I was so drawn in by the idea of us all being together, in a home with a big loft bedroom for Leo and Dennis to share, a proper bedroom for me and Scott, and a garden for us all to enjoy. It was nearer to the beach, so it took less than ten minutes to walk to the shore, and the whole place had a lovely homely, happy feel.

'I can't believe we're really going to do this,' I told him as we stood on the road outside after our viewing. Leo and Dennis were exploring the front garden, which had a seaside theme – gravel and pebbles dotted with rugged grasses and scrubby little plants like the ones found on the beach itself.

'I'll tell Vicky about our plans later today,' he said. 'Even if the house doesn't work out for some reason, you've given notice on your flat now and you'll be moving into my place soon.'

'How do you think she'll take it?'

'Badly. But it's got to be done. Perhaps the fact I keep walking on eggshells and always rushing round to help her is giving her false hope. I'm always going to have some involvement with her because of Den, but it needs to stay just as that. It's better for all of us.'

. . .

That evening, after putting Leo and Den to bed back at his flat, Scott gave me a quick kiss before heading out to Vicky's house. I sat on the sofa half-watching the TV, while fidgeting nervously. What were they saying? It wasn't likely to be going well, and I was concerned for him. He was gone maybe a couple of hours, and when he arrived home he appeared confused, more than anything.

'What happened?' I asked.

'Well, I said pretty much what I told you earlier. That I felt we both needed to move on, and that I was with you now and that was that.'

'And?'

'She threatened to stop me seeing Dennis—'

'What?' I burst out. 'She can't do that!'

He held his hand up. 'It's all right. I said I'd go to a solicitor and fight her, and she just caved in then. She was very quiet. She even said she understood, but the way she said it was kind of like she didn't understand at all. I think she just wanted me to leave. It was... it was really very strange. I don't know what to make of it.'

'It sounds like it could have gone a lot worse.'

'Yeah. Yeah, I guess,' he said, but he clearly wasn't convinced.

. . .

I got the sense over the following days that Scott feared retaliation from Vicky, but none came. 'Perhaps she really has accepted that you and me are serious,' I told him.

'I hope so,' he said. But thoughts of Vicky were soon pushed to the back of my mind. My period was late, and when I did a pregnancy test, it was positive. When Scott and I had got back together after our brief break-up, we'd been too excited to give much thought to contraception.

I sat on the end of the bed for a long time, looking at the result.

I couldn't help but remember the moment I discovered I was carrying Jay's baby, how terrified I'd been. It was different now, very different, but doubts crowded in. What if things changed between Scott and me? What if I decided I couldn't cope with a relationship with him, but I'd had his baby?

I shook my head, trying to clear it. I loved Scott, and I wanted to be a family with him, but I'd never meant to get pregnant so quickly – we'd never even talked about whether we wanted more children together. I threw the test away, making sure it was hidden under other rubbish in the bin, and tried to put it out of my mind. I had enough going on for now; I didn't want to rock the boat. And I didn't feel ready to tell Scott. I didn't want him to have any ownership of anything going on in my body. Not yet. Jay had believed that the fact I was carrying his child made me 'his', and no matter how much I trusted Scott, the fear of history repeating itself niggled away at me.

There was only one person whose opinion on the matter I could truly rely on. Leanne. She had always been vocal in her dislike of Jay. We'd fallen out over it, but I was sure that deep down her loyalty would always be for me. If anyone could support me through all the changes in my life that were happening almost too quickly for me to keep track of, it would be her.

Scott

37

'But I thought going back to Coalton was dangerous,' he said.

'I need to see her, Scott. I need someone in my life who's from… before.'

Scott searched Felicity's face. They were sitting on the beach, and she was gazing out at the ocean, arms wrapped around her legs, to try to protect herself from the slight chill. It was a blustery day, the early autumn wind whipping Felicity's hair around, though every now and again the sun broke through the clouds and warmed them pleasantly.

'Why don't I come with you?'

'It ended up being weird between me and her,' she explained. 'I don't know quite how she'll react to seeing me, so it will be better if it's just me and Leo. If you were there… she might feel like we're ganging up on her, or something.'

'Yeah, that's a good point.' He glanced down towards the sea, where Leo and Dennis were collecting shells and pebbles in a bucket. 'Everyone you see is to do with me – my friends, my family. It would be good to have someone of your own. Someone you know has really got your back.'

'It's not that I don't trust—'

'Honestly, Felicity, I'm not offended. I've got nothing against you reconnecting with Leanne. My only worry is whether it's safe for you to go to Coalton.'

'If Jay was hanging around in Coalton all this time he would have got caught,' she said. 'If he has any sense, he'll have stayed away. I'm only talking about going and staying with Leanne for a couple of nights. The chances of him finding out about that or seeing me must be tiny. The police were watching Leanne's flat after I escaped, because they knew he might try to go there.

They're not still doing it now, but Leanne would know to report anything suspicious. I don't think he's ever gone back there, and I can't see he would go back there now. I need my friend, Scott. I'm not going to let Jay stop me from having my friend.'

He put his arm around her shoulders and she snuggled her head against him. It didn't seem like the safest plan, but still, she had a point. She couldn't let Jay hold her back forever. It was a calculated risk, and the benefit of having someone else to talk to could be enormous for her. 'If it's what you want, Felicity, then I'm behind you one hundred percent. Just message me while you're there so I know everything is going okay.'

...

Felicity set off the next day, and Scott dropped Dennis off at Vicky's house for the weekend before heading to his workshop, though he struggled to concentrate on anything. He was uneasy about Felicity being away, and he kept checking his phone compulsively.

When Vicky turned up at the workshop her footsteps gave him a fright, and he stood up so suddenly that he bashed his head on a shelf. 'Vicky,' he said, rubbing his head. 'What's up? Where's Dennis?'

'He's at a friend's house for an hour or two.' Her voice was wobbly, her eyes red and puffy, and she was twisting her hands round and around each other in front of her body. 'I need to talk to you,' she said.

A heavy feeling settled around his heart, but he sat down with her on one of the two old chairs he had in the corner of the workshop. Vicky pulled hers close to him and said, 'I don't know why you keep trying to hurt me like this.'

Oh, God. He almost preferred it when she was angry with him than when she was like this.

'I'm not doing anything to hurt you,' he told her. 'Me and Felicity are together, and you...' He hesitated, then said, with a hint of desperation, 'You have to accept it!'

'Why should I accept it?'

'Vix, we were never even a couple! You... half the time you say you hate me, and the other half it's like you don't want to let me go. I don't understand what's going on with you. It makes my head spin trying to work out what you're thinking or what you're going to do next.'

She shrugged.

'Why have you come here, Vicky?'

'I told you. I want to know why you keep hurting me.'

Scott sighed heavily. 'Vicky, I... I can't do this. I'm not going to be able to say anything that will make you feel better.'

To his horror, she started to cry. 'I don't know how you can treat me like this,' she said. 'I'm so alone, Scott! I'm so alone!'

He wanted her to leave, but at the same time he couldn't help feeling bad for her. When she wasn't being defensive, she appeared to be genuinely unhappy. 'I'm not abandoning you, Vicky. We've got Dennis, so we'll always be in each other's lives, and I will always care, it's just—'

His words were cut off as she clumsily tried to kiss him, and he pushed her away. 'Vicky, no! Not this again! What—'

'You owe me!' she shouted. She stood up unsteadily and made her way towards the door. 'You ruined my life,' she said, glaring back at him. 'You ruined it, so you *owe* it to me to make things better. And if you don't...' She pointed a finger at him. 'I'll find a way to make you pay.'

'Vicky...' he said, but she'd already gone.

...

A little way down the street from the workshop, Vicky slumped down on a bench, and tried to rein in her feelings. She didn't want to give Scott the satisfaction of having her continue to cry over him, so instead she opened up some photos of him she had on her phone – mainly taken when Dennis had just been born, when Scott was visiting the house every day to help her out. There was a photo of the three of them together; him, her and the baby. She had this particular photo printed out on a large canvas at home – though she kept it in a cupboard where Scott wouldn't spot it. She touched his face on the screen. 'You're right that half the time I hate you,' she said softly to the photo, 'but I'm not going to leave you alone. You do not get to move on, Scott. Not with her, not with anybody.'

Felicity

38

I realised as I drove that there was no guarantee Leanne and her daughter Kayleigh would still be living in the same flat as she had been in when I was last in Coalton. She'd lived there for years – it was hard to imagine her anywhere else – but I'd been away a long time. Who knew what could have happened? I toyed with the idea of messaging her, but I wasn't in contact with her online as I was keeping a low profile, and I no longer had her phone number.

I stopped at some traffic lights and glanced round at Leo, who was busy trying to take his socks off in his car seat. If Leanne didn't still live in her flat, I'd either have to get a room for the night in Coalton, or just turn round and drive home again. I didn't much like either of those options, so I hoped my hunch that she'd have stayed put would prove correct.

The journey passed surprisingly quickly. Before I knew it I was no longer seeing anonymous roads but streets I recognised, places I used to go, in the town I grew up in.

Thankfully there was some space to park on the road right outside the big, white-painted Victorian house that contained Leanne's flat, which was down some steps on the lower ground floor. As I made my way towards her flat I recognised the luxurious pink voile hanging inside one of the windows, and a little purple trinket box, festooned with gemstones, on the windowsill. Relief flooded through me – there was no doubt she still lived here. I quickly dashed back up the steps and lifted Leo gently out of the car. He lolled against my shoulder, heavy and deeply asleep in his afternoon nap.

When Leanne opened her door, she didn't immediately recognise me. Her eyes flicked between me and Leo, a little crease between her eyebrows as she tried to work it out, and then her eyes widened in recognition. She reached her hands towards me, and then let them drop back down to her sides. 'Felicity?' she said, as though she thought she might be mistaken. She looked so comical, frozen on her doorstep in a pair of jogging bottoms and a black t-shirt covered in glittery stars, her red hair hanging loose around her shoulders, an astonished expression on her face, that I couldn't help but laugh. Then all of a sudden I was crying, and she threw her arms around me, a little awkwardly as I was still holding Leo, but she held on to me tightly and I breathed in her familiar scent – rich and flowery, almost like incense.

'Oh my God,' she said, 'oh my God, Fliss.' She stood back from me and looked at Leo, who was beginning to stir. 'Who's this little sleepyhead?' she whispered, touching his hand.

'Leo,' I said.

She smiled, a little guardedly, and I knew she was wondering if he was Jay's. But she said cheerfully, 'What a gorgeous name. You can put him down in my room before he wakes, if you like.'

...

With Leo asleep in Leanne's bedroom I collapsed onto the sofa and before I knew it I'd started to cry again. She put her arms around me and we stayed like that for a long time, until finally she voiced the question I had been waiting for. 'Leo... is he Jay's?' I nodded as we broke our embrace. 'The things I've heard,' she said. 'I feel terrible, the way I just abandoned you and let that man—'

'You didn't abandon me.'

'Yes, I did. I knew he was bad news. I knew it the second I met him. And when I saw how he kept that flat you shared, never a single thing out of place, not a speck of dirt, and he stopped you doing everything you loved...'

'You did try to warn me,' I said. 'Remember when you came round that time and you were so angry with him that you slapped him?'

'If I'd known what he was going to do to you I'd have done a lot more than slap him,' she said. She made a scissor motion with her fingers. 'I'd have cut his thing clean off.'

I smiled at her ferocity. 'I've really missed you.'

'God, me too,' she said. 'Why didn't you come before now? Were you... I guess you didn't want to risk coming back here.'

'No.'

She touched my hair. 'You've gone brunette.'

'Yeah.'

'So they still haven't caught him?'

'No.'

She was silent for a time. Then she drew her legs up onto the sofa and sat cross-legged. 'It's safe for you to be here, though? You don't think Jay...'

'Nobody seems to have heard from or seen Jay since I escaped from him. He's never made any contact with me.'

Leanne nodded. 'Well, hopefully he's dead,' she said bluntly. 'That's what he deserves.'

Jay

TWO WEEKS EARLIER

39

Jay sighed and stretched, trying to bring some life back into his limbs after another long day staking out Leanne's street in his van. When he had first thought of it, he'd been delighted with his plan, but now he'd been watching Leanne for a while, with no success, it was beginning to wear him down. He travelled to Coalton as often as he could, making excuses to Stephanie about what he was up to, but it was beginning to feel hopeless, and unsustainable. Today was no exception. Worse than that, when he arrived back home, Stephanie was waiting up for him in the kitchen, and from the look on her face, she meant business.

'I know you're not out working three or four nights a week,' she said, as her eyes met his. 'Not any kind of honest work, anyway.'

'Nothing I do is honest,' he said irritably. 'My whole life is a fucking lie.'

He threw himself down onto the free chair at the kitchen table. 'If you're looking to give me a hard time, just get on with it and spit it out, will you? I want to go to bed.'

'Tell me what you're really doing.'

He gave her a long look. 'It's late. I'm not talking about this now.'

She stood up and placed her palms on the table. 'Yes, you are! You're living in *my* house, and yes, I agreed to protect you, but I need to know what it is you're doing all the time.'

'*Your* house,' he said. 'What am I, then? Your pet? I thought I

160

was your boyfriend, Steph. Your equal. I thought we loved each other.'

'People who love each other tell each other the truth.'

'People who love each other tell the biggest lies,' he said. He got up too and started towards the door, but she stepped into his path. 'Please,' she said.

He looked into her insipid brown eyes, currently wide with desperation, and an idea struck him. He almost grinned. Her eyes widened further as he began his explanation, and by the time he'd finished, instead of looking cross, she was starting to look cautiously optimistic.

'I thought you said it would be impossible to turn any of your old friends in to the police,' she said. 'You told me they'd come after you, and me too, and that you'd still get in trouble.'

'Well, things have changed. I've been keeping my ear to the ground, seeing what's going on, and it's looking promising. These people I was mixed up with, they're not as strong as they once were. If I went to the police and they rounded the last of them up, I don't think anyone would come after you. And if I'm free, I'll be able to protect you, anyway.'

'You really think you'd go free? I thought you said you'd still end up going to prison, that the police were after you because of what you did—'

He waved her comments away. 'It's got to be worth a shot.'

She looked torn. Clearly she couldn't decide whether to believe him. Perhaps it did sound too good to be true, but there wasn't much he could do about that. He certainly couldn't say what he was really up to. 'And what about me?' she asked tentatively. 'I've been keeping you hidden, will I…'

'I'll smooth it over,' he told her. 'You won't get in any trouble.'

She raised her eyebrows. 'So… when can you go to the police? Are you ready now?'

'Soon,' he reassured her. 'I just need to keep on… monitoring the situation for a bit.'

'Isn't that risky? To keep going back to where you might be recognised, trying to get information about dangerous people?'

'It's fine,' he said. 'I know how to keep myself hidden.'

She still looked sceptical.

'What is it, Steph? I thought this was exactly what you wanted?'

'It is. But… after all this time telling me it's impossible…'

'Well, why would I lie now? That's what I'm spending my time working towards, Steph. I'm working towards us being together properly. Like you wanted. Like I want. You deserve it.'

After that, Jay stayed out as much as he wanted, confident that Stephanie wouldn't complain. He travelled to Coalton nearly every day, but the victory of getting Stephanie off his back was short-lived. What he was doing was such a long shot. He got sick of watching Leanne's flat. He had to be so careful, always stay a good distance away, and he never stayed for too long in one go: he'd drive around the block a few times, or go and get a coffee, then come back and park in a slightly different place. Leanne and her daughter Kayleigh would come and go, and sometimes other people would visit, though nobody of any use to Jay. Would Felicity ever visit her old friend?

Perhaps his only option was to wait until Leanne and Kayleigh were out and break into the flat to search for clues about Felicity. Once or twice when he saw them leave he told himself that he would do it, but he always stopped himself at the last minute before he got out of the van. Breaking in was so risky. What if he messed it up? What if he made loads of noise and disturbed the neighbours, or he couldn't get in through the window? Even if he managed to get in, he'd have to steal some things from her flat to make sure it looked like a burglary, but how would he have enough time to search everywhere and then mess around finding things to steal? He might end up spending so long that Leanne and Kayleigh came home – they might only be going out to the corner shop – and they'd catch him red-handed. Or, if he managed not to be caught by them, somebody on the street could look out of their window at just the wrong moment, see him leaving and watch him get into his van. If they took a note of his registration number, it would take the police straight to Stephanie's house.

Jay pressed his palms against his face. He had to stop this; he was driving himself crazy. The chances were that nobody would see anything and nobody would do anything. It would be difficult to hunt through Leanne's flat for details about Felicity – Leanne was the kind of person who wouldn't have anything tidy or organised – but what was the alternative? There was every chance that Felicity would never go to Leanne's flat in person.

Eventually, one weekend in early autumn, his patience ran out. He would have to break in. Kayleigh and Leanne would be away from the flat at some point over the whole weekend, surely, and he would seize his moment. He needed Felicity back. He'd had plenty of time to think of other options, and there were none. It was now or never.

Felicity

40

After our initial rush of words to each other, Leanne and I fell
silent. I looked around her living room, which had barely changed
from when I used to visit her in the past. There was a faded blue
carpet on the floor, a huge purple beanbag next to a striped
three-seater sofa, and an eclectic collection of art on the walls.
The place was cluttered, cosy and homely. I picked up a cushion
with an elephant embroidered on it, and hugged it in my lap. I'd
been so happy to see her, but now I had no idea what to say.

'In the news it said Jay is wanted in connection with two
deaths,' Leanne said, 'and for the false imprisonment of a
twenty-seven-year-old woman. I remember it all almost word for
word. Because the woman was you, wasn't it, Fliss?'

I didn't reply, so she nudged me gently with her knee. I nodded.

She didn't speak for a while, as though she was trying to decide
what words could possibly sum up her feelings about my ordeal.
'Well, you're here now,' she said, 'and that's all that matters. You're
safe. You got away from him.'

'Yeah,' I agreed weakly. I *had* got away from him, in any normal
sense of the word, though in truth, it didn't often feel that way to
me.

...

We spent the rest of the day talking, and playing with Leo when he
got up from his nap. Leanne said Kayleigh was going straight to a
friend's house after school, so I had plenty of time to tell her
about Scott and Dennis, and a little more about what had
happened between Jay and me. By about eight o'clock, Leo was in
bed for the night and I was exhausted. I yawned and put my head

in my hands.

'You need some rest,' Leanne said. 'I need to go and pick Kayleigh up, anyway. Do you want to sleep in my room with Leo? I can sleep on the sofa.'

'Thank you, Lee.'

'Now tomorrow, we'll talk some more if you want to. Kayleigh is here in the morning but she's going to the cinema for a friend's birthday in the afternoon, followed by a sleepover, so we'll have lots more time to catch up.'

'How is Kayleigh?' I asked. 'She must be…' I tried to work it out, but Leanne answered for me.

'Eleven. She's just started secondary school.'

'Wow.'

'Yep. She acts like she's a teenager already, so I think she's getting on just fine.'

I gave a small laugh, and she smiled at me. 'I know I've already said it, but I really am so glad to see you,' she told me.

As I snuggled up in bed next to Leo, a sense of calm overtook me. I missed Scott, but it was reassuring to be back in this place I knew so well, with my best friend since childhood. Leanne went out to collect Kayleigh, and later I heard them get home, Leanne shushing Kayleigh as they walked past my bedroom. I closed my eyes, and let myself drift off. I'd confide in Leanne tomorrow about the baby, and about my worries, though in truth I was already feeling calmer. Coming back to Coalton had been a good idea.

. . .

Woods. I was in Tatchley woods again. The trees were dense around me, and all was silent, except for the noises made by Mark and Jay as they walked just in front of me; leaves crunching, twigs snapping. Suddenly, they both stopped.

'Is that…' I whispered to Mark. 'Is that where… she…'

Mark nodded. Jay knelt down and put one hand flat on the earth in front of him, the earth where the police had found the remains of a sixteen-year-old girl; a girl whose whole life had been ahead of her, her only crime falling in love with a boy who couldn't control his temper.

Then my mind deviated from what had really taken place that day. Instead of picturing Jay kneeling in the dirt, mourning the loss of his first love, I could see an open grave, and Sammie's remains. Then the men began pushing me in too, until I fell in beside the bones. 'No!' I screamed. 'Don't leave me in here! Don't leave me in here!'

Then I was in another memory. I was on the bed in the room where Jay had kept me in Tatchley. His lips were hovering just above my skin, and I remembered some words he'd spoken. It was one of the most disturbing things he'd ever said to me, when he'd called me by her name. 'I love you, Sammie,' he said.

'Jay?' I whispered, in the darkness, frightened.

'It's okay, Sammie,' he said, 'everything is going to be okay. Everything I do is for you. For you and our baby. Just like you wanted.'

I woke drenched in sweat, shaking uncontrollably. The light came on and Leanne rushed over to me, stroking my hair and calming me down, while simultaneously talking reassuringly to Leo as well. 'Sssh, sssh,' she was saying. 'It's okay, it's okay.'

'Was I... did I wake you?' I asked.

'Don't worry,' she said.

She went over to the window to draw the curtains back, and sunlight filtered into the room from the tiny courtyard outside her subterranean home. 'It's morning,' she said. 'Let's get up now. I'll make pancakes. Or eggy bread. Or I've got a bit of bacon, and some baked beans. What does Leo like?'

Leo was still shaken and confused, but eventually he said, 'Pancakes.'

'Cool, pancakes it is then.'

She started towards the door, Leo following along behind her, but then she turned back to me. 'Nightmare?' she asked quietly. I nodded. 'Jay?' she asked. I nodded again.

'You were screaming,' she said.

'I'm so sorry, Lee—'

She gave my arm a squeeze. 'There's only one person who should be sorry, Fliss, and it's not you.' She smiled. 'Come and join us when you're ready.'

I nodded, and after taking a few minutes to compose myself, I went to find them in the kitchen.

Felicity

41

Once we'd spent a pleasant morning together, Kayleigh enjoying playing with little Leo, Leanne dropped her off at her party and we took Leo for a walk to the big play area in the centre of Coalton. To begin with Leo trotted in front of us happily, but it was a fairly long walk and when his legs got tired he flopped down in his pushchair.

'Leanne?' I said.

'Mm?'

'I think I'd like to look at my old house.'

She raised an eyebrow. 'You mean where you were with your parents?'

'Yeah.'

'Well, all right,' she said. We turned off down a side street and before long I was looking at the spot where my childhood home had once stood. The last time I'd been here, the remains of the house had still been there, a hollowed-out, blackened wreck, but now that was gone. In its place a brand new house was being constructed. The walls were up and the roof was on, but it was windowless and looked surreal; no builders were there on a Saturday afternoon. It was eerie, and somehow shocking, to see something so unfamiliar when the rest of the street was exactly as I remembered it. I even recognised one or two of the cars as ones my neighbours had had back when I'd still been at home. My parents' plot was one of the larger ones. Our house had been set back a bit from the road, the garden running down to a line of spindly trees and a little stream. Looking closer, I realised the site had been carved in two. There wasn't only one new house being built but a pair. The garden had been ripped up, and my dad's workshop – the only thing that had not been destroyed in the fire

— was gone.

'They were good people, your parents,' Leanne said once I'd had a chance to process the fate of my former home. 'And your dad, it was fucked up what he did, I'm not going to lie, but... that doesn't make him all bad. It doesn't cancel out all the good, you know?'

'You'd apply that to Jay, would you?'

'Jay's bad through and through,' she said, 'but your dad was kind, patient, clever. And he used to really make us laugh sometimes, do you remember? We'd never expect it because he seemed kind of quiet and serious, and then he'd suddenly say something so funny and we'd both just crack up.'

'Yes, I remember.'

'It's pride, isn't it?' she said. 'He must have been ashamed about all the money troubles, and when he found out they were going to lose the house...'

'That's exactly what Jay told me. That it was about pride.'

'Huh,' Leanne said. She didn't seem able to speak again, having been told she had any views in common with Jay.

'And when Jay said it, I told *him* how ridiculous it is that anyone could think burning their house down is better than admitting you need help with something. I wasn't a child! I was in my twenties and they let me live there and barely pay any rent, even though I had a full time job! I gave them something like fifty quid a month for bills and stuff. If I'd known about the shit they were in I could have given them ten times that. More. All I spent it on was clothes and going out, I just can't believe... I'm angry, Leanne! I'm so angry with them! With both of them! And my dad... my dad *killed* my mum in that fire! How am I supposed to come to terms with that? With the fact he wanted to leave me not only without my dad, but without my mum, too! I... I'm so...' I struggled for a word to sum it up and in the end repeated the one I'd used already. 'I'm so, so *angry!*'

I stared at her, shocked I'd said it out loud, but she encouraged me. 'Good,' she said. 'You've every right to be.'

I gave the building site another look. 'There's nothing here for me now,' I said. 'There's not anything of my childhood left. I don't have a single thing that belonged to either of them; it all just went up in smoke. My dad had disabled the fire alarms, did you know that? There's other houses on this street – what if it had spread before anyone realised? It was such a selfish, horrible, stupid, *senseless* thing to do!'

'I can't imagine what it was like to come back home and see what had happened.'

'I thought I was seeing things,' I told her. In truth, I couldn't remember it properly. My dad had chosen to set fire to the house on a night when I was out with my friends. I'd crashed at Leanne's place afterwards. The battery on my phone was dead and no one had been able to get hold of me, so the first I knew was when I walked up the street and saw all the emergency vehicles. The fire was out by that stage but the scene was like something from the TV, not from real life. Not something that happened in my life, to my house, and my family. I couldn't remember how I'd reacted, or much about what happened in the week that followed, apart from the fact that exactly seven days later I'd met Jay, and woken up the next morning in his bed.

'You miss them, though, don't you? I know how close you were, especially with your dad.'

'They weren't really like my parents. I mean, they were, but I felt like they were my friends too.'

I snapped back to reality. I didn't want to get lost in these memories; it wasn't helping anything. Leo was getting restless. He was whimpering and trying to climb out of his pushchair, so Leanne helped him and caught hold of his hand to stop him making a dash off down the street. She started walking with him and glanced back at me with a smile. I stayed for a moment longer, looking at the place where my family home had used to stand, and then I turned and followed Leanne and my son.

...

Leanne plonked two cups of tea onto the coffee table and sat down beside me. 'Right,' she said, 'now you are going to tell me why you've come here now, after all this time.'

She reached forward for the mugs, handed me mine and sat back against the sofa with hers. Leo had not long gone to bed, and I'd been looking forward to spending the evening talking to her, though now it had come to it I was clamming up again.

'What makes you think there's a specific reason?' I said. 'Couldn't it just be that I wanted to see you?'

'Well, was it?'

I took a sip of tea and shook my head. 'No. I mean, I did want to see you, but… there was something that triggered me to…'

'Is it the same reason you asked for tea when I offered you some perfectly respectable wine?'

I glanced round at her, and she said, 'I'm not daft, Fliss. You were pretty much asleep on my sofa by eight last night, I saw you looking queasy after breakfast this morning, and now you don't want to drink. How many weeks are you?'

'It's very early days. I only just found out.'

'Does Scott know?'

'No.'

She drew her legs up onto the sofa and crossed them. She was wearing patterned leggings today; black with red roses. I thought we must look a funny pair – her with such flamboyant outfits, while I was in nothing more exciting than jeans and a white and green floral shirt. 'Why haven't you told him?' she asked directly.

I hesitated, and then it all came pouring out. I said how scared I was that I'd somehow end up trapped like I had been with Jay, how I was worried that even though Scott had been nothing but kind up until now, things might change when I had his baby, and finally that I wasn't sure if I was ready to have another child when everything with Scott had been a bit of a whirlwind.

'Has he ever done anything to make you feel uncomfortable?'

I thought back over the months I'd spent with him. 'No,' I said. 'Things have happened fast, but he doesn't ever push me.'

'How did he react to you coming to see me? I noticed he's been texting you a bit.'

She was right: I had got a few messages from him since I'd arrived at Leanne's, but they were kind, not controlling.

'Only because he's worried about me. You can read the messages yourself if you want.' I held out my phone but she didn't take it. 'I don't need to read your messages, Fliss.' She looked at me closely. 'Are you here because you want my permission to have a relationship with Scott?'

I didn't answer straight away, but then I said, 'I think I might be, yes.'

'I warned you about Jay, so you want to know what I think about Scott before your relationship goes any further?'

I nodded.

'I've never met Scott.'

'I know.'

'Listen, Fliss, when you started seeing Jay, you were a different person to who you are now. Your head was in a very different place. You didn't want to listen to me. Perhaps you felt like you couldn't trust anyone from your life after what your parents did, and you wanted the alternative kind of life that Jay could offer you, I don't know. But you were hell-bent on spending time with him, and you accepted all the weird stuff about him. Which was fine until he started... until he turned nasty, but by then you'd already fallen for him. Look – what I'm trying to say is that you're going into this thing with Scott much more cautiously. Yes, it's happened fast, but you're thinking about him in a much more rational way to the way you thought about Jay. You might be scared to trust yourself or him, but to me it seems like you're safe. It seems like you've made a good choice.'

I didn't speak for a while, then she said, 'Show me that picture of him again.'

I opened a picture on my phone that I'd showed her the day before. It was Scott with his arm around Leo, both of them grinning widely. 'I know it's only a photo,' she said, 'but I can see how he is with Leo. They look so natural together. And I think he makes you smile, too, am I right?'

'Yeah. He makes me laugh, too.'

'What's he like in bed?'

'Leanne!'

She spread her hands wide. 'I'm just asking.'

A shadow fell over me. 'To be honest, I… after Jay… it's not… I don't find it easy.'

'Of course,' she said. 'I've got such a big mouth. Sorry, Fliss.'

'I find it difficult to forget how things ended up being between Jay and me. Sex isn't… it often doesn't feel how it's supposed to. It's like this switch just goes in my head sometimes. I'm okay, and then all of a sudden I think I'm back with Jay, and no matter how much I tell myself I'm with Scott and it's okay, once that switch has been switched, I…'

She touched my hand gently. 'Does Scott understand?'

'Yeah.'

'Good.'

'There was… one time, with Scott, the time that ended up getting me—' I waved vaguely at my stomach. '*That* time was…' I couldn't think of a word to describe it adequately.

'That good, huh?'

I nodded.

'In that case, I think your body is trying to tell you what your mind is too scared to admit,' Leanne said. 'You obviously love Scott, and you want to be with him. You don't need my permission. You know your own heart. But if you want me to come and visit and give him a good grilling on your behalf, I'm more than happy to. I'd like to meet him.'

I put my tea down. I suddenly felt fidgety.

'You're ready to go home and talk to him now, aren't you?' she said.

'I still feel scared. I'm scared all the time. I jump at shadows.'

Leanne took my hands. 'Fliss, you endured *months* trapped in some godforsaken house with Jay. You ran away from him, literally had to run through the woods while you were seven months pregnant. But you've still managed to bring up Leo on your own, find yourself a job, and do all of that while knowing that Jay might turn up on your doorstep. Just give yourself a break. You deserve to be happy with somebody new if that's what you want.'

As if on cue, my phone beeped and I saw I had a new message from Scott. I read it and showed it to Leanne.

'I hope you are enjoying catching up with Leanne,' she read out loud. 'I miss you ever so much, but don't come back if you're not ready. I understand if you need some time to talk things through with her, so take as long as you need, and I'll be here waiting. I love you.'

Hearing the words out loud filled me with a surge of emotion. Suddenly all I wanted in the world was to be back with him again, and it must have been written all over my face. Leanne stood up and starting pulling me up from the sofa. 'Go back to him,' she said. 'Go, now. It's not too late, Leo will stay asleep while you're driving, won't he? And you can get back there by midnight.'

'No, it's silly, I can't...'

'Are you going to be able to sleep if you stay here?' she asked. 'You want to go to him and tell him about the baby, so do it now while you feel fired up, don't leave it.'

'What about you? I feel like I only just got here...'

'Don't worry about me. Just call me tomorrow and tell me how it went, okay?'

My mind made up, I didn't hesitate a moment longer. I loaded our bags into the car and transferred Leo into his car seat, and when I hugged Leanne goodbye it was as if some of her strength was transferred to me. Leanne stood briefly at the top of the steps and waved me off, the breeze playing with her colourful hair, and I smiled. I wanted to be with Scott. I wanted my life back. I wanted it more than anything. It was as though I was waking up. I'd spent so many years in a fog, but now I was going to fight for what I wanted, and I wasn't going to let Jay, or what had happened with my parents, or my fear, hold me back any more.

Jay

42

Jay watched as the door to Leanne's flat opened. It was Saturday afternoon, and he'd been waiting on her street on and off for the past couple of days. He shook himself to try to shift some of the lethargy that had settled into his body. He was so bored his eyes had begun to glaze over. Leanne made her way up the steps, her ridiculous red hair streaming over her shoulders. God, why had Felicity ever been friends with such an irritating, opinionated woman? The answer was simple: she was weak. That's why she needed people who would take her under their wing – but she was much better under the wing of a man like him, someone who could look after her properly, not a woman who looked like she deliberately dressed to repel anyone of the opposite sex. How on earth Leanne had managed to have a daughter Jay couldn't imagine.

Leanne had reached the top of the steps now, and Jay sat bolt upright. She wasn't alone! Another woman was with her, holding hands with a small boy. He narrowed his eyes as he watched the small group make their way to a car parked outside Leanne's flat. The woman took a pushchair from the boot, and the three began making their way down the street away from him. He peered closely at their receding bodies. The other woman. There was something familiar about her. She was too far away for him to get a close look. Surely, she couldn't be... But the way she moved, the shape of her body, the child too, a child who seemed about the right age. Every one of his hairs stood on end. It was Felicity! He was certain now. She had short brown hair, not the lovely straight blonde hairstyle he'd adored on her – which reminded him so much of Sammie – but it was unmistakable.

Jay looked at the little blond-haired boy, walking along beside his mother. That boy was his son! His body went hot and then cold, like he had a fever. What should he do? He wanted them so badly he was tempted to go and snatch them from the street, but it was broad daylight. Leanne was there. Other people were walking around too, there were cars on the road – people everywhere.

Staring at the small group, he opened up his phone camera, zoomed in as much as he could and snapped several pictures. His heart hurt as they made their way further down the road, finally disappearing from sight, but what else could he do? He needed to wait for a better opportunity – he'd be patient and see what happened next. At some point Felicity would be on her own, or some chance would present itself for him to follow her, or discover more about her. He'd waited over two years for this; it wouldn't kill him to wait a little longer. Patience was of the essence.

As the afternoon wore on, he moved his van a couple of times, spending a few minutes driving around and then parking again in a slightly different location. It killed him to think that one of the times he left could be when the opportunity he needed would present itself. After all, he hadn't seen Felicity arrive – that must have happened at a time he was away from the street. But, equally, he simply couldn't risk always staying in one place. He'd just have to make sure he was never away for too long.

At last he caught sight of the group returning from wherever they had been, and they all went straight inside again.

...

It was early evening. He was beginning to give up hope, when Felicity finally emerged again, and she made her way along the pavement to her car. He watched her closely, his heart pounding. What now? What should he do? She had bags with her that she was loading into the car, and Leanne had come out now too, holding a box of children's toys that Felicity must have brought for her – his – *their* son to play with. The two women talked for a moment and hugged, then Felicity placed her handbag on the passenger seat of her car and the two women went back towards the flat. Jay's mind raced. Felicity must be going back inside to fetch the boy, and then she'd presumably drive back to wherever it was she actually lived. Should he rush over and confront her? Could he hide inside her car? It didn't look like she'd locked it. He began to sweat.

No, he told himself, *you're being crazy. Think sensibly.* He couldn't confront her, and neither could he snatch her and the boy right now – he had nowhere to take them, no plan, and Leanne might decide to stand on the street and wave them off. Following the car was an option, but he wasn't keen on that either. Felicity had a lot of stuff with her – she'd been staying overnight, which meant she must not live locally. Following her for a long journey would be difficult. If he lost her he'd be left with nothing, and if she realised she was being followed she might call the police.

Suddenly, he remembered her handbag on the passenger seat. If she hadn't locked the car – and he was sure she hadn't – he could rush over, and look through her bag for her address. She'd almost certainly have her driver's licence in her purse. If he took a photo of it, then he'd have her address. He quickly opened his door. He was scared – petrified, in fact – that he would be caught, but it was now or never. He had to take the risk.

Jay

43

Jay sprinted towards the car. Running made him more conspicuous, but he had no choice. Unless he moved as fast as possible, Felicity would spot him.

When he reached out for the door handle he had a moment of doubt, worried the car would be locked. His hand closed around the cool metal, and he gave a tug. The door opened, and he squatted down in an effort to stay out of sight. With a surge of adrenalin, he frantically pulled the zip of her handbag open. It was a large bag, and inside was an overwhelming jumble of stuff – a packet of tissues, hand cream, old receipts, vouchers, a small hairbrush. He shoved it all aside and his hand closed around a pale blue leather purse. Among the loyalty cards, bank card and credit card he spotted her driver's licence and slid it out.

He paused, surprised, when he saw the name. *Felicity Hart.* Hart? What was that all about? Had she changed her name? Of course that made sense, if she was trying to hide. Was the little boy's surname Hart too, rather than Kilburn, like it should be? He took out his phone and snapped a couple of pictures of the front of her licence.

Then he froze. Were those women's voices he could hear? He quickly put everything back how he had found it. After closing the car door as slowly and quietly as he could, he risked poking his head up high enough to see if it was Felicity and Leanne who were coming. He immediately ducked back down behind the car again. It was them. The little boy was in pyjamas with a blanket wrapped round him, sound asleep against Felicity's shoulder. The two women were immersed in conversation and paying little attention to anything else, but even so, he needed to get away from the car. With Felicity nearby, running across the road was out of the question, but it was a busy street with plenty of cars parked along the curb, so there was a more discreet way of escaping.

He shuffled carefully along the road until he was squatting behind a different car, then he edged around to the front of it, and stayed out of the way between the car's bonnet and the back of a van. He rubbed his face with his hands and felt beads of perspiration on his forehead. Although he was hiding, he felt very exposed. He was out of sight of Felicity and Leanne, but what would anyone else think if they spotted him hiding like this? He'd look like a criminal – which was, of course, what the world thought he was.

Eventually, he heard Felicity open the car door and close it again. She must have been putting the little boy inside. Then Felicity and Leanne exchanged all sorts of mushy sentiments about how glad they were to see each other and that they should meet again soon. He rolled his eyes. 'And I loved meeting Leo,' Leanne said. Jay's ears pricked up; that was the name of the boy! Leo. He quite liked it. At least Felicity hadn't given his son a stupid name, even if she believed Leo didn't deserve to know his own father. 'Go home to Scott,' Leanne continued, 'and be happy. God knows you've earned it.'

Scott? Blood rushed to Jay's head. Who the fuck was Scott? Did Felicity have a boyfriend? No. She wouldn't dare, would she? His rage made him reckless and he peeped out from behind the car, up at the two women. They were hugging. He hid again. Why didn't Felicity just go? Why did they have to drag it out like this, on and on and on? He needed to be away from here. He needed to think, and cool down, and get his head clear.

But the name kept going round and round in his brain. Scott. Surely she didn't have a boyfriend. What man would want her anyway, with a toddler in tow, and a whole lot of unfinished business with the boy's real father? Finally, thankfully, he heard her get into the car and start the engine. As her car pulled away, he sighed and checked the photos he'd taken of her driver's licence. Alstercombe. He'd never heard of the place. He peeped out to see whether Leanne was still on the pavement, and saw her disappearing down the steps to her flat. Thank God.

Safely back in the van, he tried not to think about Scott, but questions about him kept intruding anyway. Could she really be with somebody else, *love* somebody else? No. It was impossible, a mistake, maybe even some kind of revenge against him, to make him jealous. Once he finally got a chance to speak to her, it would get sorted out. He'd make her see how ridiculous she was being. It was him that she truly loved. No other man could ever come close.

Stephanie

44

Stephanie jumped at the sound of Jason's key in the door. She turned off the history documentary she'd been watching on TV – she hadn't been able to concentrate on it anyway – and now Jason was home she was keen to talk to him. Since his admission about how he was spending his time, her head had filled with questions. If he was telling the truth about wanting to give information to the police, she was proud of him, but would he really be safe? She didn't want him to put himself in danger. On the other hand, if he was actually doing something else... But what? Stephanie sighed. She couldn't bear to think about it any more.

When Jason came and found her, his mood was odd – as though he was excited, yet with an edge of anger. 'Do you want to talk about it?' she asked him.

'No.'

'Okay. Well, you know I'm here for you.'

He gave her a strange look. Then it was as if he couldn't be bothered to even try being civil with her. 'I don't want to talk to you right now,' he told her. 'I'm going to bed.'

'It's early.'

'I'm knackered.'

She let him go. There was no point trying to force him to spend time with her. She turned the TV back on, and wiped away a stray tear from her cheek.

When she went upstairs a little later, Jason wasn't in the bedroom. She went back out into the hall. The bathroom door was closed, and there was a strip of light showing under the door. Perhaps he felt ill or something. She moved towards to the door, and froze when she heard some sounds from inside. She leaned a little closer, and then her cheeks grew warm as she realised what she had overheard. Jason wasn't ill, he was masturbating.

She took a step back, wondering what to do. If she retreated back downstairs, he might hear her going down the steps, and then he would realise he'd been overheard. She made her way quietly into the bedroom, and sat down on the bed. Jason's needs were a lot more complicated than hers, and she'd realised pretty early in their relationship that he watched a lot of porn – not that she'd ever mentioned anything to him about it, and she didn't really mind that much – but she was surprisingly sad about the whole thing tonight. Why did there have to be so much of his life she was excluded from? Why did he get so little out of their relationship, when to her, being with him – especially being intimate with him – had always meant so much? Was the way he acted towards her normal? Was the way he treated her her own fault somehow? She'd never been in a relationship before, so she had nothing to compare her experience to.

Even though she told herself it was a silly, childish thing to do, she opened a drawer to take one of his t-shirts out. If she could only hold it against her, bury her face in the fabric, it might make her feel a little closer to him. She grabbed a t-shirt furtively, mindful of the fact that he didn't like his things being touched. He did all the washing and ironing, and putting clothes away. But she paused when she caught sight of a piece of notepaper in the back of the drawer. She took it out, meaning to throw it away because it must be a piece of rubbish, but it had something written on it:

Keith Vinney
56a Travis Road
Graycott
Wrexton

Her heart missed a beat. Keith Vinney – her father? What on earth was Jason doing with her dad's address? Had he somehow discovered where he lived? Was he going to surprise her with the information? She held the paper in her hands, staring at it in astonishment. What did this mean? Could she see Dad? At last, after waiting for so long.

The bedroom door opened, and she held up the paper. 'How did you get this, Jason?'

Was that a flash of anger on his face? She must have imagined it, because it was gone as quickly as it had appeared, and when he sat down beside her he spoke softly. 'I was going to tell you, Steph, honestly I was.'

'What do you mean?'

'He came to the house. He wanted to see you, and I told him to leave you alone.'

'You... you did what?' She stared at him incredulously. What was he thinking? He'd been there after her granddad's funeral; he'd *seen* how upset she was that her dad had never shown up. She'd told him more times than she could remember how much she wanted her dad to come knocking at the door one day, and now he was telling her that that exact thing, the thing she dreamed about, had actually *happened?*

'I don't want him to get suspicious about me,' Jason continued, as if he hadn't noticed her horror. 'It could blow everything I'm working towards.'

'You... you turned him away?' She had a sudden urge to slap him, but she didn't. 'How could you?'

'I did it for us! I made sure he gave me his address, so that you'll be able to see him in the future. Once I've sorted everything out and I'm not trying to hide any more, the first thing I was going to do was tell you about him. I was looking forward to it. All I want is for you to be happy, for us both to be happy.'

'You could still have told me. I don't know how you could keep this from me! This wasn't your decision to make!'

He grabbed her hands. 'To keep us safe. I knew how much you'd want to see him, but I couldn't risk losing everything we've worked for. Please, Steph, listen to me. Once I've sorted everything, you can have a relationship with him – of course I won't stand in your way. I want to know him too. I want... I want to show him I'm a good man, and to ask him if I can marry you.'

She gave him a long look. Was he joking? He went from one extreme to the other, avoiding her one second, coming out with things like that the next. He was desperate for her to believe him, and it made her suspicion deepen. 'Why should I trust you?' she said. 'If you hide something as big as my dad coming here to find me, why should I believe a word you say?'

Felicity

45

Back in Alstercombe I made my way straight to Scott's flat. Now I'd made my mind up, I was full of excitement to tell him about the baby, but once I turned onto his street I heard a commotion. He was out in the street, and Vicky was there too. They were arguing loudly. I parked a little way away and turned the engine off, unsure what to do. I didn't particularly want to get in the middle of an argument, but I needed to get Leo into bed and I was desperate to talk to Scott. As I opened the door, some of their words drifted over to me. 'It's not like Felicity's had an easy time either,' Scott said, 'so don't make out like she doesn't deserve to be happy.'

'What's she had to deal with that's so hard?' Vicky shot back at him, her voice slurred. 'Is the love of her life dead?'

Scott raised his hands to his head in a gesture of utter despair and frustration.

'Why doesn't she go back to her boy's dad, and leave you alone?' Vicky continued. 'Why does she need *you*? *I'm* the mother of your child, Scott—'

'And where is Den?' he said. 'Being looked after by a friend, while you've been spending all weekend getting drunk.'

'I need time to deal with everything.'

'Then go home and deal with it! You're not helping yourself by constantly coming to see me. Give yourself some space from me, Vix, for God's sake, or you're going to drive yourself crazy.'

'Just because *Felicity* can move on so quickly from Leo's dad, doesn't mean all women can—'

I started to get out of the car, but I froze as Scott shouted, 'Felicity's ex is a violent, sadistic rapist, Vix. That's why she's not

185

with him, not that she needs to justify herself to anyone.'

I frowned. I didn't particularly want Vicky to know my business, but equally, I couldn't blame Scott for snapping and wanting to shut her up. They still hadn't noticed me, so I carefully took Leo out of the car and held him close, his head heavy on my shoulder as he nestled against me. I didn't catch their next few words, but as I made my way towards them, still unnoticed, Vicky said, 'I don't care what her ex did to her, Scott. You're not a charity worker, you don't have to look after her because she's some sort of *victim.*'

A stab of pain went through me at her words, and I froze. Scott said, 'She's not a victim. She's a survivor.'

For some reason this infuriated Vicky. She stumbled on the pavement as she stepped towards Scott, and screamed, 'She's not the mother of your child! I *am.*'

I got close enough that Scott spotted me, though it took Vicky a little longer. When she eventually turned, she said, 'Oh, look, here she is.'

'I am too,' I said, the words spilling out before I could stop them. Even though it was bound to aggravate her further, I couldn't help myself.

'What?' she spat. 'What are you talking about?'

'I'm pregnant,' I told her. She stared at me, then she and I both turned to Scott. He was watching me with an expression of wonder, his anger evaporated. Vicky, however, was enraged. 'I don't believe this,' she shouted at Scott. 'You've known her *five minutes!* What is wrong with you? Haven't you heard of condoms?'

His attention turned back to her. 'Vicky, you're drunk. We shouldn't be yelling in the street, it's ridiculous. And Leo is asleep.'

Vicky glanced at the little boy asleep on my shoulder and said, 'Like I give a shit about that.'

'I'll call you a taxi,' Scott told her.

'Save yourself the trouble. You don't care what happens to me. You've made that clear over and over again.' She pointed her finger at me. 'You be careful, Felicity. Scott is not the nice guy he makes himself out to be. When it comes down to it, he couldn't give a shit about anyone other than himself. Why don't you get him to tell you exactly what he's done to me? Like how he tried to ruin things between me and Tim—'

'Ignore her, Fliss,' Scott said quickly. 'She doesn't know what she's saying.'

'*She* does know what she's saying,' Vicky said. She glared at both of us, and then began to stumble away. 'This isn't over,' she said.

...

'Are you really pregnant?' Scott asked as soon as I'd put Leo to bed and joined him in the living room.

I laughed. 'I'd hardly lie about it.'

He put his hand on my stomach, and then he lifted my top up and kissed my tummy until it began to tickle me. I dropped down onto the sofa giggling, trying playfully to push him away. 'I love you so much,' he told me. 'You've made me so happy.'

'I love you too.'

'Are *you* happy about the baby?'

'Yes. I… I'm a little scared, but I'm happy too.'

'Did it help to talk to Leanne?'

'Yes. It made me realise – well, how much I want this. All of it. You, the baby. Our family.'

He kissed my cheek. 'Move in here. Move in straight away. Tomorrow. You don't have much stuff, it won't take long. It's a Sunday, I can rope some people in to help. I know a couple of guys with vans. I'm sure one of them will be free.'

I didn't answer straight away. 'Only if you want to,' he added. 'But you'll be leaving your flat soon anyway. I just thought you could bring it forward a few weeks.'

'I do want to,' I said. 'We can start moving my stuff tomorrow. I don't really feel like I live there any more; I feel like I live here already. And… and hopefully soon we'll have the house. A proper home together.' I smiled, but then I looked at him squarely. 'There is something that is worrying me.'

'What's that?'

'What was Vicky talking about when she said you messed things up between her and Tim? Martin hinted at something similar when he came to speak to me. I thought he just meant you were discouraging Tim from being with Vicky, but... was there something else?'

Scott sighed, and nodded. 'Yeah. I've been wanting to tell you, actually, but I'm embarrassed about what I did. It was such a stupid thing. It was... almost like a prank, really, but it was cruel. Martin and I shouldn't have done it. It was a terrible way of getting our point across. It almost cost us our friendship with Tim.'

'So,' I pressed him, 'What was this... prank? What did you and Martin do?'

Scott

4 YEARS AGO

46

'Someone's popular,' Martin said, as Tim's phone bleeped for what felt like the hundredth time that night. In reality, it had probably happened somewhere between fifteen and twenty times. And each time, Tim's frown had deepened as he'd glanced at the message. He now looked positively harassed.

'Is it Vicky?' Scott asked.

'Why would you assume that?' Tim shot back, with unexpected hostility.

Scott held his hands up. 'All right. Sorry.'

Moments later, Tim slipped away from their table, taking his phone with him and saying he'd be back in a second.

'He's gone to call her,' Martin said.

'Yeah, I know.' It happened every time Tim went out anywhere with them – whether it was to the pub, as tonight, or whether they went somewhere during the day. The three of them had gone mountain biking the previous weekend. Tim had checked his phone as they stopped for a break and Scott had seen he had eleven missed calls. Whenever they tried to talk to Tim about Vicky, though, he would act like he didn't know what they were talking about, or get defensive. It wasn't like him at all. They both hated how much he'd changed.

'Everything okay?' Scott asked when Tim returned. To his surprise, Tim threw his phone down on the table and said, 'I wish she'd just leave me the hell alone for five fucking minutes.'

'So... it is Vicky?' Scott pressed him.

'Why don't you just turn your phone off?' Martin said.

'Because then she'll get suspicious.'

'Suspicious of what?'

'You know what.'

'She thinks you're cheating on her?' Scott said.

'Nothing I say or do ever convinces her otherwise.'

Martin picked up Tim's phone as it beeped again. 'Why can't you just come home?' he read from the screen. Tim snatched it back off him. 'She just gets... wound up,' he said. 'She doesn't mean anything by it.'

Martin took out his own phone and started writing a message. 'Vix, Tim's with us, chill the hell out,' he said as he typed.

'Don't send her that—'

'Sent.'

Tim gave Martin a long look. 'I'm going home,' he said in the end.

'You should never have moved in with her,' Martin said as Tim began to walk away. 'She's taking over your life.'

...

'Well, that was subtle,' Scott said once Tim had left. 'I thought we agreed a softly-softly approach was going to be best for this. You know how touchy he gets about Vicky.'

'The whole thing does my head in,' Martin said. 'Why is she like this? Did she have some boyfriend in the past who was a real dick to her or something?'

'There was Ollie, he cheated on her in the end, but... I think she was already paranoid before that.'

'Well, someone's really fucked her head up.'

Scott shrugged. He didn't know why Vicky was the way she was. He wondered about it himself, why she assumed nobody would be faithful to her. Did she just not trust anybody, or did she feel deep down that she didn't deserve anybody's love in the first place? Either way, her beliefs were a self-fulfilling prophecy. If she carried on like this, she would drive everybody away.

'Tim needs to open his eyes,' Martin said. 'In fact, I've got an idea.'

'Okay…' Scott wasn't sure he liked the sound of it, especially as there was a mischievous expression on Martin's face.

'Something that should make all this crap between Tim and Vix stop for good.'

'You mean, a plan to break them up?'

'Hopefully.'

'I don't know… I think perhaps we should leave them alone. Tim's a grown man, he can make up his own mind. If we keep pushing him, he might decide he'd rather stop seeing us than stop seeing her.'

Martin didn't say any more about it, but Scott knew that he wouldn't be easily dissuaded from his plan, whatever it was.

…

For two weeks, Scott heard nothing more about it. He hoped the whole thing had been forgotten, but at a house party for Tim's birthday a couple of weeks later, Martin took him to one side to show him something.

'What on earth?' Scott said, as Martin pulled something pale blue and lacy from his jeans pocket.

Martin grinned, pleased with himself. 'Isn't it obvious? We hide these under their bed upstairs. You know what'll happen if Vicky finds women's underwear up there. She'll go ballistic and throw Tim out. It'll be the end of all this nonsense.'

Scott took a closer look at the item in Martin's hand, a blue lace thong with a little white bow on the front. 'For God's sake, put it away,' he said. 'The whole idea is crazy. For all you know, Vicky might have underwear like that anyway. She might just think it's hers.'

Martin put the thong back in his pocket. 'I don't think she'd have these.'

Scott raised an eyebrow. 'How would you know?'

'Come on, she wouldn't, would she? She'd wear black or red or bright pink or something. Not pale blue.'

'I can't believe we're even talking about this. This is just… it's weird. And wrong.' Despite his words, though, he had to admit the idea of Vicky finding the underwear, the look on her face, wasn't entirely unappealing. He remembered all the looks he'd seen on Tim's face recently, how withdrawn and unhappy he'd become.

'You're thinking about it,' Martin said. 'I can see you are. You haven't said no.'

'I'm getting another drink,' Scott said. 'Let's see how the evening plays out before we make any rash decisions.'

Scott

PRESENT DAY

47

Scott waited for Felicity's reaction. She'd be disgusted with him, surely. 'Did you do it?' she asked him. 'I'm guessing you did, if that's what Vicky means when she says you messed up her relationship with Tim.'

Scott nodded. In the end he'd done the deed himself, creeping into the bedroom while Martin kept watch on the landing. He'd put the underwear just out of sight beneath Tim and Vicky's bed. In the end, it had felt like the right thing to do.

'It was the way she treated him that night,' he said. 'The party was for *his* birthday, but she kept putting him down. Not in ways that were really obvious, but all these little things. It all added up. And then Martin and I overheard her talking to Tim in the kitchen – she was angry with him for inviting us. To his own birthday. I just saw red.'

Felicity put her hand on his leg and he looked at her in surprise. 'You're not horrified, then?'

She shook her head. 'Leanne hit Jay once. She slapped him across the face.'

'How did he react?'

'He tried to put me off seeing her. He said she put ideas in my head about him.'

Scott winced as he remembered what had unfolded after Vicky had found the underwear.

Felicity gave a small smile as if she understood. 'How long did it take for them to realise you and Martin were behind it?'

'Tim turned up at my door. I think it was the evening after the party, maybe the day after that, I can't remember exactly. He was really shaken up. Vicky had thrown him out, they'd had an almighty row, and he was so angry because he hadn't done anything – he was saying he thought she'd done it herself, that *she'd* hidden the underwear. He was telling me that he was seriously worried about her, that he thought she needed professional help. I couldn't not say anything. I admitted what I'd done. I tried to tell him that I thought Vicky needed help regardless. I mean, surely no one treats their partner like that unless they've got a lot of bad stuff going on in their own head. Something in her was driving her to keep checking up on him, to get so paranoid. It was hurting them both, it was so destructive.'

'Did he listen?'

'Of course he didn't, not after what I'd done. He was furious. He said he never wanted me or Martin to come near him again, and then he left. He did forgive us eventually, but it took a long time, and a fair bit of grovelling on our part.' Scott thought back to the months Tim had completely blanked them. 'Which is saying something,' he added, 'because Tim wasn't really the sort of person to hold a grudge. He hated conflict, he just wanted everybody to get along. It's no wonder Vicky sucked the life out of him. I think what we did began to open his eyes about her. Not straight away, but after a while. It wasn't worth it, though, and I really regret it. He'd have come to the same conclusion on his own, without us interfering.'

'What conclusion?'

'He was going to break up with her. He told Martin and me, just a few days before he went climbing with me and… you know.'

'Just before he died.'

Scott nodded. 'He said he'd told Vicky several times that she needed to get some help. She'd agree, but she never followed through. Or she'd turn it around and make Tim feel like all her problems were his fault. She really got inside his head – he spent hours going through it all with us. I think he needed us to confirm to him that he wasn't losing his mind, that it really was her being unreasonable.'

'And he concluded they'd be better off apart.'

'Yeah. He said he'd given her too many chances already, and that he couldn't take it any more. He loved her, but he was miserable with her.' Scott hesitated. 'The thing is, Vicky doesn't know he made that decision. He died before he ever said anything to her about breaking up.'

Felicity nodded. 'So… what I don't get, if she hates you so much for what you did, how on earth did you and her end up having a baby together?'

'I can give you the answer to that in a couple of words,' he said. 'Grief and alcohol.'

'The same way I got together with Jay.'

'I guess so. Except I already knew Vicky, so when I woke up with her the next day, I already knew what a huge mistake I'd made.'

'Does she feel that it was a mistake?'

Scott thought about it. Honestly, he had no idea how Vicky felt about that night.

'I mean, she seems very possessive of you for somebody who claims not to like you,' Felicity continued. 'It… it's kind of weird, isn't it?'

'Well, no matter how we feel about having slept together, we both love Dennis,' he said at length. 'We wouldn't change him for the world. I tried to be there for her as much as I could while she was pregnant. I went round to help her every day when Dennis was a baby, or sometimes I'd take the night shift with him so she could rest. I think she got used to me being around, and when I started to distance myself, she didn't like it. Perhaps I let her get too close to me. But… I just wanted to help her. I felt guilty. I never purposefully blurred any boundaries. Half the time when I went to help, she'd go and lie down; we weren't even in the same room together. I guess I must have confused her feelings for me though, by doing all that. She tries things with me sometimes. While you were away she came to the workshop and tried to kiss me. Every time it happens I don't think I could be any clearer that I don't want it.'

Felicity frowned. 'She tried to *kiss* you?'

'I think she's scared of losing me. She wants to feel like she has somebody there for her. In the past, I have been, but now I wonder whether trying to be her friend has done more harm than good.'

'So you don't have any feelings for her? None at all?'

Scott almost laughed at the idea. 'I really don't, Fliss,' he said. 'I never have, and I never will. I don't want to have any interactions with her that aren't to do with Dennis, I can promise you that. Sometimes…' He almost said that he wished she wasn't Den's mum, but he couldn't let himself think that. No matter what he thought of her as a person, she'd given him a wonderful little boy.

It was like Tim had said: he just wished Vicky would leave him the hell alone for five minutes.

Vicky

48

Vicky woke with a jolt. What was that sound? She rubbed her eyes, and the noise came again. It was somebody knocking on her door. She squinted at the time on her phone – nine a.m. With a sigh she dragged herself out of bed, and when she opened the door she was stunned to find Felicity there.

'What the hell do *you* want?' she asked. Felicity was taking in the sight of her hot pink pyjamas and tangled heap of hair. Why hadn't she at least brushed her hair before she came downstairs? The last thing she wanted was for Felicity to see her looking like this, especially as she was so composed. She was wearing jeans and a striped white-and-navy-blue top, a thin silver bracelet around one wrist. She smelled of fruity shower gel, and seemed to be alone.

'May I come in?' Felicity asked.

'I'd rather you didn't.'

'Listen, Vicky, I'm sorry for just coming out and saying I'm pregnant the way I did last night. I shouldn't have said it to try to score points in an argument.'

Vicky didn't reply. So, Felicity was trying to be civil. It just made her even more irritating.

'I'd like us to all try to get along,' Felicity continued.

Vicky almost burst out laughing. 'Did Scott send you here to say this?'

'Scott doesn't know I'm here. He's taken Leo to the play-ground, while I go back to my flat and start packing. I'm moving in with him today.'

Vicky froze. What the fuck was this? Had Felicity come round so that she could savour delivering this news herself? Vicky was on the verge of lunging at her to scratch her eyes out, but she caught herself. That's probably what Felicity wanted. Instead, she dug her nails into her own palms until the pain cleared her head. 'I thought you weren't trying to score points,' she said, as calmly as she could.

'I'm not.'

'So why did you come round to tell me you're moving in with him?'

'You already knew I would be soon. Look, that's not why I came. We're going to have to find a way to tolerate each other at least, for Dennis's sake if nobody else's.'

'So now you're telling me what's best for my son?'

A line appeared between Felicity's eyebrows. She fussed with her bracelet. 'If anyone knows how out of hand things can get when there's... jealousy, it's me, Vicky.'

'You mean because of your ex?'

'If you let Scott go, you and him could get on a lot better than you do now.'

Vicky's irritation boiled over. Her head was pounding, and Felicity's voice was like nails down a blackboard. 'Just... just go away, Fliss! Leave me alone!'

Felicity's right, the little voice piped up in Vicky's mind. *You're your own worst enemy, Vix. So hot-headed and idiotic, you've driven everybody away.*

Felicity had taken a step back, startled by her outburst. 'I'm sorry if I've made things worse,' she said quickly. 'I didn't mean to. I've had enough drama and conflict to last me a lifetime, and I don't want to fight you. I don't think we need to be fighting. Scott's told me about how things have been difficult for you, with... anxiety and things. I... since my ex, I've struggled myself.'

Vicky stared at her. Was she for real? 'Well, why didn't you say so before?' Vicky taunted her, 'All this time, we could have been best buddies.'

Felicity gave her a hard look. 'I came here in good faith,' she said. 'I'm trying to be honest with you, and make a bad situation better. I didn't mean that you and I are the same. What I went through and what you've been through are completely different—'

'You're damn right,' Vicky said. 'I don't have any sympathy for you. If a man hit me, I'd get him out of my life so fast it would make his head spin. I wouldn't keep going back for more.'

Felicity visibly recoiled, as though Vicky herself had hit her.

'I've not come here to talk about what happened to me,' Felicity said when she'd recovered. 'Or to justify anything I did or didn't do. I came here because I thought we could all come to a better understanding. I can see I was wrong. But let me say this. If you want to make mine and Scott's life difficult, fine. We can handle it. The one who's really going to suffer because of all this is Dennis, and I'm sure that's not what you want.'

'Don't bring my son into this! You're not his mother, I am!'

Felicity looked exaggeratedly round Vicky's shoulder into the house. 'Where is he, then? He's not even here. You got someone else to look after him while you went out on some sort of bender last night.'

'So I'm not even allowed to have a bit of time to myself now? A bit of fun?'

'Were you having fun arguing with Scott in the street last night? It didn't look fun. It looked pitiful, frankly.'

Vicky's skin prickled with anger as Felicity turned to leave. 'Is your ex in prison, then?' she asked on a sudden whim. 'If he's as bad as Scott says he is?'

Finally, Felicity lost her upper hand. Her eyes flicked over Vicky's face. There was fear in them. 'No, he's not.'

'Where is he, then? Is he not interested in his son?'

'I think I should go now. I've said what I came here to say.'

Felicity took a step back and Vicky said, 'Are you hiding from him? Is that why you're so keen to be with Scott, to protect you from your ex?'

'I'm with Scott because I love him,' Felicity said. 'I don't need protecting.'

Vicky smiled. Everything about Felicity's body language was saying otherwise. The woman was diminished now, nervous and unsure. Joy surged through Vicky's body. She'd got the better of

Felicity. She'd discovered her weakness. 'Well, I hope he does manage to track you down,' Vicky said, 'and I hope he really hurts you.'

She slammed the door in Felicity's face.

Felicity

49

The rest of the day was so busy I barely had time to think about my conversation with Vicky, or to talk to Scott about it. Going to see her had been a spur of the moment decision – even I hadn't really known I was going to do it until I found myself standing at her door. I just wanted to make peace, and for life to be simpler. If only she hadn't found out I was pregnant the way she did. I had to conclude, though, that my visit had been a miscalculation. She obviously hated me, and there was little I could do to break through a wall like that.

Scott roped in a couple of friends to help move my stuff to his flat, and by late afternoon my belongings were all safely inside his four walls. Although I didn't own a lot, and I'd rented my flat ready-furnished, the addition of all my clothes, Leo's toys, pots and pans from my kitchen and other bits and bobs made Scott's flat look suddenly very small.

'We can go for a second viewing of the house next week,' Scott suggested.

'Are you having second thoughts about having me and Leo here now you've seen all the clutter?' I asked him light-heartedly.

He smiled. 'It's not clutter,' he said, with a glance around at the boxes and bags in the living room. 'It's just stuff that isn't unpacked yet.'

I rubbed my face with my hands, suddenly exhausted. 'I'd better try to sort Leo's stuff out, at least,' I said. 'He won't like it if he can't find anything.'

By the time I got into bed I was so tired I fell asleep instantly, but sometime in the dead of night my dreams took a turn for the worse. I was in Scott's flat on my own, when there was a knock on the front door. A sense of dread overtook me in my dream, and

LK CHAPMAN

yet I made my way to the door. I turned the handle, making no attempt to check who was there, though a little part of my mind was screaming at me to be careful. I swung the door fully open, and there in front of me was Jay.

I turned away, trying to shut the door in his face, but it was too late. I ran into the bathroom and locked the door, but Jay said, 'I know you're there, Fliss. I'm coming to get you.' Those last words had an eerie ring to them, like something from a childhood game gone wrong. He started to kick the door – one, two, three, four times – until it crashed open and I screamed.

I woke to darkness. Or near darkness. As I scanned around the room, my breath still catching in little gasps, sinister forms emerged in the uncertain light: bags of clothes became crouching figures, boxes morphed into intimidating black towers. I tried to regain control of myself but it was as though the room was closing in around me, until I reached out and turned on the light. Immediately, the shapes resumed their true form. Scott, who'd managed to stay asleep up until this point, woke up and blinked. 'Fliss?' he croaked at me.

I was about to turn the light back off, but couldn't bring myself to do it. 'I got a bit scared,' I told him, embarrassed. 'The shapes of all the things in here.'

He squinted around the room in confusion, and then he finally grasped what I was getting at. 'There's no monsters in here,' he told me. 'I'm good at checking for monsters. Just ask Den.'

'Don't make fun of me! I feel ridiculous enough.'

He put his arm around me. 'I was just trying to make you laugh. I have only just woken up.'

'I'm sorry.'

'Were you dreaming about him?'

I quickly outlined my dream to Scott, and he gave me a squeeze. 'Are you sure nothing out of the ordinary happened in Coalton?'

'I didn't notice anything. I felt fine while I was there. I felt good. Safe.'

'Still, it must have been a big deal to go back to where everything started. Perhaps you're having a delayed reaction to going back there.'

'I don't usually dream about him finding me. I usually dream about things he's already done. I dream that I'm back there with him.'

'Perhaps it's some sort of progress,' he suggested. 'At least you're thinking about the future and not the past.'

'I don't want to think about him *finding* me!'

'It doesn't mean he will, just because you thought about it. Fliss, you had a nightmare, that's all. Jay is gone, you've really no reason to think otherwise.'

I paused briefly. 'Vicky said she hopes he'll track me down and hurt me.'

'What? When were you talking to *her*?'

'This morning. I wanted to try to smooth things over with her. I thought she would be upset after that argument.'

'Did you smooth anything over?' he asked, once he'd digested what I'd said.

'Well, I just told you what she said to me about Jay, so what do you think?'

He sighed. 'The stuff that comes out of her mouth,' he said. 'She doesn't really mean it. I don't think even *she* would genuinely wish for Jay to get his hands on you, no matter what she feels in the heat of the moment.'

'I don't really care what she thinks. But… it did rattle me a bit to hear her say it.'

'She won't stay angry like this forever. She just can't. Nobody could sustain it for that long, it's too exhausting.'

'Do you think that's true of Jay, too?'

'Perhaps. Hopefully. But listen to me, Fliss, you're safe here. Alstercombe isn't a huge place. If he comes here and starts asking questions, it's going to get back pretty quickly to someone who knows me or my family. Somebody like him won't be able to hide in any shadows here. Not in Alstercombe, and' – he gestured around the bedroom – 'and certainly not in this room.'

Jay

50

Jay wanted to drive down to Alstercombe as soon as possible, but a job came up on Sunday – one that would take all day and earn him a nice bit of cash. It was too good to pass up. What difference would a day make, after all? He'd waited this long. Instead he made his way to Alstercombe on Monday morning, going straight to her address.

He watched her block of flats all day. It wasn't a huge block; nine flats in all, with a car park out the front. He never saw her come and go. Her allocated parking space was empty. Of course, during the day on a Monday, that wasn't entirely surprising. Perhaps she was at work, and Leo was at nursery. But she didn't return in the evening. Neither was she there when he visited the next day, nor when he went again later in the week. Unease began to spread through him. Where was she? Surely she couldn't be on holiday, when Leanne had specifically talked about her going home to see Scott. More unsettling still, there was a To Let sign next to her building. After over a week of frequently watching her flat, a heavy feeling settled around his heart. Felicity didn't live there, that was for sure. She had moved out, and recently too. But where to? Had she moved in with Scott? *Scott!* His skin prickled with anger. Why was she doing this to him? It was unbearable.

He opened up the pictures of her on his phone, the ones he'd taken when he saw her in Coalton. He gazed first at the pictures of her with Leo, then, as he began to think about how much he wanted to screw her, he stared instead at the picture of her face on her driver's licence, imagining how he'd push her down onto a bed, or maybe up against a wall. Once he was inside her she'd remember all her feelings for him. She wanted him just as much as he wanted her, no matter how much she was trying to pretend otherwise. He quickly closed the photo. It was no good getting worked up like this. He needed to find her first; all his energy needed to be focused on that. The fact she'd just moved out of her flat was a blow, a bad one, but it didn't necessarily mean he was back where he'd started. If she had met Scott in Alstercombe, and she had moved in with him, chances were she *still* lived somewhere in Alstercombe. And if he kept going back, one day, surely, he would spot her.

Scott

51

Despite the reassurances he'd made to Felicity, as the weeks passed Scott began to pick up on her mood. Though they made an offer on the house, and Felicity and Leo were happy in his flat, she continued to be jumpy. She became increasingly obsessed by the idea she was being watched or followed, though she had no evidence to support it, and said she had a feeling something bad was coming. One night, after the weekly pub quiz, Scott brought it up with Martin. 'The thing is,' he explained, 'I'm almost starting to feel the same.'

Martin gave him a critical look. 'You can't let him get inside your head. Think how happy it would make him to know he was freaking the two of you out like this. And you, especially. This isn't like you.'

'Felicity is certain something is going to happen.'

'Could it just be because she's scared something will mess up your plans? You're going to move house soon. Everybody finds house moves stressful, but on top of that she's adjusting to living with you and Den. *And* she's pregnant. It's a lot to take in for anybody.'

'It does my head in that they haven't caught him. I don't tell Felicity how much it concerns me, and a lot of the time I'm okay, but sometimes I'm scared shitless he's going to get his hands on her.'

Martin was quiet for a time. The pub was a little busier than usual, and Scott was comforted by the buzz of conversation that filled the air around them. 'I bumped into Vicky the other day,' Martin said. 'She was asking about Jay.'

'About *Jay*?'

'Well, she didn't call him by name. She just mentioned Felicity's ex, seemingly in passing, but when I looked back afterwards I think she might have been trying to draw a few more details about him from me.'

'Why would she want to know about him?' Scott asked, confused.

'I don't know. She's probably just looking for something she might be able to use against you and Felicity someday.'

'It feels like we're being attacked from all sides sometimes. Vicky. Jay.'

'Jay isn't really here, though.'

Scott must have looked as exhausted as he felt because Martin said, 'You should go home and get some sleep. Stop thinking about Jay. You're going to drive yourself nuts.'

. . .

The next morning, when Vicky came to drop Dennis off at his flat, he was given further reason to question her motivations. Dennis's favourite soft toy was missing. Vicky had been looking everywhere for it, without success, and she'd concluded in the end that it must not have come with Dennis to her house at the weekend. 'You need to check here,' she said. 'I promised him he could have it when we got to Daddy's house. He's going to kick up a fuss if you can't find it.'

'Sure,' he said, though the whole thing was odd. If Den had been that upset about it at the weekend, why hadn't she just called and asked him to take the toy round?

Vicky went into the living room with Dennis while he gave the boy's bedroom a search. He was just on the point of giving up, when he found the fluffy toy lion wedged down the side of the chest of drawers. He pulled it out triumphantly, just as Dennis came into the room. 'Here,' Scott said, 'Mummy said you've been looking for this?'

Dennis took the toy lion without much interest, and put it down on his bed.

Scott frowned. It was as if Vicky just wanted to get him out of the way for a minute. In the hallway he paused. He could hear Felicity moving around in the kitchen, probably making sand-wiches to take to work with her, and then came Vicky's voice. 'I realised something,' she said. 'He's told you that me and him were just a one-time thing, hasn't he?'

Scott's blood ran cold. He was right! Vicky had sent him off on a so-called urgent errand in Den's room so she could drip poison in Felicity's ear. 'I don't have a lot of time to talk, Vicky,' Felicity said.

'Neither do I. But you should listen to what I have to say. It wasn't one night. We were together for *months*.'

Scott froze in horror and disgust. She was lying!

'I don't believe you,' Felicity said calmly. 'And I don't like what you're trying to do.'

'Why don't you believe me? I'm telling the truth. He knew I was pregnant when he left me. He told me it was over just after I had my twenty-week scan. It all got too real for him. He may well do the same to you, you know.'

Scott's rage boiled over. 'I can hear what you're saying,' he said as he joined them in the kitchen. 'How dare you, Vicky?'

He became aware, suddenly, that Dennis had followed him and was now looking at him curiously. Leo had heard, too, and was looking round at him from where he sat at the dining table eating a bowl of cereal. He didn't want to argue in front of the two children. 'Fliss, can you stay here with the children for a minute? I'm going to talk to Vicky outside.'

Felicity nodded, and Scott fought the urge to physically drag Vicky out of the door. The second the front door was closed he faced her across the top of the stairs, and a red mist descended. To begin with, he shouted at her for lying to Felicity, trying to make her think he would leave her while she was pregnant. Vicky gave as good as she got, screaming back at him, until he found himself saying, 'Tim was going to leave you, you know.' The second the words were out of his mouth, he wished he could take them back. Vicky's face turned white. 'You're lying,' she said, narrowing her eyes at him. 'That's a sick, *sick,* lie, Scott.'

Scott took a deep breath. Telling Vicky was going to cause all hell to break loose, but he'd done it now. He couldn't take it back, so the best thing he could do was stick to the truth. 'It's not a lie. Ask Martin if you don't believe me.'

'Martin? Like I'd believe him either. The two of you have it in for me. You always have. Always sticking your oar in with me and Tim, dragging him away from me—'

'What the—' Scott caught himself. He wasn't going to start swearing at the mother of his child. 'Vicky, you smothered Tim. You know you did.'

'Because I knew you and Martin would do whatever you could to split us up.'

'No, Vix. That's not why. It's not normal to behave the way you did. Tim told us. He said what it was like for him. He said he asked you several times to get help, that he didn't want things to carry on the way they were, but you never got any help. He couldn't take it any more. He wanted his life back.'

'He was *not* going to break up with me,' she said, pointing her finger at him. 'That's a filthy lie. He loved me. I'd still be with him now if you hadn't...'

'Go on. If I hadn't what?'

She held his gaze. 'He never wanted to go climbing with you that day. He wanted to stay with me.'

'That's not true.'

Vicky was still and silent, paralysed with anger, then she flew at him. She lashed out at him with her hands, her nails, and he put his arms up to try to fend her off, but as abruptly as she started, she stopped. There were tears on her cheeks. 'Vicky, I'm sorry,' he said. 'I never meant for you to hear about it like that. I was angry. But... perhaps it is better that you know. You could change things now. Make sure nothing like this happens to you again.'

She swiped angrily at her tears. 'I know it's not true. He wasn't going to break up with me.'

'Vicky...'

'No,' she said, shaking her head. 'No. No.' She was making her way down the steps now.

'Don't you want to say goodbye to Den?' he said.

She didn't reply. She took the last few steps at a run, and was gone.

Vicky

52

Vicky had noticed, on a couple of occasions, the man in a white van who parked near Dennis's nursery and watched the children being dropped off and picked up. He'd been doing it the past few weeks; he was there when she collected Dennis on Friday afternoons to take him to stay with her for the weekend. Most people wouldn't notice, but something about the man had caught her eye. He parked a good way away, and was usually doing something, like eating, or he'd be busy on his phone, but keeping a careful lookout, his eyes on the children and parents leaving the nursery. Vicky's gut instinct, reinforced when she gathered a bit more information about Felicity's ex, was that Scott and Felicity were concerned he would turn up in Alstercombe. Her conversation with Felicity the previous day had confirmed it. And this man looked like he was searching for something, or someone.

After her argument with Scott, she drove to the nursery where Dennis went a few times a week. Most of the kids had been dropped off by now, and she was going to make herself late for work, but she hoped the man she suspected was Felicity's ex would be there – that it wasn't only Friday afternoons that he chose to stake the place out. He was in the wrong place, of course. Leo didn't go to the same nursery as Dennis. But she suspected his plan was to watch all the nurseries until he discovered the right one. There weren't many in Alstercombe, so it was a good plan.

She scanned the street, initially thinking he wasn't there, until sure enough, she spotted his white van parked just around the corner. She parked her car behind his van, and marched straight up and knocked on his window.

The man nearly jumped out of his skin. He was in his early thirties, his hair dark and shoddily cut, and his face might have been attractive if it wasn't for the pair of odd thick-framed glasses he wore. Was he trying to alter his appearance? The rest of his colouring wasn't dark like his hair, and those glasses were part of a disguise if ever she'd seen one.

He opened the window and looked her up and down. Was he checking her out? She would have thought he'd be too preoccupied to think about that, but his gaze lingered for a moment on her chest. Then he met her eyes. 'Yeah? What is it?'

'I think I know who you are.'

Was that a flicker of fear? 'Oh yeah? Who's that then?'

'I think you're Felicity Hart's ex.'

His eyes widened, but he said, 'I don't know what the hell you're talking about.'

'I think you do.'

'I'm here doing a delivery, all right? I don't know who you think I am, but you've got it wrong.'

'Why do you never get out of your van, then? I've seen you round here before, and I've never noticed you get out and deliver anything.'

She watched his face carefully. Was she putting herself in danger by talking to him? She really hadn't thought this through – she'd let her anger at Scott take over. It wouldn't be in this man's interest to harm her, though. Surely he would be grateful for any information she could give him.

'I'm going now,' he said.

'Just hear me out. I think I can help you.'

He looked exasperated, and more than a bit nervous. It was clear he was scared about the fact he'd been spotted, so he must be exactly who she thought he was. Now she needed to reassure him, show she was on his side.

'What do you want?' he asked.

She smiled. 'It's more about what we both want.'

He didn't reply, and she continued. 'Felicity,' she said. 'You want her back' – she lowered her voice – 'and I want her gone.'

Jay

53

Jay stared at the woman in astonishment. Was she for real? This was surely too good to be true. Could she be a police officer? Was it some sort of trick? He looked at her again, more carefully this time. She was slightly older than him and Felicity, in her mid-thirties, he estimated. Her strawberry blonde hair fell around the shoulders of her black padded jacket, which she'd left unzipped, showing off a fuchsia pink shirt with buttons slightly strained across her chest. Jay quite liked the look of her, if he had been in the market for that sort of thing. In fact, a bit of casual sex would do him a world of good with the mood he'd been in recently.

But that was beside the point, and it wasn't why she had come over to him. Why *had* she? He couldn't quite bring himself to believe that the solution to his problem of finding Felicity would just fall into his lap like this. On the other hand, why would she bother to try to trick him? If she wanted him caught, all she had to do was call the police. Why try to prompt him to act against Felicity unless it really was in her own interest?

'So,' he said cautiously, 'you're going to tell me where she lives, are you?'

'If that's what you need to know.' She looked around, a little uneasy now. 'We need to make this quick. I don't want anyone to see me talking to you. I don't want any of this to come back onto me, okay?'

He didn't answer so she said, '*Okay*?'

He shrugged. 'Yeah. Whatever. I don't even know who the fuck you are, do I?'

'You ready to write this down?'

He took out his phone, and quickly typed in her words as she

213

told him the name of Leo's nursery, the dentist's where Felicity worked, and finally her address.

'You must really hate her,' Jay said. 'What's she done to you?'

'Nothing.'

It was a lie, clearly, but what did that matter? If these details were correct, and he really would be able to find Felicity, everything he'd been working towards could suddenly become a reality. But doubt nagged at him. 'Tell me why you're doing this,' he asked her again.

'You don't need to know.'

Jay drummed his fingers on his knee. He might as well check the addresses out. But would it really be safe? What if it *was* a trap, and the police would swoop in as soon as he went anywhere near Felicity?

'When are you going to take her away?' the woman asked abruptly.

'Take her?'

'Yeah. You need to get her away from here, isn't that your plan?'

He raised an eyebrow. 'Where am I supposed to take her?'

'What do you mean?'

He watched her, and something dawned on him. This woman didn't know as much as she thought she did. 'You don't *really* know who I am, do you?'

'Yes, I just told you—'

'I'm not in a position to just take her somewhere.'

Her face twisted through several emotions. She kept glancing around, desperate to be away from him. 'Look, I can't talk any longer. People know me round here. Meet me later. At the White Hart in Ratchford. It's a fair way from here, no one will know us. Meet me at eight-thirty.'

She turned and quickly made her way back down the pavement, heels click-clacking on the tarmac. He watched for a second, and then he looked down at the address on his phone. If she was genuine, and he'd really been given the exact locations for Felicity, it was like being handed a pot of gold. The past few weeks had been a nightmare. He'd made so many trips to Alstercombe that he knew every street of the coastal town, though he'd not caught so much as a glimpse of Felicity or Leo.

...

The hours until eight-thirty couldn't go by fast enough for Jay, until finally he was sitting in the White Hart. The pub was an old-fashioned place, with wooden beams and a red and green patterned carpet, and it was quiet but not empty. Since he wanted to keep a clear head, he bought himself an orange juice and sat down at a small table in the back corner, well out of the way of prying eyes.

The woman – Jay realised he still didn't know her name – arrived a few minutes later. She spotted him straight away and joined him, slipping her arms out of the black coat she'd been wearing earlier. Underneath she was now wearing a shimmery grey knitted top with a scoop neck that showed a distracting amount of cleavage, and he wondered how much thought she'd put into the change of clothing. He had to admit he was fascinated and excited by the whole situation, especially as a part of him thought the police might have come to meet him in the pub instead of her, and he was so thankful to see only her that he was almost giddy with relief.

'I'll get you a drink...' he said, starting to stand.

'I'll get it myself, thanks.' She placed her coat carefully over the back of her chair and went across to the bar. Jay swirled his drink around in the glass, nerves fluttering in his stomach. Yes, he was glad the police hadn't walked through the door, but he was still unconvinced about her motive. He wanted to trust her, but with his freedom potentially at stake, it was a huge risk. He needed to play it cool, for the moment at least.

Vicky

54

Vicky stole glances at the lone man at the table in the corner. He was clearly still jumpy, and took frequent, small sips of his juice. A pang of guilt made her voice crack a little as she ordered her drink. She swallowed hard. She'd started this now, she couldn't go back. Yes, if she gave him a way to get Felicity back he would probably hurt her again, but was that really her responsibility? And did she *really* care? It wasn't actually her doing the hurting after all. It would be him.

She paid for her small glass of white wine, and made her way back over to him. He wasn't that much to look at – he was moderately attractive, despite the odd haircut, and kept himself in decent shape – but he wasn't really intimidating. She found it hard to imagine him hurting Felicity. Perhaps he changed a lot when he got in a rage. Or maybe Felicity was exaggerating to get sympathy from Scott. That would hardly be a surprise.

They sat in awkward silence for a few minutes, as though they were both too scared to cut to the heart of the matter, until the man said, 'What's your name, anyway? You never told me.'

She hesitated. Should she give him her real name? She probably should, if she wanted him to trust her. 'Vicky.'

'Do you know my name?'

She shook her head, but instead of enlightening her, he said, 'So, do you want Scott back, then? Is that why you're doing this? Are you his ex or something?'

'You know about Scott?'

'Yeah. Am I right, is he your ex?'

Vicky's insides twisted uncomfortably at his question. It made her sound jealous and petty. *You are jealous and petty, Vicky. Always have been.* She dug her nails briefly into her palm to silence her thoughts and she glared at him. She didn't have to justify her actions to this man, who as far as she was concerned was little more than a common criminal.

'That must be what it is,' he continued. 'I've been wondering why you could possibly want to help. I know Fliss has a new boyfriend, so I guessed it's him you want.'

'I don't see why you need to know.'

'I'm allowed to be curious why you'd want to help me.'

An idea came to her, though it made her nervous. She didn't want to implicate herself any further in whatever he would do with Felicity, but she really did want Felicity to go. And she really did want her to suffer. 'Look, I don't want this to drag on,' she said. 'If you need somewhere to take Felicity until you get things sorted, I *might* know a place you could go.'

'I'm listening.'

'It's a little cottage, way away from everything. My cousin and her husband were doing it up, but then she got ill and everything is on hold. It's not far off finished, but I don't think they ever go there.'

He took a sip of his drink. He wasn't as keen as she expected. Why wasn't he just saying he'd take Felicity and go? She already regretted telling him about the house, but her wish for Felicity to be gone and for the whole situation to be over was intense. She was beginning to feel ill – hope, triumph, guilt, worry and shame were all tangled up together into one painful ball.

'Look, I'm not sure about this,' he said. 'I appreciate you giving me her address. If this really is her address.'

Blind panic surged through her. Was he seriously going to back out? No. She couldn't let him, not when she'd gone this far. 'You need to—'

'I don't *need* to do anything,' he said. 'I don't know what game you're trying to play, but I don't want to get my fingers burned.'

'Felicity's pregnant!' she said, in desperation. She hated herself as soon as the words were out of her mouth, but it had the desired effect. His face went rigid with anger. It transformed him entirely. It was like he'd grown physically bigger. His presence was suddenly so menacing, frightening. 'How pregnant?'

'Not very, I don't think.'

He slammed his fist on the table. 'How dare she?'

Vicky looked around nervously. Nobody seemed to have noticed, but the last thing she wanted was for him to make a scene. Why had she said it? Why had she wound him up like this? 'Don't worry,' she said. 'I'm sure when you talk to her—'

He grabbed her hand. 'Let me tell you who I really am,' he said through gritted teeth. 'I'm wanted for murder. *That's* the truth.'

Vicky's blood ran cold. Had she heard him right? He'd *killed* somebody? Her heart was pounding. This was wrong. This was all wrong. It couldn't be happening. Why had he even told her? Was he crazy? Was he trying to scare her? She wanted to scream for help, or run out of the door and call the police, but how could she? She'd invited him here. She'd tried to help him! How could she possibly explain what she had been doing without sounding like a criminal herself? She tried to pull her hand away, but he wouldn't release her.

'I can't just go and snatch her without thinking it through,' he continued. 'I have to be careful, even though she…' His voice rose again. '*She* can just do whatever she wants.'

Vicky finally managed to get her hand away from his grasp. 'This was a mistake…'

'Write down the address of that cottage. And your phone number, in case I need you.'

'I think I should go.'

'Now!'

'I'm not giving you my number. And I'm not giving you that address.'

She watched him anxiously. A little nerve was twitching in his cheek. 'What are you going to do?' she said, her voice almost a whisper.

'I don't know. I need to think. And if I need more help from you, or if I need that address, I'll come and find you in Alstercombe. It won't take me long to track you down.'

Vicky swallowed hard. How could she have got herself into

this? This was a nightmare. Beyond a nightmare. 'Look, I don't think we should have anything more to do with each other—'

'Are you thinking about going to the police?'

'No,' she said. 'I don't want anyone to know I've been talking to you.'

'Good, because I won't think twice about hurting you if you mess me around.'

With that, he stood up and walked out of the pub. Vicky gulped down the rest of her wine. She was trembling all over. What had she done? She'd wanted Felicity to get back with her ex – whether it was willingly or not – but he had been right earlier. She hadn't known who he really was. She'd known Felicity's ex was violent, but *murder*?

Then another thought occurred to her, one that made her livid with anger. Scott obviously knew the truth about him. And yet he was allowing Dennis, *her* son, to live in a flat with a woman who was being pursued by a murderous ex-boyfriend. He was putting Dennis in danger, placing Felicity's life and Leo's life above the life of his own son. She couldn't bear it. Did he really care so little for her and Dennis? Or *that* much for Felicity? She rubbed her face with her hands. How had it become such a mess? What was going to happen now? What if Felicity's ex came after *her* for some reason – perhaps in anger over her telling him about the baby?

Vicky got up shakily. He had surely driven away now. She could go quietly out to her car, drive home, and try to pretend none of it had ever happened. Her stomach lurched as she stepped outside the door. It had taken her years to regain some control of her fears of being in public places, of being outside on her own, but tonight had brought it all back. She fixed her eyes on her car, darting across the car park at a near run, fear coursing through her with every step, the empty space around bearing down on her, like it was filled with invisible eyes.

Once she was inside the relative safety of her car, she closed her eyes and focused on getting control of her breathing. She'd made a pretty bad error of judgement, there was no doubt about that. But Scott and Felicity deserved it. They fucking deserved it.

219

The way Scott had relished telling her about Tim wanting to break up with her, the way Felicity had looked down her nose at her. Vicky was sick of people looking down their noses at her, making her feel small. Scott and Felicity were vile. They made her sick. They'd driven her to do what she'd done. Whatever happened next they'd brought on themselves.

Stephanie

55

Stephanie sat in her car, building up her courage. She'd waited a little while before visiting the address she'd found in Jason's t-shirt drawer. Not for his sake – she was so furious at him for hiding the address that her desire to help him was at an all-time low – but because she was nervous. What would she say to Dad, after all this time? What if she found him, and ended up wishing she hadn't? She was trying to be realistic in her expectations of him, but what if a part of her was secretly hoping for a fairy-tale ending? If so, the reality would almost certainly be a let-down.

She clutched the notepaper in her hand, watching what was going on around her. People tended to mutter things about this area, though she hadn't been to Graycott herself. Sure enough, it was run-down. Several houses were boarded up. In fact, if anything, the street was eerily quiet. A group of teenagers had passed her a few minutes before, giving her a fright when they suddenly burst into loud laughter as they walked alongside her car, but she hadn't seen anybody since.

She took a deep breath. She was being ridiculous, hiding in her car like this, too frightened to go and meet a man she'd spent most of her life longing for. After all, what was the worst that could happen? He obviously wanted to see her, so he wasn't going to slam the door in her face. The worst thing would be that he somehow disappointed her – but if she didn't try, she'd never know.

Tentatively, she got out of her car and made her way to her dad's flat. It was in a small block, and she had to ring nearly every buzzer before somebody let her into the building. She made her way slowly inside and found 56a, her dad's flat, almost immediately. She swallowed hard. *It's now or never.*

She knocked decisively on the door, and waited, her pulse racing.

Nothing.

She knocked again, and still there was nothing. She tried to listen for sounds inside the flat, but there was only silence. How had she managed to pick a time he was out? After all this build-up, she was almost on the verge of tears at this anticlimax. She knocked again, desperately, and the door of one of the neighbouring flats opened. A dark-haired young woman popped her head out.

'Who are you after?' she asked.

'My dad... uh, I mean, Keith. Keith Vinney. Do you know him?'

The young woman shook her head. 'There was some old guy here a while ago. He started out the perfect neighbour, then he kept coming back home pissed and started messing the place up.'

Stephanie's heart missed a beat. 'You mean he's... he's *gone*?'

The woman raised an eyebrow. 'You not in touch with him then?'

Stephanie shook her head.

'I don't think he'll be back here. No one stays around here too long if they can help it.'

Stephanie stared helplessly at the closed door in front of her, then back at the woman, who was watching her curiously. 'Thanks for your help,' she said. The woman disappeared back inside. Stephanie rested her forehead against the door of her dad's former home, and closed her eyes.

...

'I don't want to talk about this *again!*' Jason shouted. It was probably about the tenth time in the past two weeks that she'd brought up the fact he'd lost her that one chance to see her dad. Every time they argued, he'd repeat over and over that he did it for the good of them both, but she was so hurt and angry that she thought the pain would never go away.

'How could you do this to me?' she yelled back. 'The one thing

I wanted more than anything else in the world—'

'I thought you wanted *me* more than anything else in the world.'

He fixed his eyes on her. They were the colour of slate, and had an unpleasant gleam in them. It unnerved her, and she didn't reply.

. . .

Jason continued his frequent trips away in his van for another one or two weeks, until one night he came back late, while she was in bed reading. She jumped out of her skin as he slammed the front door behind him, and he called out her name. She sat up slowly, placing the fantasy novel she'd been reading down on the bed beside her. Something told her that right now she didn't want him to find her, though she didn't have much choice. He was coming up the stairs, and there was nowhere to hide.

He burst into the bedroom, and nodded grimly when he saw her. 'Jason,' she said as calmly as she could, 'what's happened—'

He got onto the bed beside her, sweeping her book onto the floor. 'Take your clothes off,' he told her.

'What?'

'You heard me.'

She wrapped her arms around her body. 'Jason, no. I don't want to have sex. I'm still too upset with you. Haven't you even noticed how unhappy I am—'

'I'll put a smile on your face then.'

'Jason—'

He shoved her so hard, and so unexpectedly, that she fell down onto the bed. She tried to sit up but he pinned her down, and covered her mouth with his. She pushed at him. What the hell was he playing at? 'Jason, stop it,' she managed to say. 'I said I don't want to!'

He kissed her harder, and a knot of fear formed in her stomach. 'Stop it,' she said, turning her face to the side. 'Get off me. You're scaring me.'

He pressed his mouth over hers again, and released one of his hands from her wrist, bringing it up between her legs. She tried to speak, to tell him to stop again, but his mouth was pressed too firmly over hers. In fear and anger, she bit his lip.

He moved away from her with a yell, raising his hand to his mouth, and when he saw the blood on his fingers he slapped her. 'Why did you do that?' he shouted. 'What's wrong with you?'

'What's wrong with *me*?' she said, as her eyes filled with tears. 'What's wrong with *you*?'

'I'm going to do it,' he said. 'How unpleasant it is – that's up to you.'

Panic welled up inside her. 'Jason, stop this. You're really frightening me.'

'Why are you like this?' he shouted at her.

'I don't understand,' she said. Her voice shook. What was wrong with him? He'd never done anything like this before. At this moment she barely recognised him, she'd never seen him so angry, so out-of-control. 'Please Jason, just—'

'I said, why are you like this?'

A tear spilt out from the corner of her eye. 'I don't know what you're asking me.'

'I'm talking about women!' he said. 'You're all fucking sluts, until times like this when you decide that for once you want to keep your legs closed. Where does that leave me? Huh? You're supposed to be my girlfriend, aren't you? You haven't let me fuck you for weeks. You use all that shit that happened with your dad as an excuse, but I know what you're really doing. You're just trying to drive me crazy.'

She tried desperately to push him away, but he held her down and shouted in her face. He'd completely lost the plot now – the words and threats horrible, obscene, like nothing she'd ever heard from him before. She was too shocked to move. Her body froze in fear as his words washed over her, many of them barely registering, but the one that remained with her was "slut". He said it over and over while he raped her, as if he thought saying it cancelled out what he was doing. Stephanie didn't make a sound. She didn't move, she barely even breathed, until it was over. And when it was over Jason was, if not calm, then at least less crazed.

'I'm sorry if I hurt you,' he said roughly. He gave her a handful of tissues, and she wiped them between her legs, before rolling onto her side to face away from him.

'There's only so much I can take, Steph,' he told her. 'I had some bad news tonight. I was angry. You need to be here for me, not against me all the fucking time. Do you understand?'

She nodded.

'Get some sleep,' he told her.

Jay

56

Jay slammed his hand against the bathroom tiles, over and over, until finally the pain was bad enough that his head cleared. Stephanie was the one person he really couldn't afford to mess with right now, and he'd hurt her. He'd done to her what he wanted to do to Felicity. He'd let his anger over Felicity's pregnancy get the better of him.

Slowly, he made his way across the hall and back into the bedroom. Stephanie was curled up on her side, eyes open and staring. She hadn't moved since he'd left the room. He tried to get his head together. Maybe this wouldn't work out so badly. Stephanie had been getting more difficult to control, so having her fear him might work in his favour. He'd get her flowers – a big bunch of flowers backed up by some pretty words, and a great deal of apologising. That should be enough to get her back on side.

A heavy, sick feeling spread through his body. He hated what he'd just done to her. She'd sacrificed so much to help him, and she was harmless really, just a friendless young woman. When she wasn't buried in her video games or her books, she buried herself in the fantasy that he was really her boyfriend. That he really loved her.

He turned away from Steph. This was Felicity's fault! The thought of the baby inside her, *Scott's* baby, had made him lose his mind. He couldn't believe that she had done it. He slipped back out of the bedroom onto the landing and looked at Felicity's address, workplace and the name of Leo's nursery on his phone. It made him feel a little better, but it also made him feel powerless. He knew where she was, and yet he couldn't go and get her. She'd be with Scott, and Jay would have to get past him to get to her. On top of that, Vicky hadn't given him the address of the cottage that she'd dangled in front of him, and if he went on the run with Felicity and Leo without a proper plan he'd end up getting caught. Managing to outrun the police once was lucky; trying to do it again was foolhardy. He couldn't take Felicity and Leo until he had a place to take them to.

He peeked round the door into the bedroom. Stephanie still hadn't moved.

'Do you need anything?' he asked her. 'Do you want a drink? Hot chocolate? You love hot chocolate.'

Stephanie made a tiny noise. He went and stood beside her. 'Did you say something?'

'Leave me alone,' she whispered.

Jay nodded. He could do that easily enough. He kissed her gently on the cheek. 'I'll see you in the morning,' he told her.

. . .

Inside his van, Jay gave himself a firm talking-to. He had to change. He wanted to show Felicity he was a better man, not some sort of maniac. It was stupid, impulsive actions that kept getting him into trouble, and no matter how much Felicity provoked him with her new boyfriend and her pregnancy, he had to rise above it. He had to show he was better than her. He had to make sure she understood that she was the one in the wrong, and that all he'd ever done was love her. He'd drive back to Alstercombe straight away. Not to do anything to Felicity, not yet, but just to try to catch a glimpse of her. Seeing her again with his own eyes would remind him what all this pain was for. It would make him feel alive.

He started the engine, his heart already lighter, and began the drive back to Alstercombe.

Stephanie

57

The sound of the front door closing carried up the stairs, and relief flooded through her. He was gone. Jason had gone. She was alone. She squeezed her eyes shut tight. For a long time, she was still.

She wasn't sure how much time passed, but eventually she got up from the bed. She washed herself, and pulled on her dressing-gown. After that, more blank, dark hours slipped away. The time disappeared without her doing anything to fill it. She just lay in the bed, awake. She was numb. In shock. What should she do? She couldn't get her thoughts together, she couldn't process it. She'd let Jason into her house, into her life. She *loved* him. Perhaps it hadn't been as bad as she thought. Maybe she'd confused him somehow, brought the whole thing on herself.

He raped you.

No, Stephanie said to the little voice in her mind. No. He'd said he was sorry for hurting her. He'd never done anything like this before. He had moods, he was unkind, sometimes, or thoughtless. But he didn't mean anything by it. He just struggled sometimes. He struggled, and tonight he'd lost.

He'll do it again.

'Shut up,' she said out loud to herself. 'Stop it. Stop it!' She couldn't believe that. If she believed that, she'd have to take action. She'd have to throw him out of her house, or confront him. And that would be awful. If everything was okay, she didn't need to act, and so everything *had* to be okay. She had to believe he was honest, and decent, and good. She had to. She had to. She wasn't ready to be on her own, and, in any case, she was too afraid to try to make him leave.

As dawn began to lighten the sky, she went back over her whole relationship with him, questioning every word. Was he really planning to turn in his former friends to the police? Perhaps his crimes were something other than what he had said they were. Perhaps the police wanted him for something else.

Perhaps he's hurt other women.

No, she told herself firmly. No. Stop.

It was eight o'clock in the morning. She went downstairs to make herself a cup of tea. She'd just act normally. If she acted normal, everything would become normal. It would all just go away.

But after sitting quietly at the kitchen table, warming her hands on the mug and drinking it slowly, using each mouthful to swallow down the swirling, dangerous feelings inside her body, she came back upstairs and began to search through Jason's belongings inside the fitted wardrobe. He didn't have much. He'd arrived in Wrexton with little and not bought much since. There were clothes, shoes, underwear. There was the bag that he'd brought with him right at the start – a large grey backpack that didn't look like it had much in it. She opened it.

To begin with, she thought it was empty, but in fact there was a black bin bag inside. Carefully, she opened it up, and drew in a breath when she saw there was cash inside. Not huge amounts, but enough that he was either saving for something, or keen to hide it from her. She held some of the notes in her hands. Was there really anything suspicious in this? There weren't thousands here. He couldn't open a bank account and she knew he didn't give her all his money for housekeeping, so perhaps this was simply where he kept his cash because he had no other option. She put the notes back in the bin bag, then lifted it out. There was something underneath it.

She peered closer. There were clothes at the bottom of the bag; jeans, and a polo-neck shirt. She took them out, and immediately dropped them with a cry. The clothes were spattered with reddish-brown stains. Not huge patches, not like there would be if the wearer had been stabbed or badly injured. These clothes belonged to the person doing the injuring. They belonged to Jason.

A tear splashed into her lap. The clothes sickened her. She knew Jason had been violent in the past – he'd pretty much told her that he'd beaten guys up while he was embroiled in his old life – but seeing the physical evidence of it was horrifying. Why did he have these clothes? Why hadn't he destroyed them? Whose blood was it? Had he *killed* somebody?

She snatched the clothes back up, careful not to touch the bloodstains, and shoved them back into the backpack, followed by the bin bag of money. More tears were coming now. Was she hiding a murderer? She put her hands over her face and rocked back and forth. *It's just Jason,* she told herself, *and Jason loves me. He loves me. He loves me.*

She couldn't be without him. She didn't want to be alone. She wished she could make all of it go away.

I just won't ever talk about it, she told herself. *I'll pretend none of it happened. I'll just be normal.*

She placed the backpack deep inside the wardrobe, and closed the door. Perhaps she'd confront all this another day. But that day was not today.

Jay

58

Jay drove straight to Scott and Felicity's address: 12a George Street. He arrived at four in the morning, and quickly found the flat, above an accountant's office on the corner of the street. The curtains were shut, with no light on behind. Felicity was sleeping soundly just a few metres from where he was standing. She had no idea. He smiled to himself. He'd find somewhere to park and have a rest until morning, and then he'd see if he could catch a glimpse of her.

He found a discreet spot to park, further down the road, under a large tree. Too excited to sleep, he passed the time imagining over and over what it would be like to catch a glimpse of her. At seven forty-five, his wish came true.

He was too far to see her very clearly, but she was there on the street corner, pausing as a bike went past, before dashing across to her car with Leo's hand held tightly in hers. She was dressed in work clothes, clutching a little green backpack that must be Leo's. The street was busier now, and he risked leaving his spot under the tree, driving a little closer and pulling over again, in time to watch her struggling to get Leo into the car. He could hear the little boy protesting, but after a few minutes she stood up again, and ran her hand through her brown hair. Jay shook his head. Why had she messed her hair up like that? It was such a shame. One of the first things he'd get her to do would be to dye it back to its natural colour again, that lovely blonde that had first drawn him to her.

He sat up straight, alarmed. Felicity was holding her phone up to her ear, while she looked down the street. Shit! Had she seen him? Jay's palms began to sweat and he glanced nervously around. No, it wasn't him she was looking at. With his different hair and glasses, she'd have to be pretty close to him before she would recognise him, and he was too far away for that. He rubbed his hands on his jeans and took a deep breath. He'd probably stayed long enough. He'd seen her, he'd proved that the address Vicky had given him was definitely correct – that was all he'd wanted.

He started the engine, but paused as a man rushed over to her car holding a pair of small boy's wellies. He held them out to Felicity, who grabbed them, kissed the man, and got into her car.

Jay swallowed hard. *Bitch! How dare she?* She was driving away now, but the image of her kissing the man – Scott, presumably – kept playing over and over. He shook himself. *Get a grip!* He narrowed his eyes as Scott made his way back towards the house. He'd assumed Felicity's new boyfriend would be someone pathetic, a loser who couldn't find anyone better than a woman with the kind of baggage Felicity had. But this man didn't match that description. He was tall, athletic-looking. Jay certainly wouldn't fancy getting in a fight with him. Scott had obviously rushed outside without pausing to get a jacket, as his bare arms were folded over a mustard yellow t-shirt, and he had flip-flops on his feet. Flip-flops. How fucking ridiculous. Jay hated him with every fibre of his being, and he glared at Scott's back as he made his way back inside the building.

What now? After how excited he'd been to see Felicity, he didn't want it to end here, to have to go back home and face Stephanie. It would be better to remain in Alstercombe a little longer. He'd stay where he was, see if he could get another look at Scott. He had a kind of grim fascination with the man now he'd seen him. What was so great about him? What did Scott have that he hadn't?

He waited perhaps an hour, and then Scott came back out. Jay fixed his eyes on him, waves of anger rippling through his body. The flip-flops had gone and Scott was wearing trainers with his jeans now, plus a green hoodie, zipped up to his chin. Under one arm he held a football, and holding on to his hand was a young boy. He was a similar age to Leo, but a little taller, and with dark hair. Jay blinked. Another boy? What was this all about? Eventually it dawned on him that this boy must be Scott's son.

The boy started to walk right along the edge of the kerb, and Scott awkwardly picked him up and carried him along to keep him out of the way of the cars. Jay smiled to himself. *Now* it made more sense. Scott already had a kid to care for, so having Felicity around probably made life easier for him, even with Leo in tow. More realisations flooded in. Vicky had met him because he was waiting around outside a nursery. It was *this* boy's nursery. This boy was her son – the reason Vicky was so bothered about Scott was because they had a child together, that had to be it! This new knowledge would certainly come in handy. Vicky had proven a very useful ally so far, but if he had to start intimidating her, threatening her son would be a great bargaining chip.

Happy with the work that he'd done, Jay stopped at a florist and bought a large bunch of flowers to give to Stephanie when he got home. He drove by Leo's nursery, though he didn't stop – there was nothing to see, and he knew better than to try and get inside. Instead, he made his way to the dentist's, where he immediately spotted Felicity's car in the corner of a small car park. To his delight, just as he paused across the road he caught sight of her walking behind one of the windows, carrying some leaflets. His skin tingled with goosebumps. It was a thrill, watching her like this. She appeared behind the window again, her hand now empty. She turned her face towards him, but she didn't see him. It was just an idle glance, and then she passed immediately out of sight again.

He grinned, and picked up the bunch of flowers from the seat beside him. As he breathed in their scent, he looked over at her car with giddy excitement. He'd found her! He'd found where she lived, he'd found where she worked. He could hardly believe it. At last, after all this time, she was nearly in his grasp.

Felicity

59

When I saw the rose on my car, I stopped and stared at it dumbly, uncomprehending. With a frown, I reached out my hand towards it, and then I stopped. I took a step backwards, every one of my hairs standing on end, my body cold all over. I looked around me, at the car park, the road, the shops beyond. 'No,' I whispered to myself. 'No, no, no!'

A woman walking by gave me a funny look. 'Hey,' I said, 'you didn't... did you see anyone put this rose on my car?' She paused and stared at me blankly. 'This rose...' I gestured towards it. The woman muttered a quick no and hurried away.

I forced myself to move closer to my car again, where the single red rose had been carefully placed under one of the windscreen wipers. 'No,' I said again. 'No. No. Please God, no.' My throat began to constrict, and I leant against my car, trying to calm down and get my breathing under control. But panic swept through me. I was almost certain who had left it there, but there was another possibility, and one that I hoped like hell would turn out to be true. It wasn't his style, but if there was any chance this was a romantic gesture from Scott, my fears would all be unfounded.

I took out my phone and called Scott. Some concern crept into his voice before I even spoke. 'Fliss, are you all right? What's—'

'Did you put a rose on my car?'

'What?'

'A rose. There's a red rose on my car.'

'A... what do you mean?'

I almost screamed in frustration. Why didn't he understand? 'A rose! A red rose, under the windscreen wiper. Somebody put it on my car.'

There was a pause. 'Could it be somebody from your work?'

'What?'

'Maybe it's some clumsy attempt at showing they're interested in you.'

'It's not somebody from work,' I cried, and the ground seemed to lurch under my feet. 'Scott, it's... it's...'

My breath escaped me. I dropped to my knees, and my phone fell to the ground beside me. I grabbed it and lifted it back up to my ear. 'Scott—'

'Have you called the police?'

'No, I... not yet—'

'I'm going to call the police from the home phone,' he said. 'Can you go back inside the dentist's? Get someone to wait with you until they come.'

I forced myself to my feet. There was a chance some of the staff might not have gone home yet, so I knocked on the door, which was locked, and, when there was no answer, on a couple of the windows. I could hear Scott talking on the other phone. 'Scott,' I said, 'Call Anne, too.'

'Who?'

'Anne! I mean DI Miller. After you... get someone to come here. Please.'

'I will.'

'There's a number,' I said. 'A crime reference number. It links to Jay, I...'

'I've got it,' he said. We kept all the information close to hand back at the flat. 'Just get inside the building in case... in case he's there.'

An awful thought struck me. 'Leo!' I cried.

I ended the call with Scott and ran to my car. I unlocked it and yanked the door open, and then I paused to rip the hateful rose off the windscreen and throw it on the ground. I reversed out of my space and pulled out into the road with a screech of tyres, heading straight for Leo's nursery.

When I arrived, I was in tears, stammering out my fears that Jay was in the area, though they swiftly reassured me that Leo was safe. I finally found Leo playing outside in the sandpit, and I ran to him and wrapped my arms around him, holding him close and kissing his hair, though he tried to push me away, keen to get back to playing with his beloved sand. 'I'm so glad you're safe,' I whispered, 'I'm so glad you're safe.'

I squeezed my eyes closed tight and breathed in the scent of Leo's golden hair. That red rose – every detail of it was burned into my mind, from its delicate petals down to the curved spines on its stem. The gesture had Jay written all over it.

Tears overflowed from behind my eyelids. He was coming. I was sure of it. Jay had found me. And now he'd found me, he was going to come and get me. It wasn't a question of *if*, any more. It was a question of *when*.

Never Let Her Go

Book Three in the chilling NO ESCAPE psychological thriller series (coming 2019)

All he wants is his family…

After escaping her ordeal at the hands of her obsessive ex, Jay, Felicity thought she was safe, building a new life with Scott and son Leo in a seaside town. Little does she know that Jay has tracked her down and wormed his way into the confidence of Vicky, a woman from Scott's past who has her own very sharp axe to grind…

In the gripping final book of the No Escape trilogy, Jay's obsession with Felicity pushes him to ever more desperate lengths to get her back. Felicity soon discovers that he'll stop at nothing, and history begins to repeat itself as she finds herself terrified, alone, and at Jay's mercy once again. Can she escape him before it's too late, or will she be destroyed by his determination to never let her go?

Author Note

If you liked Found You and you're keen to read more of my books in the future, I invite you to join the LK Chapman Reading Group. I send only occasional emails with information about new releases, offers and giveaways – no spam. You will also be able to download a free copy of my short story about a one night stand gone wrong, 'Worth Pursuing' (a prequel to Anything For Him that's now available exclusively to Reading Group subscribers) when you sign up!

Visit my website, www.lkchapman.com or any of my social media pages to sign up to the reading group.

Thank you so much for supporting me by buying my book, it means a lot to me, and I hope you enjoyed reading Found You. If so, please consider leaving a rating and review on Amazon, as even a few words can make a big difference!

I also want to say a few words about why I decided to continue Jay and Felicity's story. It wasn't an easy decision. Although I felt like both characters had more to give, I also felt a little uneasy about writing a story where Felicity, after escaping the ordeal she went through in *Anything For Him*, is then hunted and stalked by her violent ex, Jay. I wanted to try to do justice to a nightmare situation that can sometimes, sadly, be a reality. I wanted this story to be more than just Jay chasing Felicity; I wanted to explore how Felicity's experiences with Jay continue to affect her life, and to show more about Jay – how he thinks and feels, and how he justifies his actions to himself. There is so much about Jay that was only very briefly touched on in *Anything For Him*, and I welcomed the opportunity to explore his past and his present more fully in *Found You*, and to give him a voice with scenes from his perspective. Likewise, I wanted Felicity to have an opportunity to reflect on what happened to her in *Anything For*

Him, and to show her building a new life on her own terms.

Anything For Him was never originally intended to be the first of a series, but I kept going back to it and thinking about it, as I suppose I felt that the story wasn't over. I'm so glad I created this series, and I hope that you enjoyed your journey with Felicity and Jay – a journey that concludes in the final book of the series, *Never Let Her Go*.

Help and support for issues covered in Found You

UK
Refuge
Support for those who have experienced violence and abuse
www.refuge.org.uk
Call 0808 2000 247

Respect Phoneline
Help for people who inflict violence
www.respectphoneline.org.uk
Call 0808 802 4040

US
The National Domestic Violence Hotline
www.thehotline.org
Call 1-800-799-SAFE (7233)

Other books by LK Chapman

No Escape series:

Worth Pursuing (short story)

Anything For Him

Found You

Never Let Her Go (Coming 2019)

Psychological thrillers/suspense

The Stories She Tells

Sci-fi thrillers

Networked

Too Good for This World (short story)

Acknowledgements

Writing sequels to Anything For Him turned into a much bigger project than I originally anticipated! Initially I was going to write one sequel, but it expanded into two, and has been an exciting, challenging and rewarding experience for me (and occasionally a little daunting too!) For their support and encouragement while writing the sequels, I'd like to thank my husband Ashley and all my family and friends who are so enthusiastic and positive about my career as an author. It means a lot to have people believe in me.

Thank you to my wonderful editor Carrie O'Grady, your suggestions and advice have been invaluable. For my fabulous cover thank you to Stuart Bache at Books Covered.

A huge thank you to the lovely people who helped me with my research for Found You: Helen Rossall and /r/climbing on Reddit for helping me with my questions about rock climbing, P.R. for helping me with my questions about police procedure, and Katie Chapman for your help with my questions on crime reporting in the media. Having people to turn to for help with my research makes such a difference, and I'm so grateful to all those who assisted me. I hope I have done justice to all your advice, and if any there are any mistakes or inaccuracies in Found You I take full responsibility.

Last but not least, thank you to my readers. It was hearing all the positive things my readers had to say about Anything For Him that inspired me to continue Felicity and Jay's story, and I loved every minute of continuing their journey in Found You.

About LK Chapman

My full name is Louise Katherine Chapman, and I am a psycho-logical thriller author (although I've also written a sci-fi novel!) I have always been fascinated by the strength, peculiarities and extremes of human nature, and the way that no matter how strange, cruel or unfathomable the actions of other people can sometimes be, there is always a reason for it, some sequence of events to be unravelled.

After graduating from the University of Southampton in 2008 with a degree in psychology, I worked for a year as a psychologist at a consultancy company. In 2009 I had to give up work after developing chronic fatigue syndrome (CFS) – a long term health condition that causes debilitating physical and mental exhaustion. After a few years I thankfully managed to regain enough energy to spend some time volunteering for the mental health charity Mind, and eventually to begin writing. Although my life is still very limited by having CFS I am so grateful to be able to write and for the support of my readers.

Mental health is often a topic I explore in my books. I suffer from bipolar disorder and OCD myself, and I find writing very helpful and therapeutic.

I live in Hampshire with my husband and young son. When I'm not writing I enjoy walks in the woods, video games, and spending time with family and friends.

You can find out more about me by visiting my website **www.lkchapman.com**.

Connect with LK Chapman

Keep up to date with the latest news and new releases from LK Chapman:

Twitter: **@LK_Chapman**

Facebook: **www.facebook.com/lkchapmanbooks**

Subscribe to the LK Chapman newsletter by visiting **www.lkchapman.com**

The Stories She Tells

A psychological page-turner by LK Chapman

A heartbreaking secret. A lifetime of lies.

When Michael decides to track down ex-girlfriend Rae, who disappeared ten years ago while pregnant with his baby, he knows it could change his life forever. His search for her takes unexpected turns as he unearths multiple changes of identity and a childhood she tried to pretend never happened, but nothing could prepare him for what awaits when he finally finds her.

Rae appears to be happily married with a brand new baby daughter. But she is cagey about what happened to Michael's child, and starts to say alarming things: that her husband is trying to force her to give up her new baby for adoption, that he's attempting to undermine the bond between her and her child, and deliberately making her doubt her own sanity.

As Michael is drawn in deeper to her disturbing claims, he begins to doubt the truth of what she is saying. But is she really making it all up, or is there a shocking and heartbreaking secret at the root of the stories she tells?